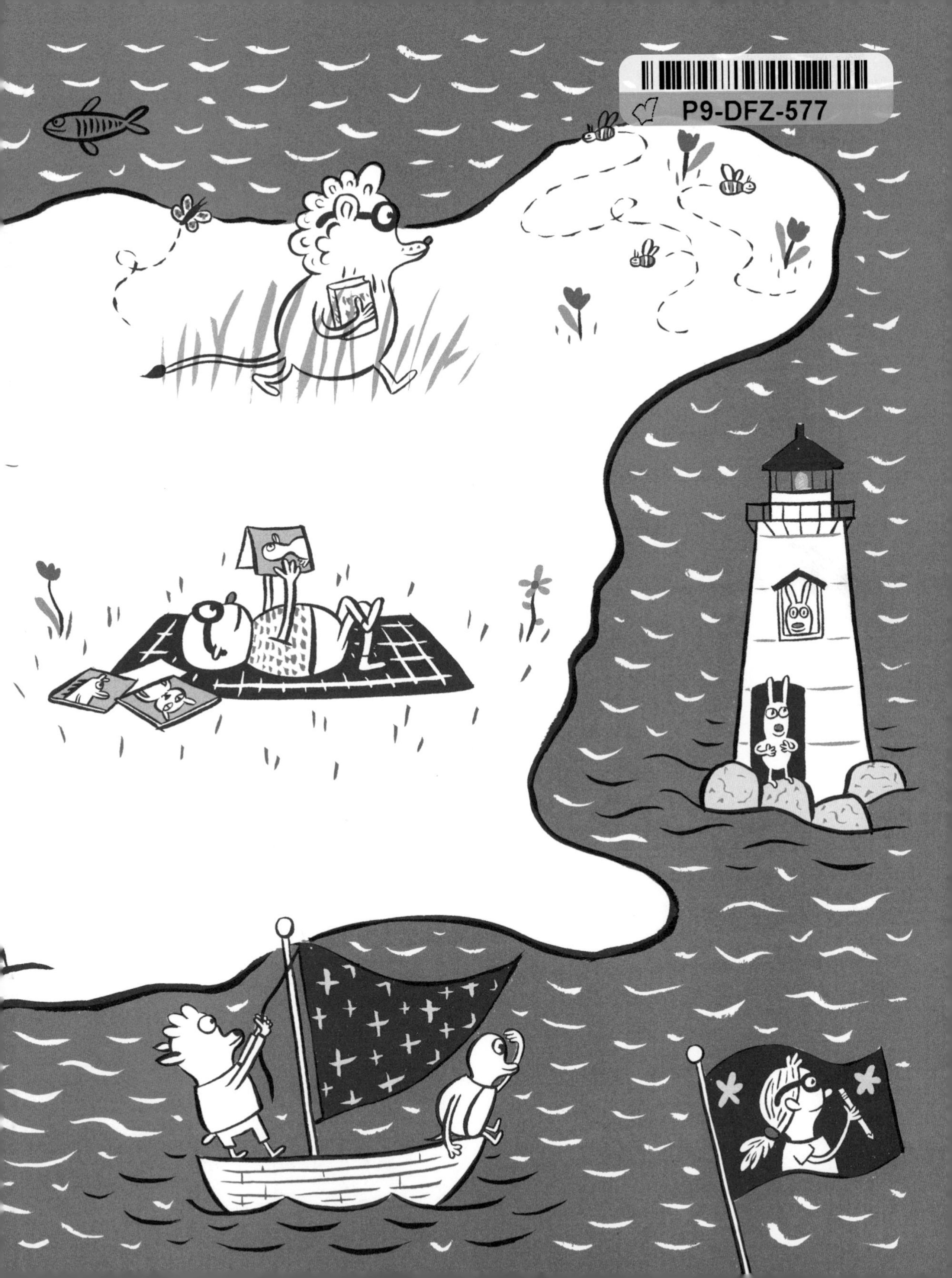

Sweaterweather

SARA VARON

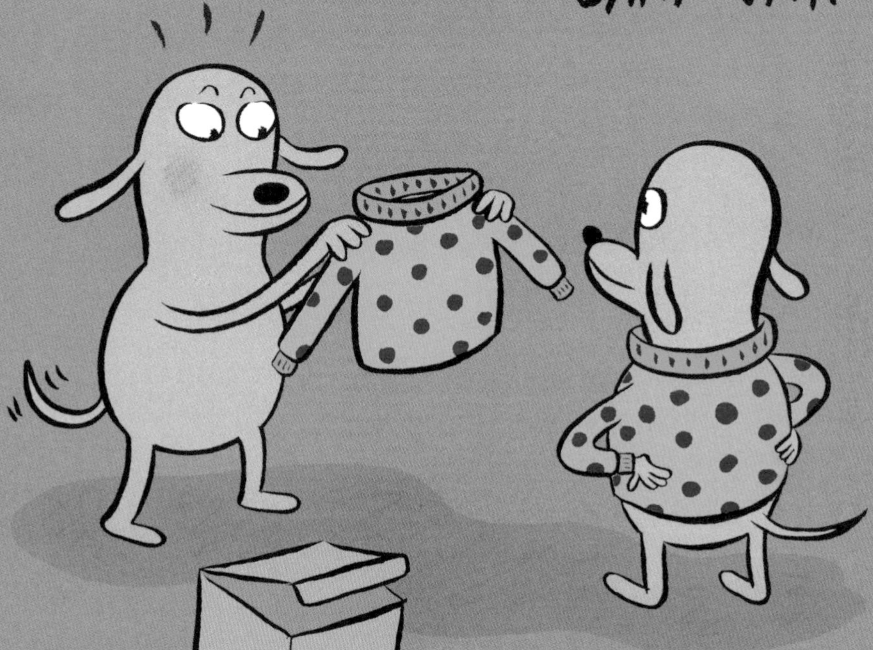

First Second
New York

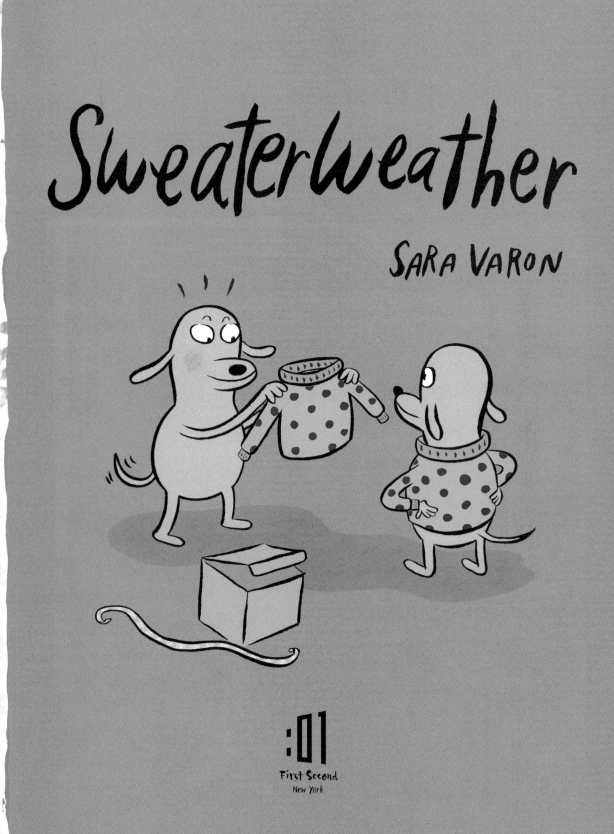

contents

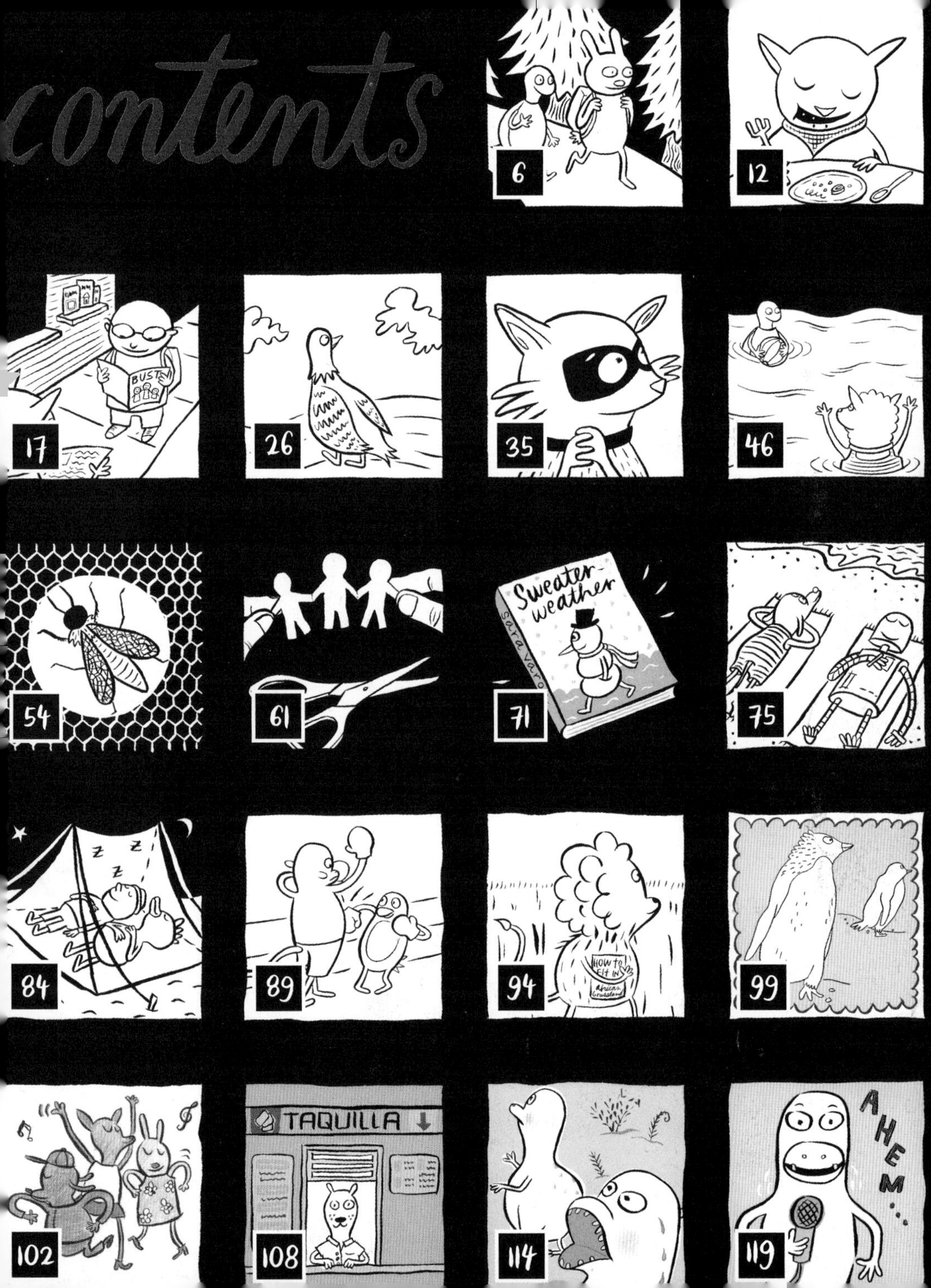
BUST
Sweater weather
Sara Varo
HOW TO FIT IN
African Grassland
TAQUILLA
AHEM...

The First eight stories in this book were originally published in 2003 as part of my very First book, "Sweaterweather." It was the beginning of my comics career, so my drawing style and choice of materials have evolved a little over the years.

Turtle and Rabbit Comic, February 2002
    I can't remember anything about how I came up with this story. I wish I could, because in some ways it's a lot more original than what I'm doing now. The idea that the characters could change size at their convenience to hang out inside a turtle shell is much more magical than what I'm doing these days, which is pretty grounded in reality. If I could remember, I would put more of these magic tricks in my current work.

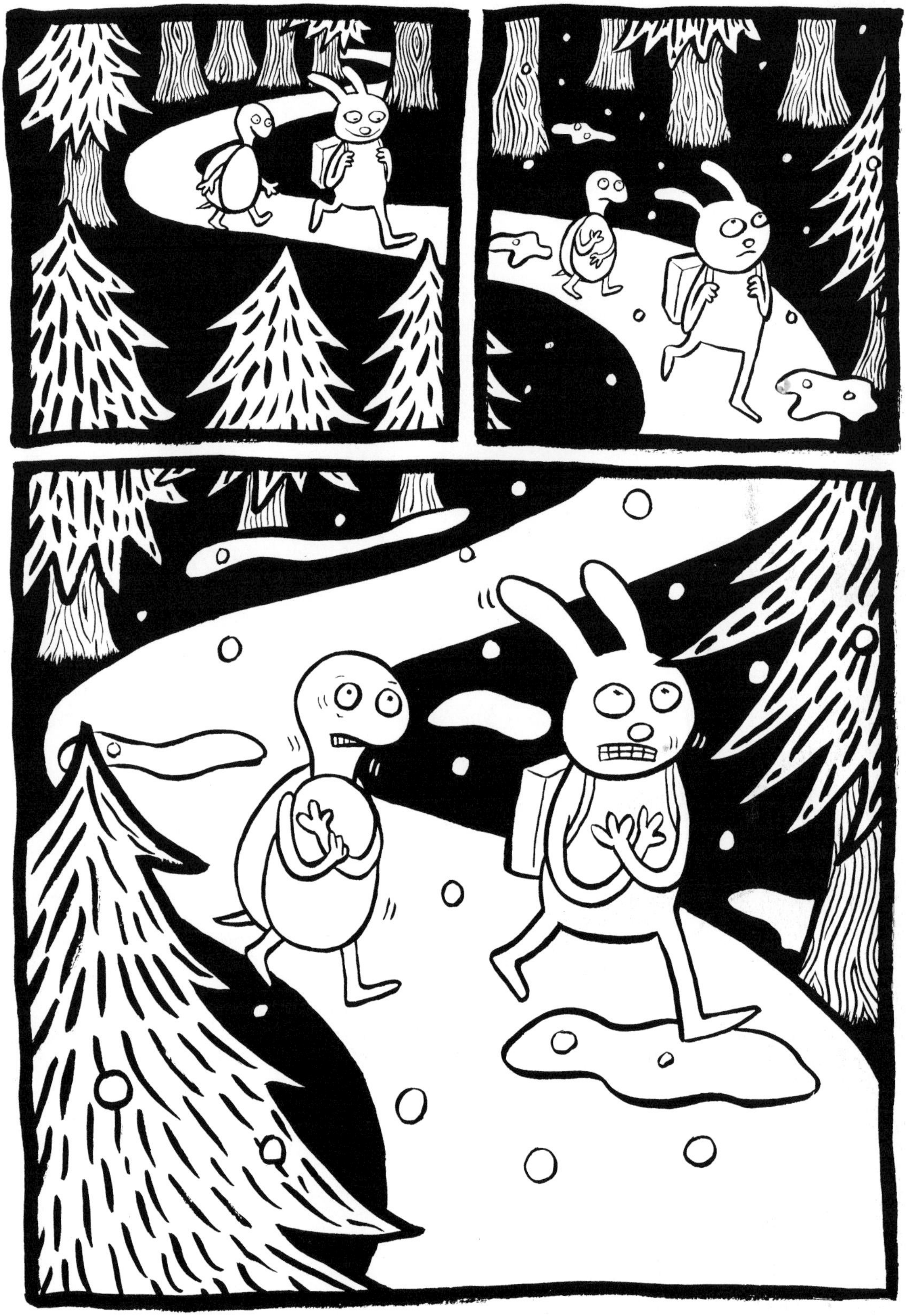

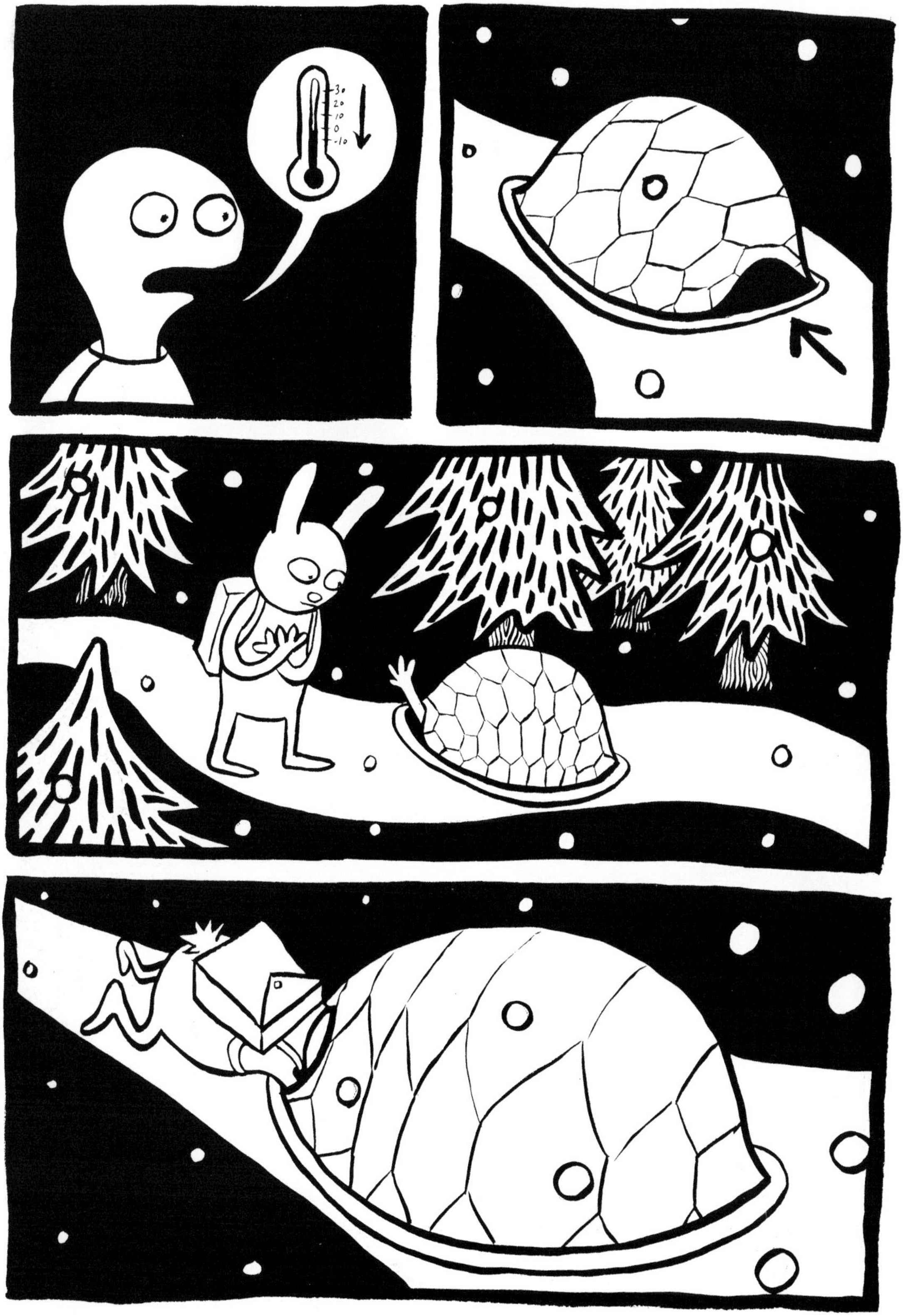
30
20
10
0
-10

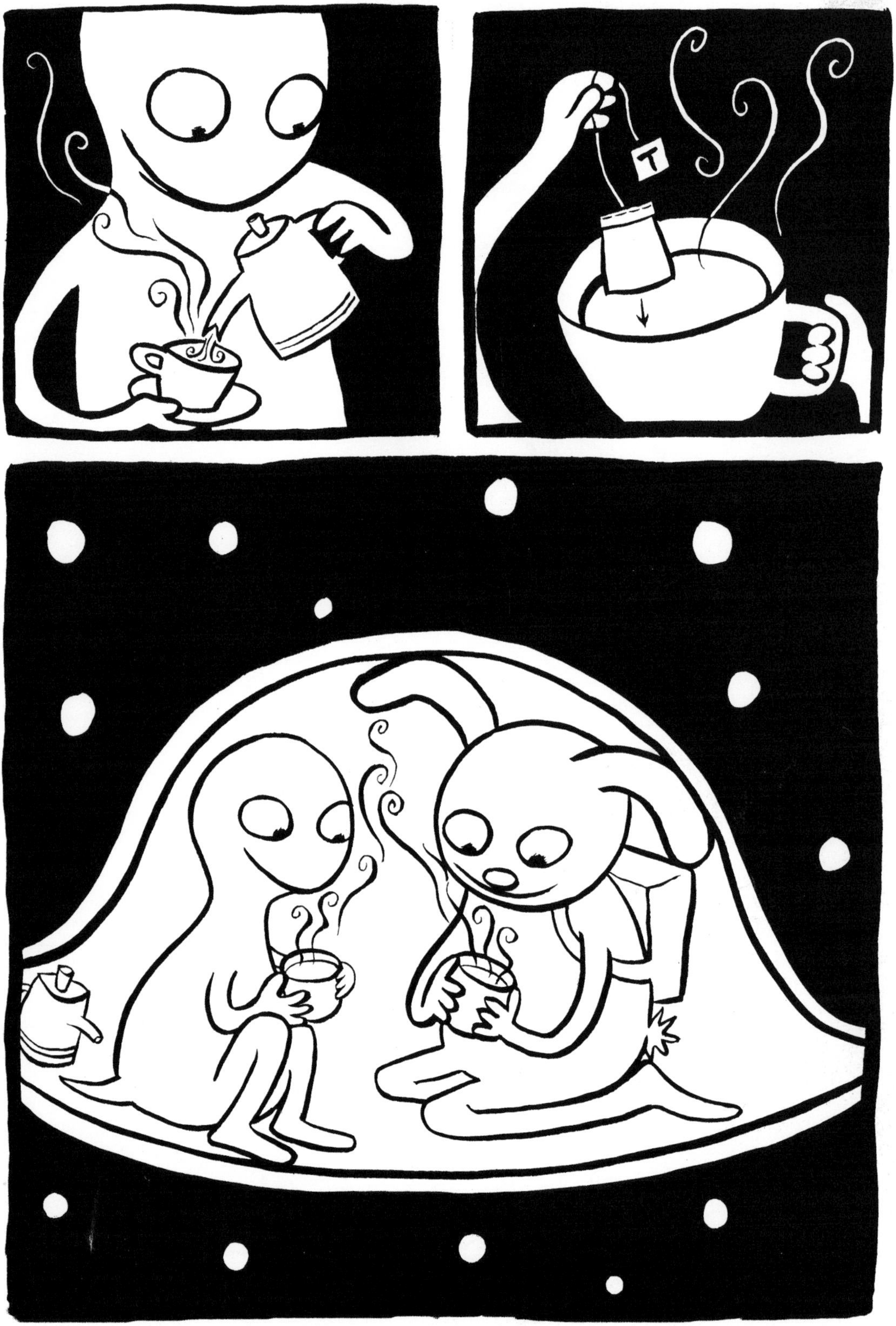
T

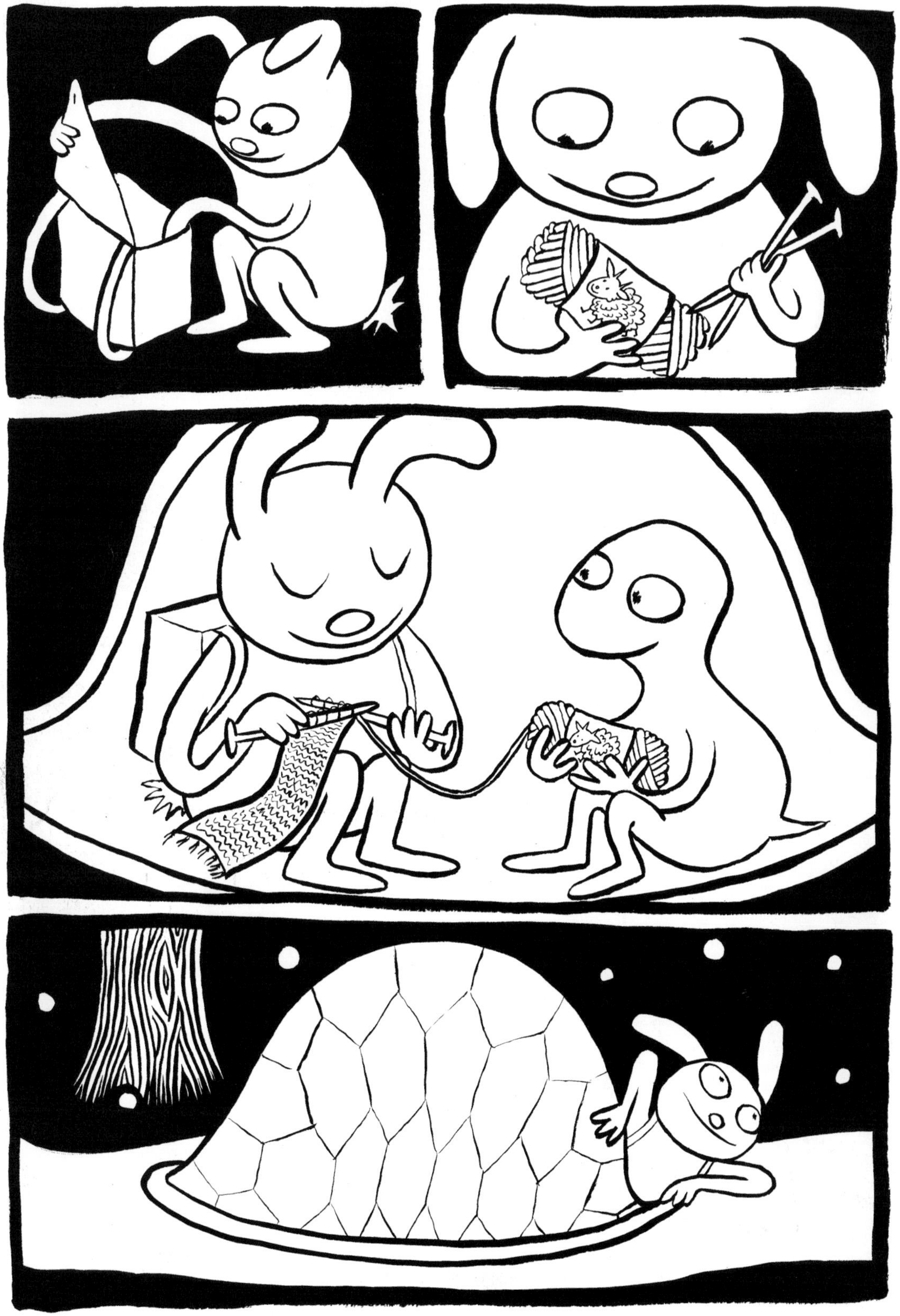

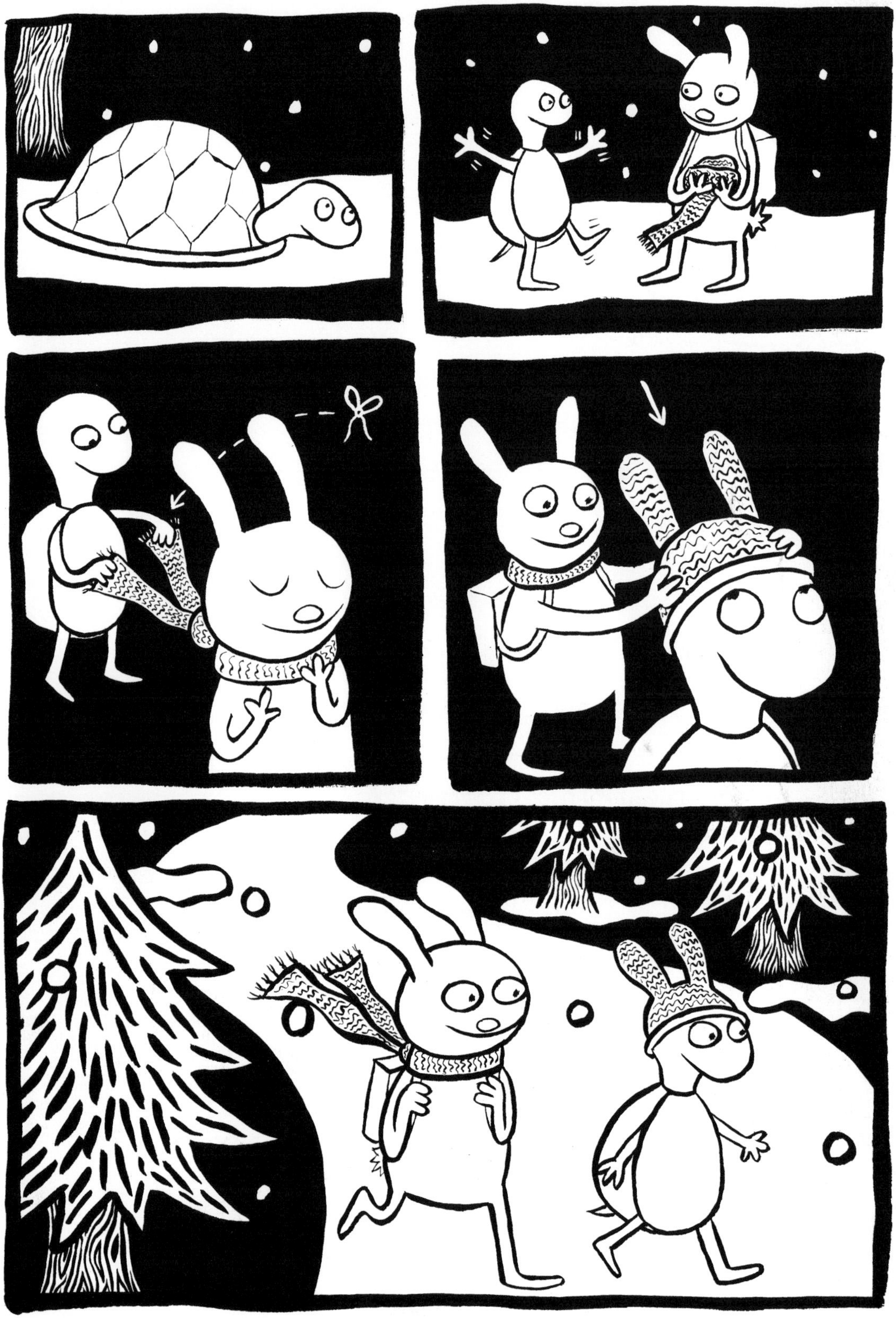

(various nibs
for a dip pen)

The Dinner Guest, February 2001
   This was my very first comic that was
more than a panel or two. Someone must've
told me that real cartoonists use dip pens,
because it seemed important that I try
them. After this comic, I switched to using
a brush, which was a better fit for me.
Since this was my first longer comic, I
also tried experimenting with panels a bit,
which I don't do much anymore.
   I'd also add that I'm often at least
one of the characters in my comics. In
this one, I am the person, and my
Dalmatian, Violet, is the dog.

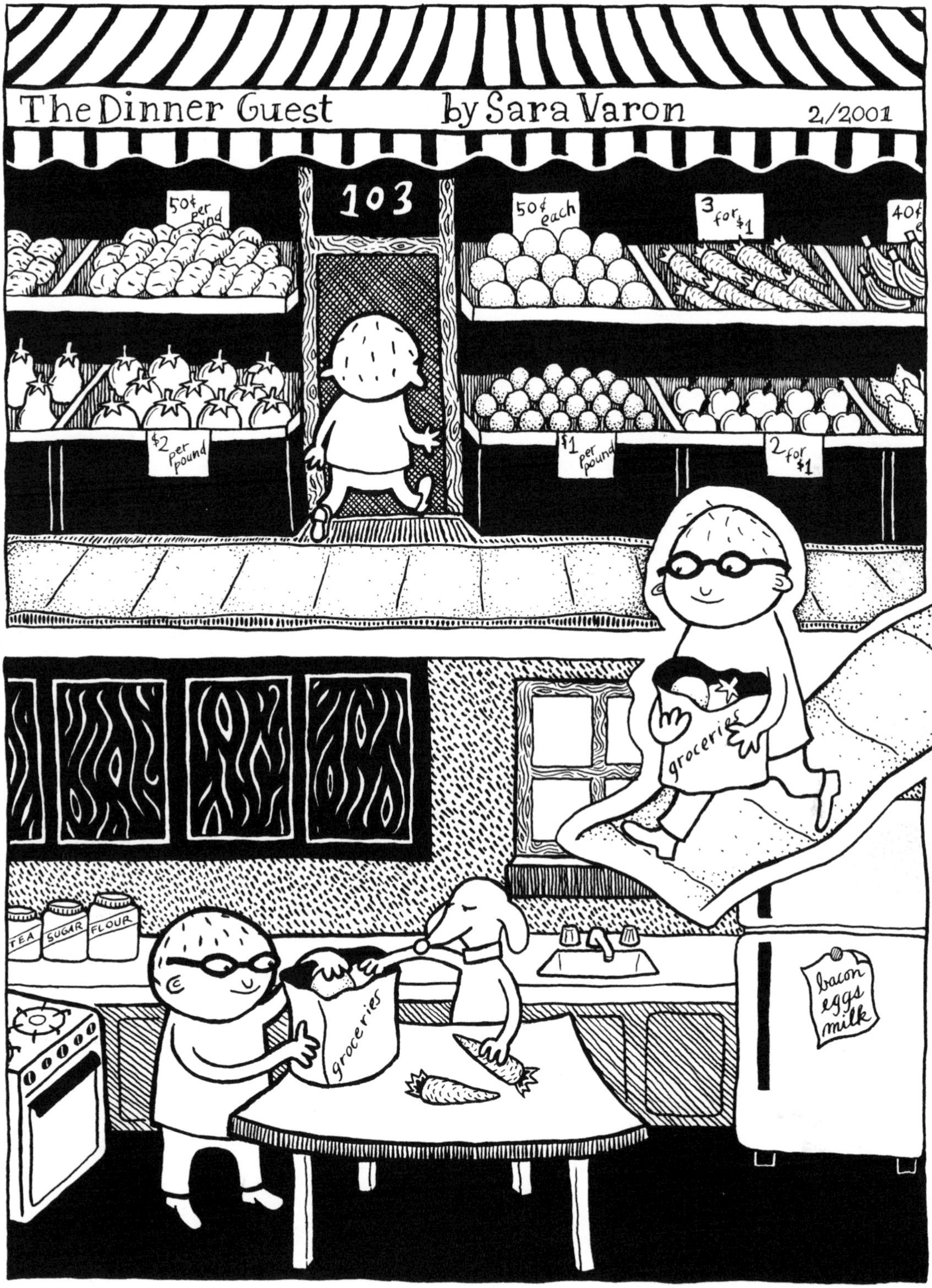
The Dinner Guest
by Sara Varon
2/2001
103
50¢ each
3 for $1
$2 per pound
$1 per pound
2 for $1
groceries
TEA
SUGAR
FLOUR
groceries
bacon eggs milk

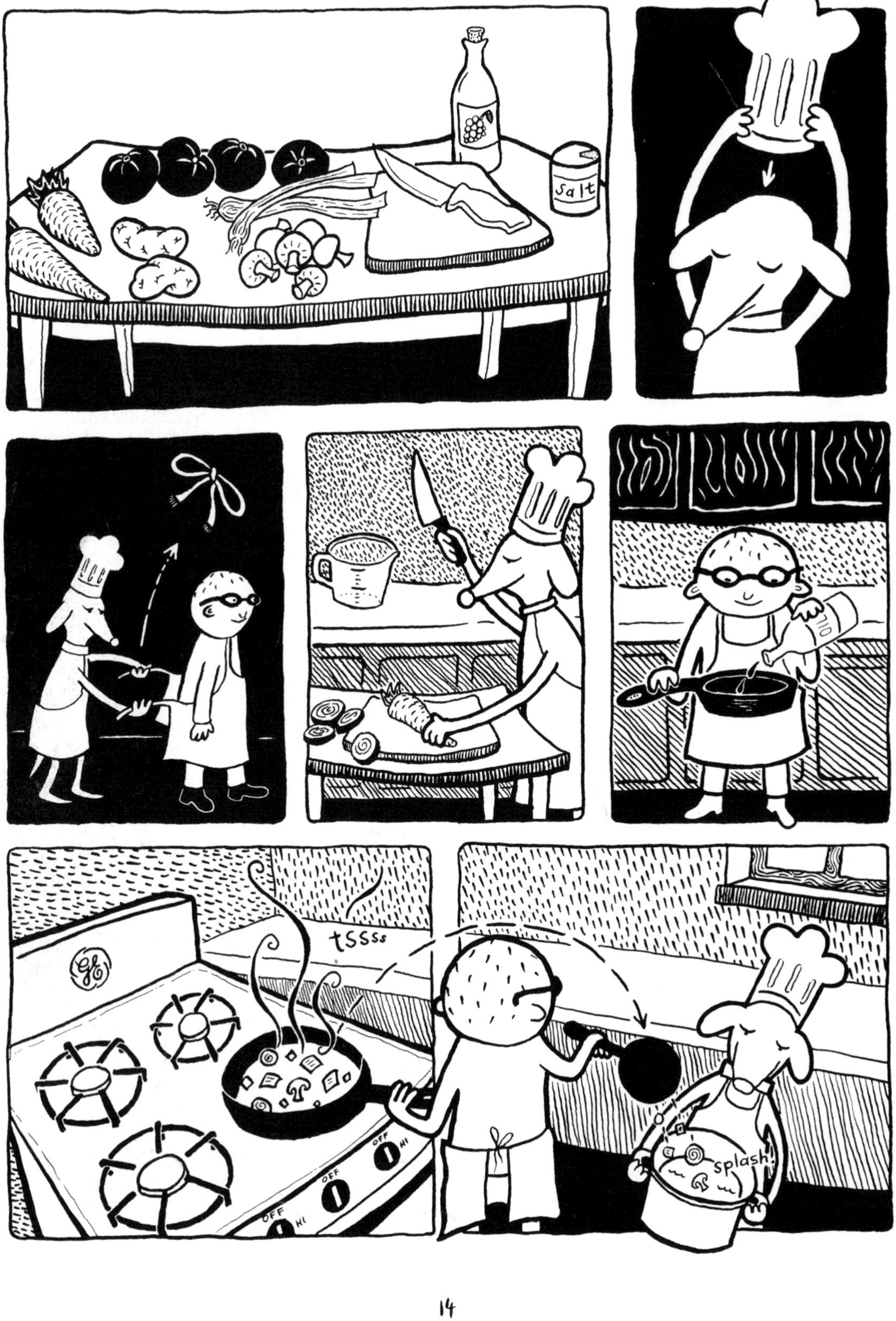
Salt
OIL
tssss
splash!
OFF
HI
OFF
OFF
HI

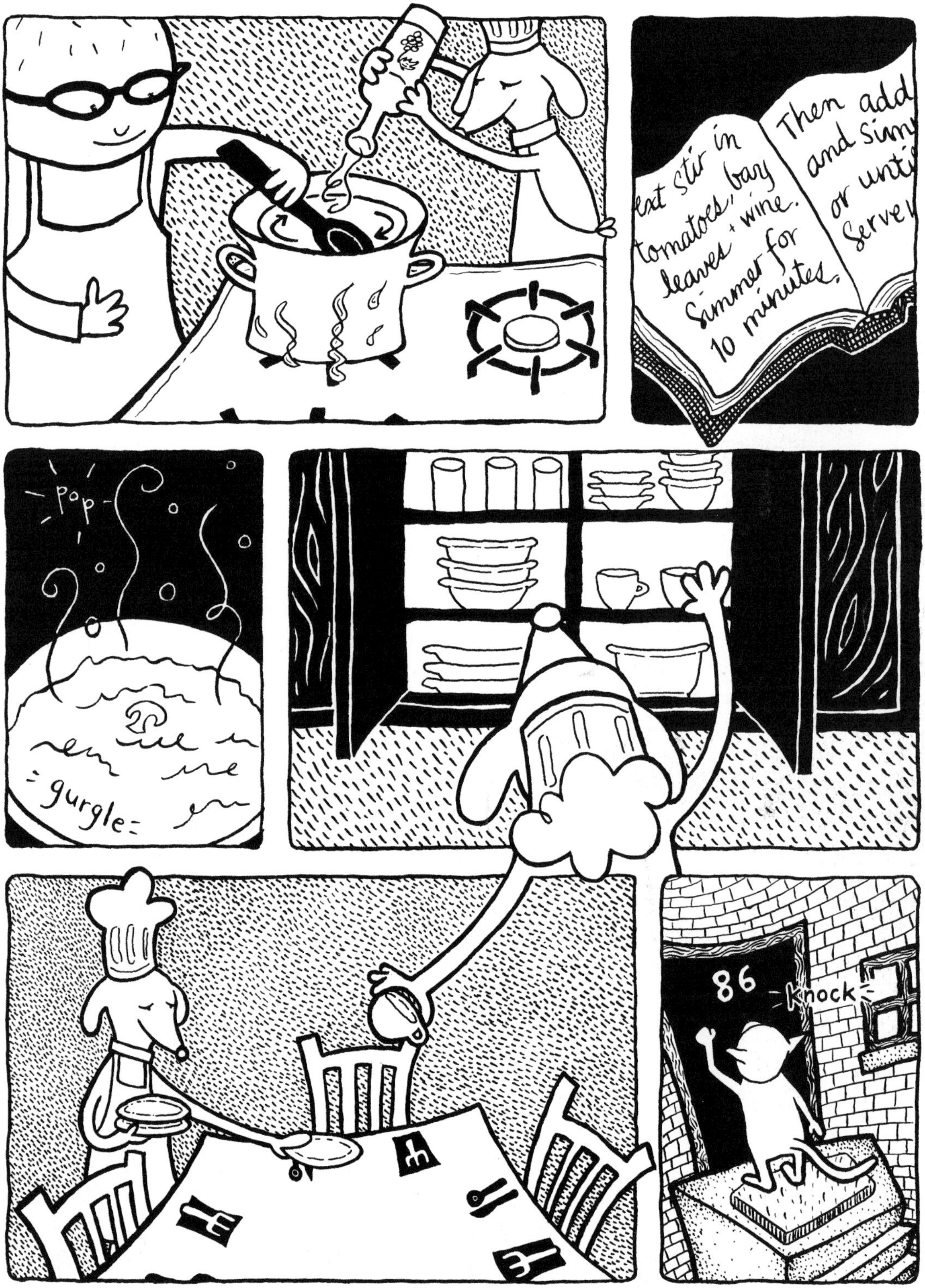
ext stir in tomatoes, bay leaves + wine. Simmer for 10 minutes.
Then add and Simm or unti Serve
pop
gurgle
86
knock

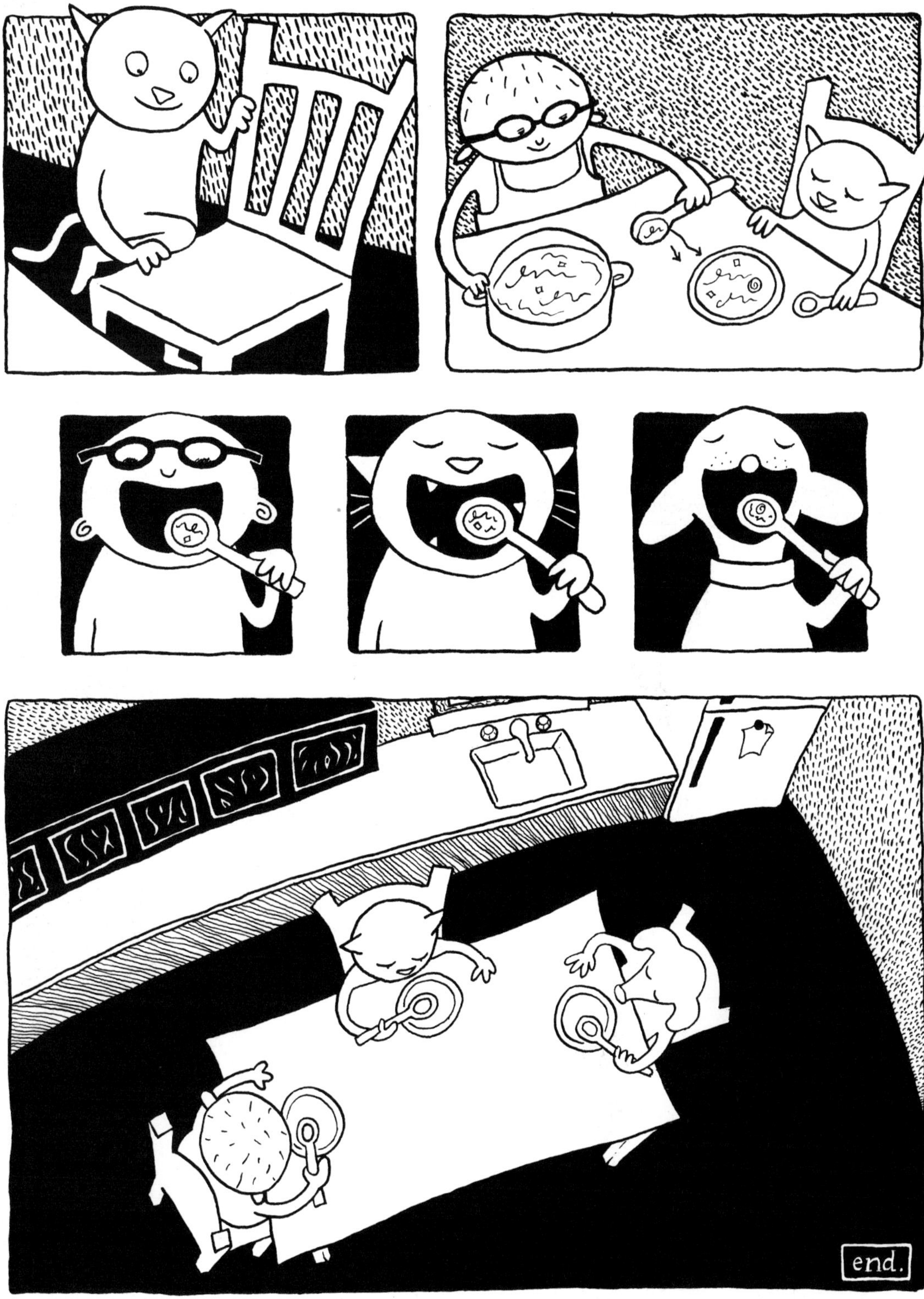
end.

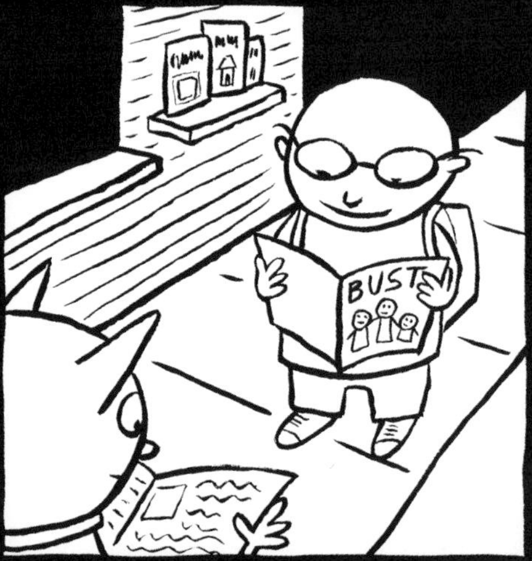
BUST

Alphabet Comic, November 2001

This was an exercise that Tom Hart put out there, back in the days when I did exercises for the sake of doing exercises. It's a reflection of the things I was doing in 2001, a sort of "day in the life." I see the magazines I was reading at the time. (There were so many great magazines back then.) I see the old neighborhood Key Foods Supermarket on Grand Street in Williamsburg. In this one, I think I'm both characters—the person and the cat.

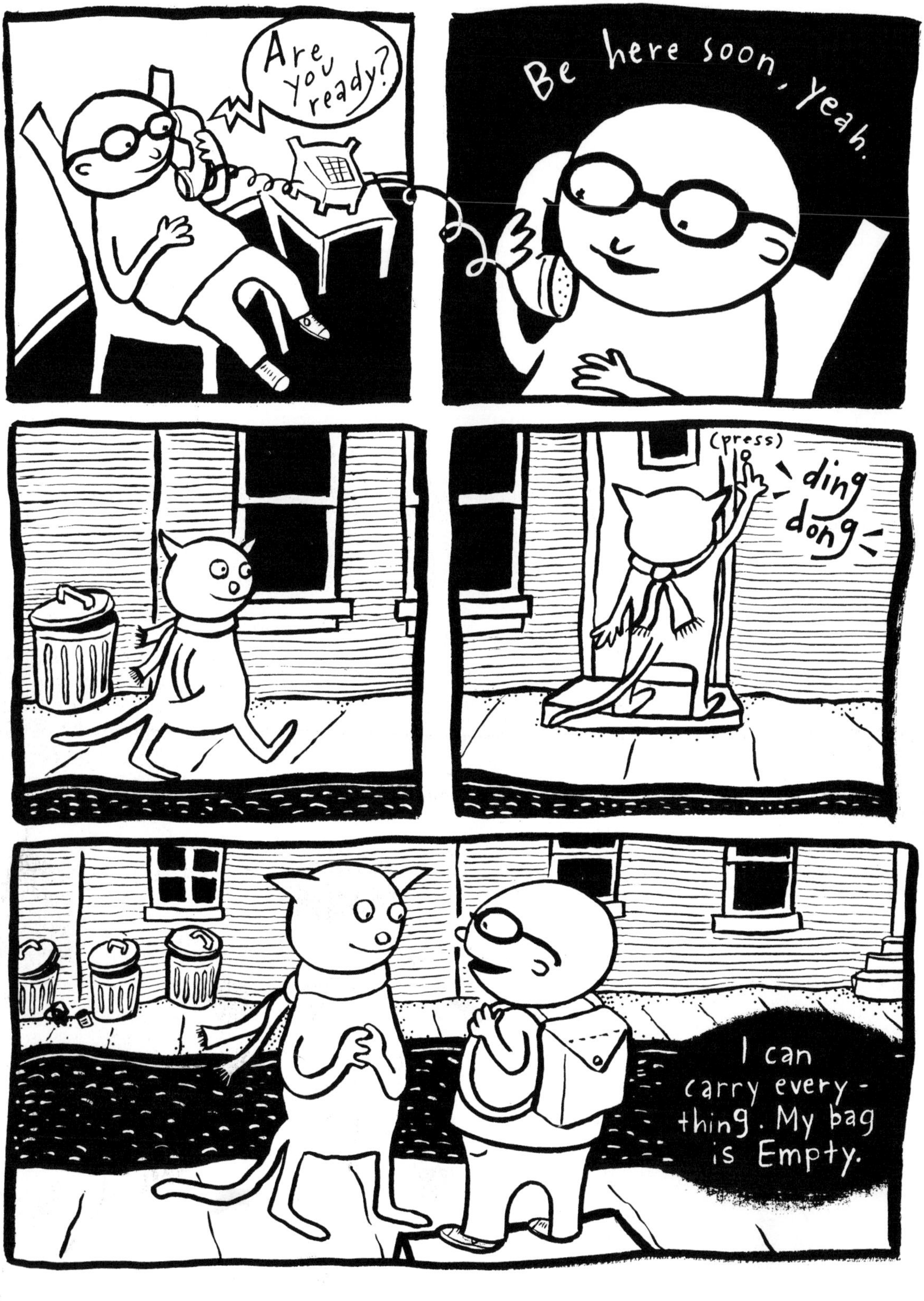

Are you ready?
Be here soon, yeah.
(press)
ding dong
I can carry every-thing. My bag is Empty.

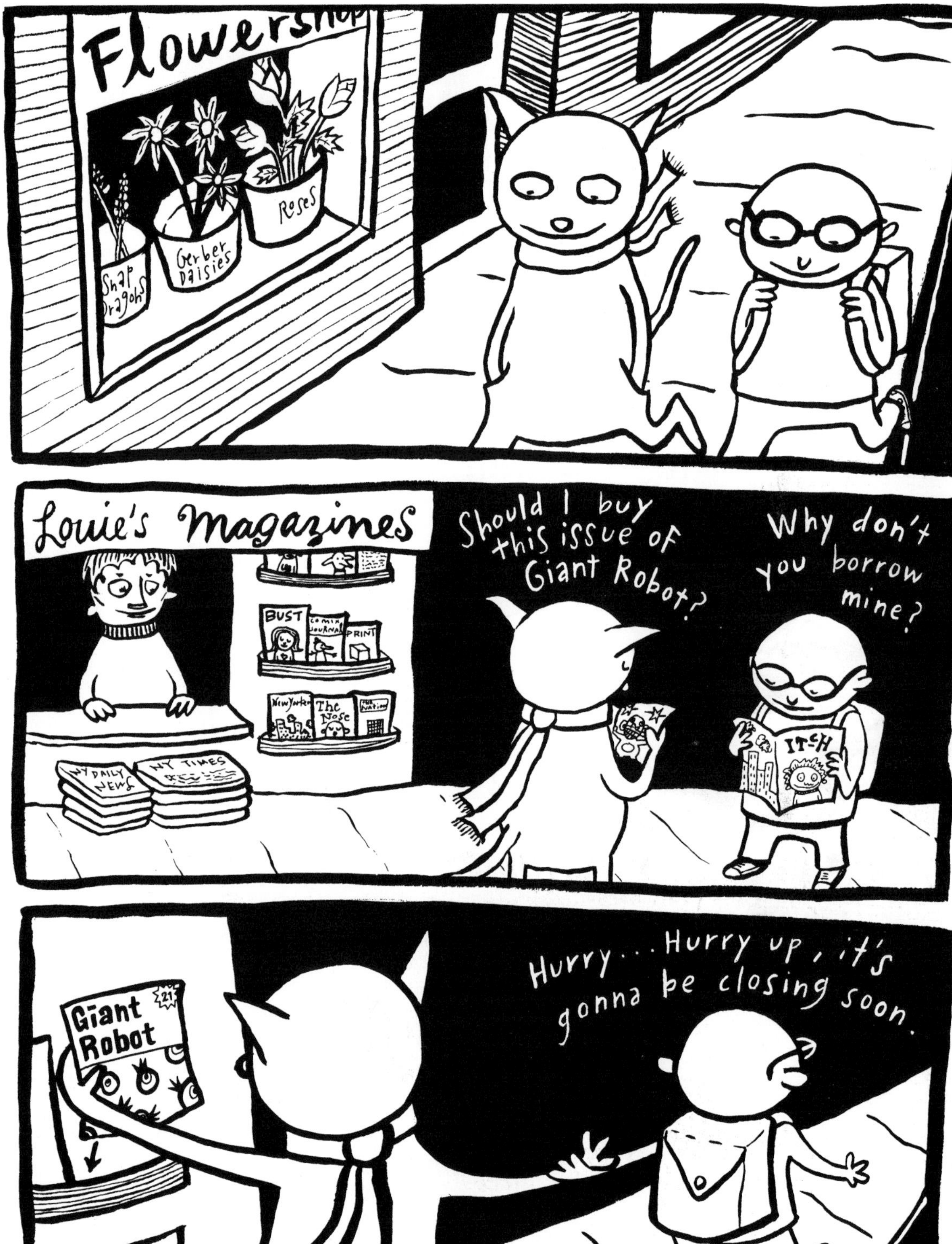

Flowershop
Snap Dragons
Gerber Daisies
Roses
Louie's Magazines
BUST
COMIX JOURNAL
PRINT
New Yorker
The Nose
NY DAILY NEWS
NY TIMES
Should I buy this issue of Giant Robot?
ITCH
Why don't you borrow mine?
Giant Robot
21
Hurry... Hurry up, it's gonna be closing soon.

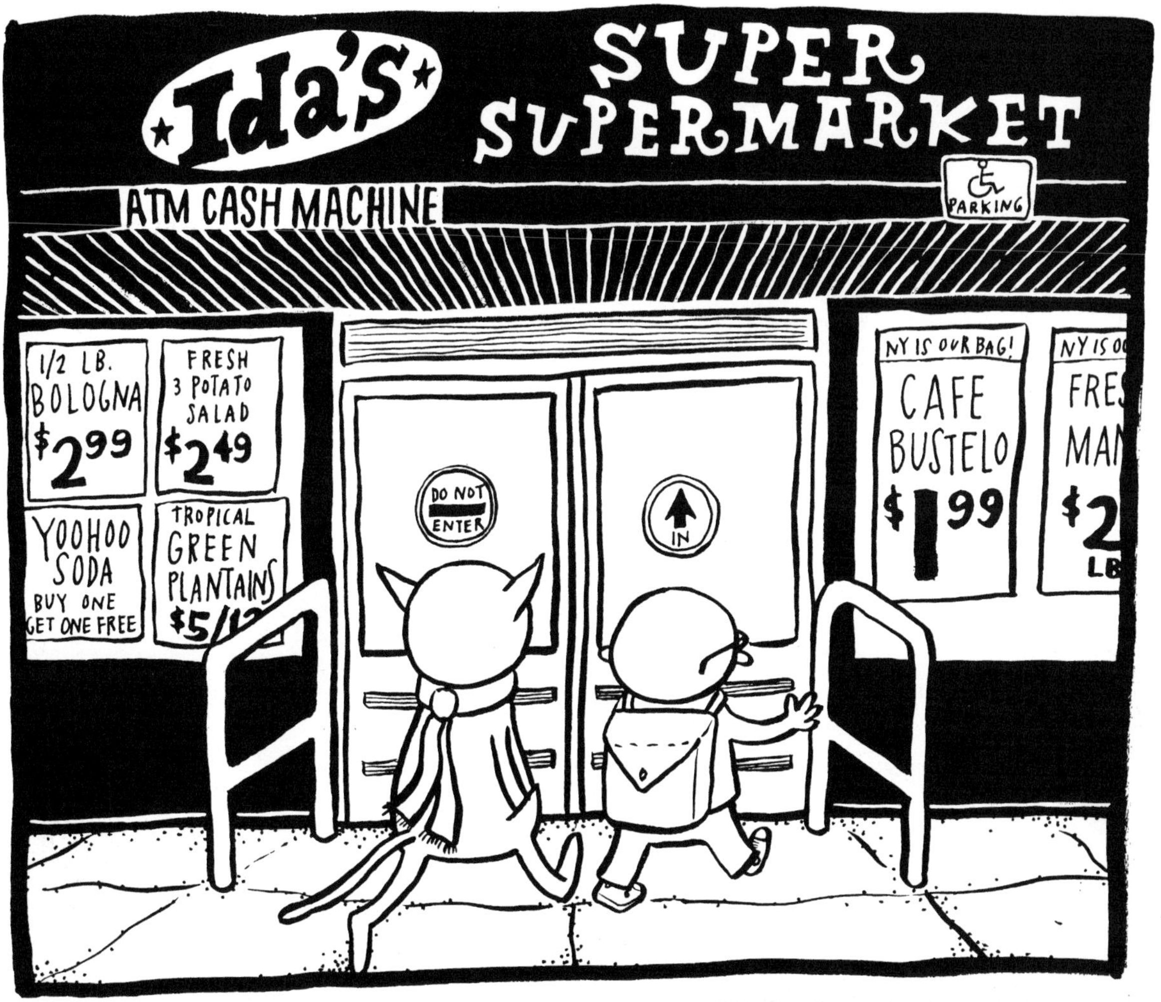
Ida's
SUPER SUPERMARKET
ATM CASH MACHINE
PARKING
1/2 LB. BOLOGNA $2.99
FRESH 3 POTATO SALAD $2.49
YOOHOO SODA BUY ONE GET ONE FREE
TROPICAL GREEN PLANTAINS
DO NOT ENTER
IN
NY IS OUR BAG!
CAFE BUSTELO $1.99

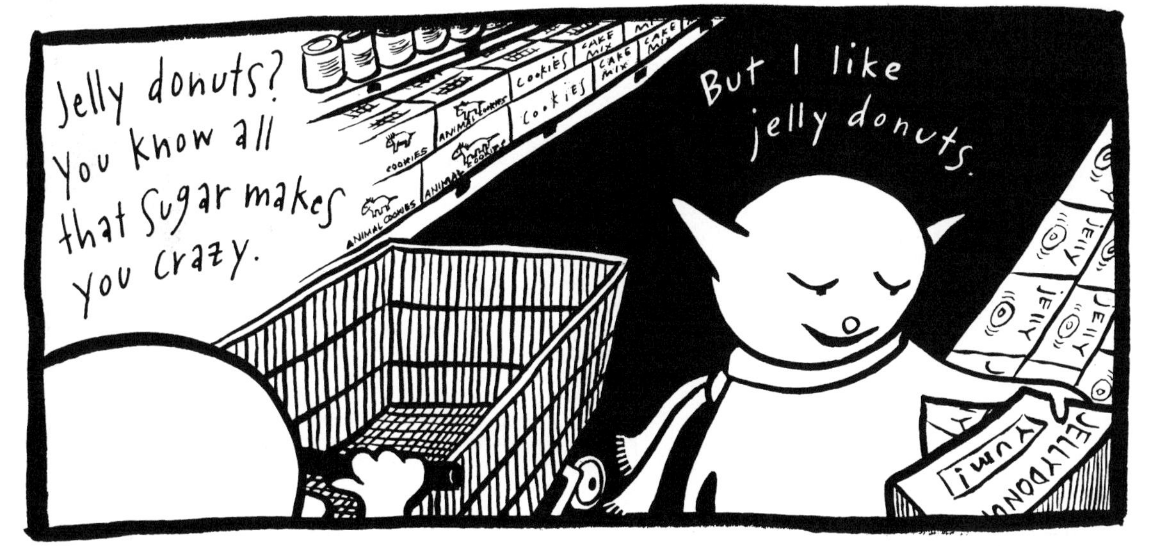
Jelly donuts? You know all that sugar makes you crazy.
But I like jelly donuts.
COOKIES
CAKE MIX
ANIMAL COOKIES
JELLY
YUM!

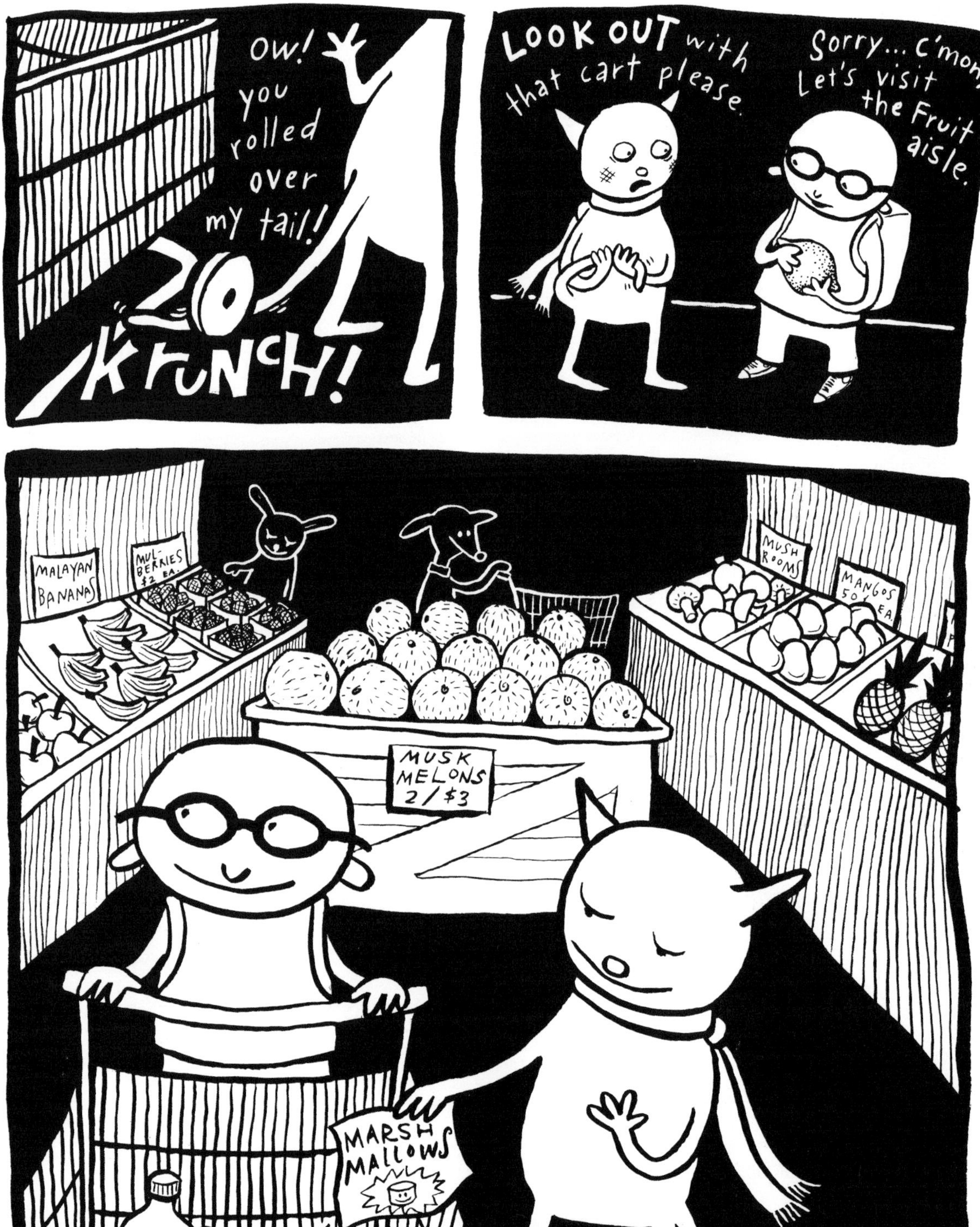
Ow! you rolled over my tail!
KRUNCH!
LOOK OUT with that cart please.
Sorry... c'mon, Let's visit the Fruit aisle.
MALAYAN BANANAS
MUL-BERRIES $2 EA.
MUSH ROOMS
MANGOS 50 EA
MUSK MELONS 2/$3
MARSH MALLOWS
MILK

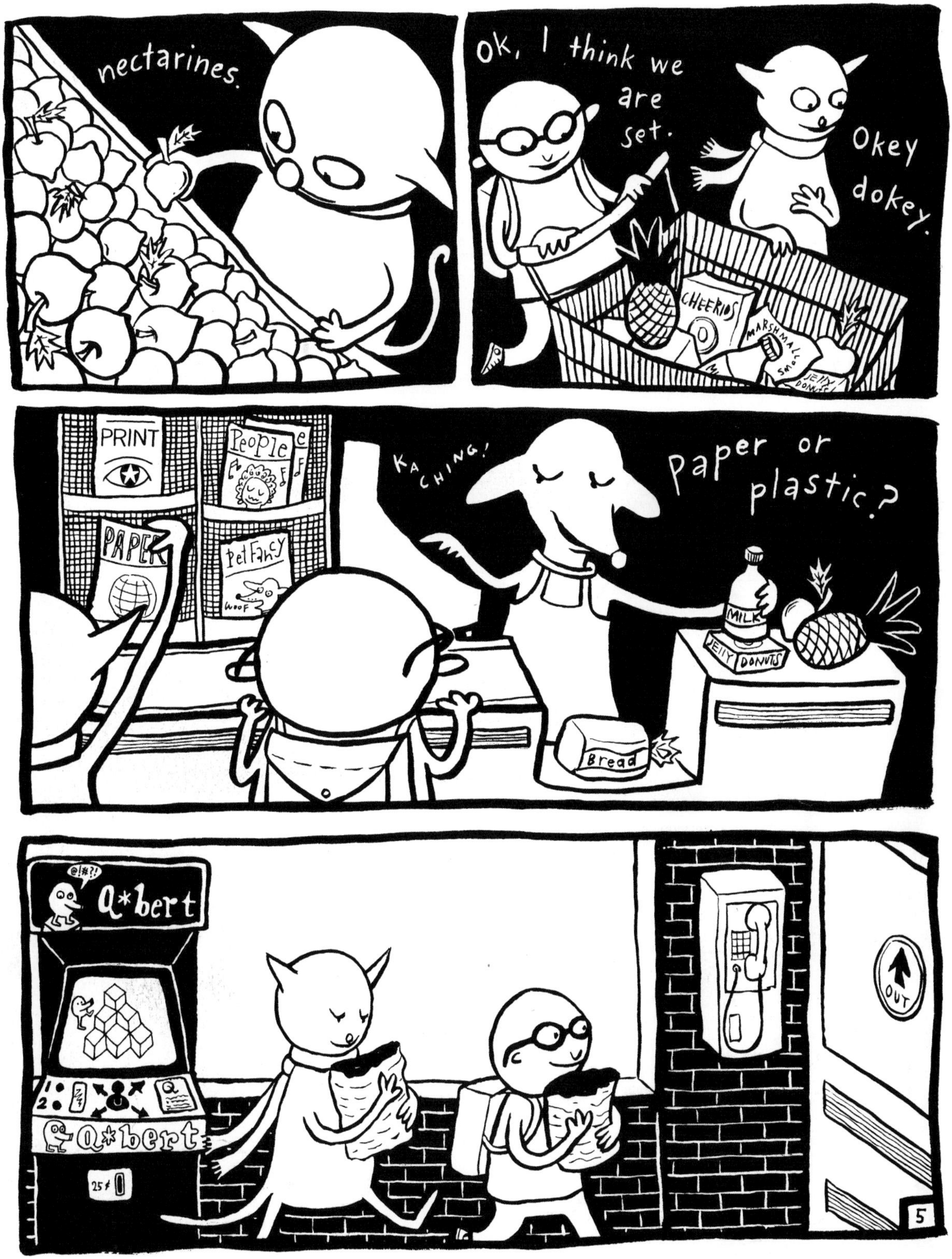

nectarines.
Ok, I think we are set.
Okey dokey.
CHEERIOS
PRINT
People
PAPER
Pet Fancy
WOOF
KA CHING!
paper or plastic?
MILK
JELLY DONUTS
Bread
@!#?!
Q*bert
Q*bert
25¢
OUT
5

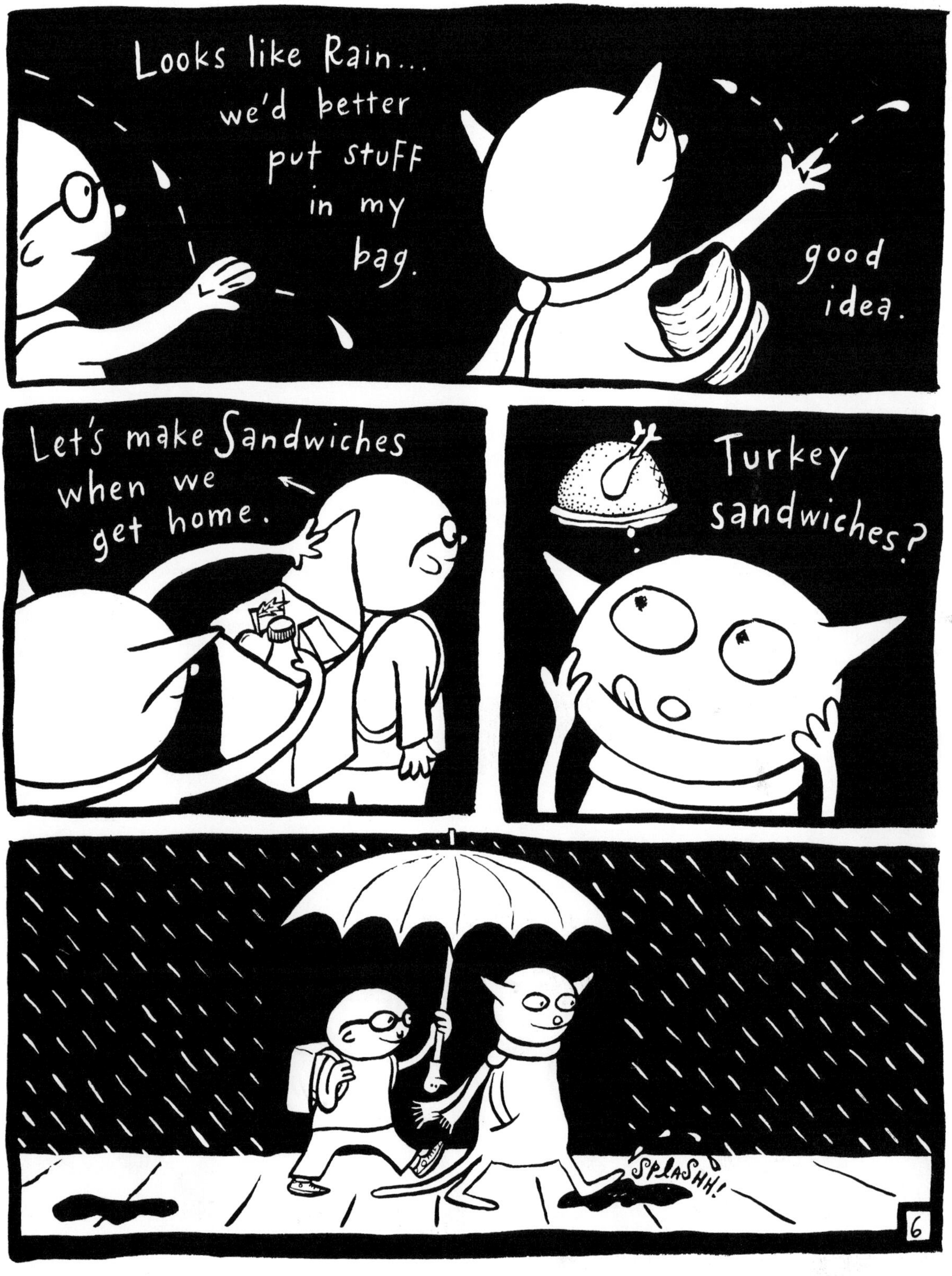
Looks like Rain... we'd better put stuff in my bag.
good idea.
Let's make Sandwiches when we get home.
Turkey sandwiches?
SPLASHH!
6

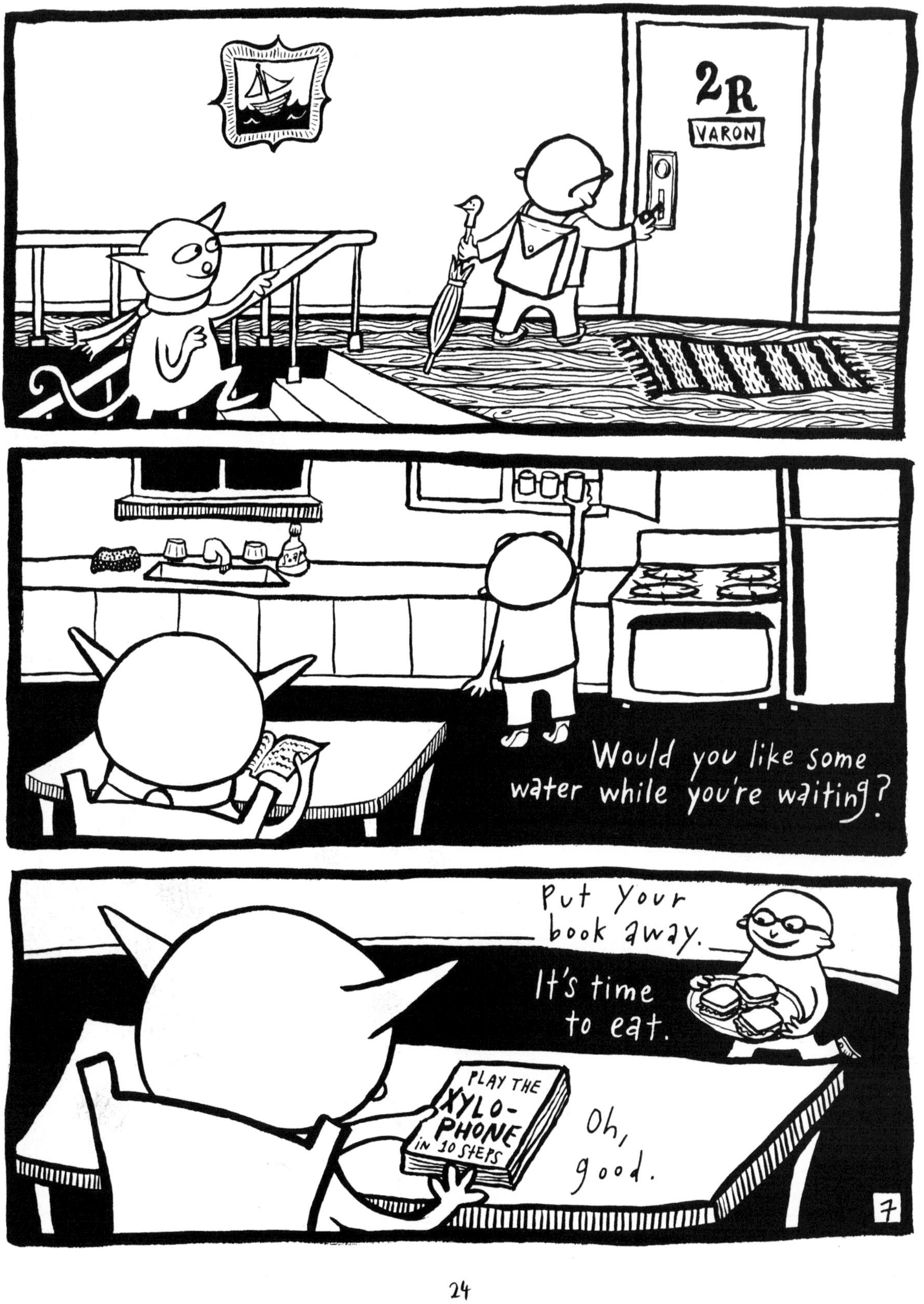
2R
VARON
Would you like some water while you're waiting?
Put your book away.
It's time to eat.
PLAY THE XYLO-PHONE IN 10 STEPS
Oh, good.
7

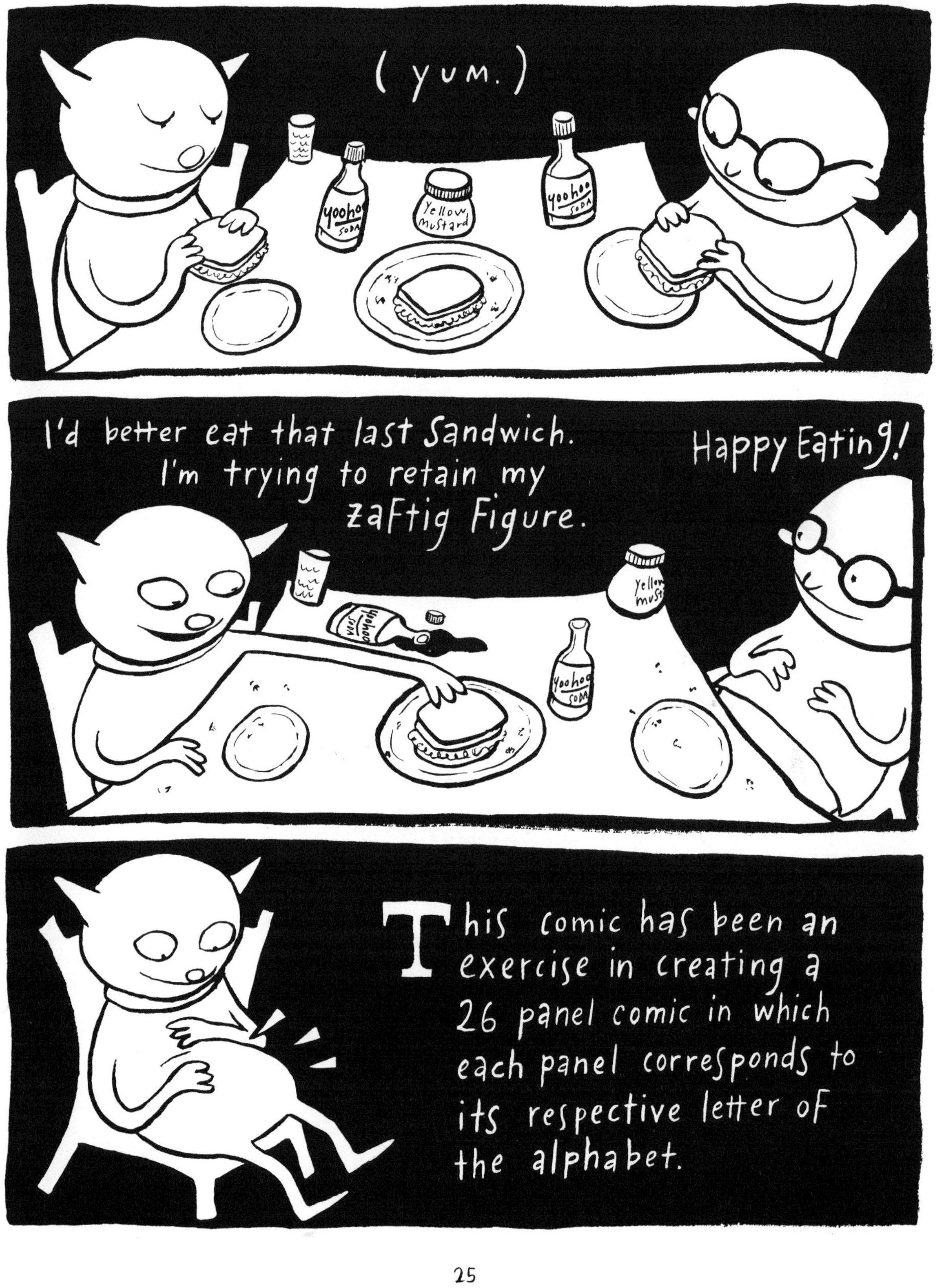
(yum.)
yoohoo SODA
Yellow Mustard
yoohoo SODA
I'd better eat that last Sandwich. I'm trying to retain my zaftig Figure.
Happy Eating!
yoohoo SODA
yoohoo SODA
This comic has been an exercise in creating a 26 panel comic in which each panel corresponds to its respective letter of the alphabet.

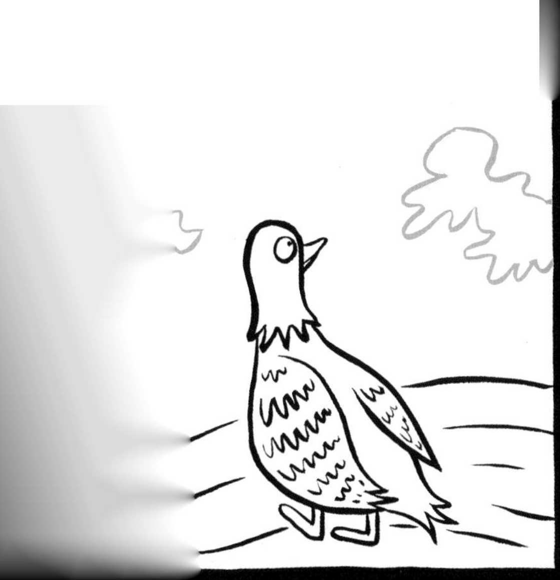

The Flight, Spring 2001

I took a continuing education comics class while in the illustration program at the School of Visual Arts, and I originally made this as a mini-comic for that class. (It was laid out differently — one picture on each of 16 pages.) I remember using my Gocco printer to print the covers, and I remember laying out all the slightly sticky prints on my kitchen floor to dry and trying to keep my dog (in her perpetual effort to be as close to me as possible) from stepping on them. I think the story was inspired by Eun-ha Paek's story of a flying elephant, which I'd seen on her website.

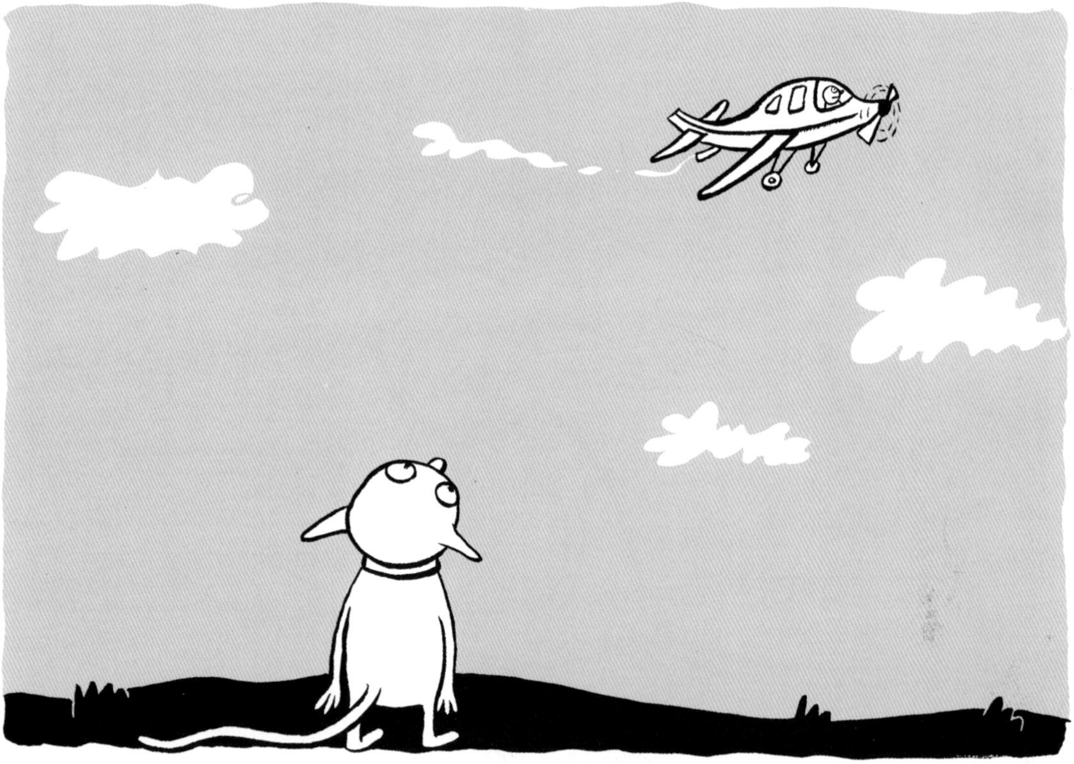

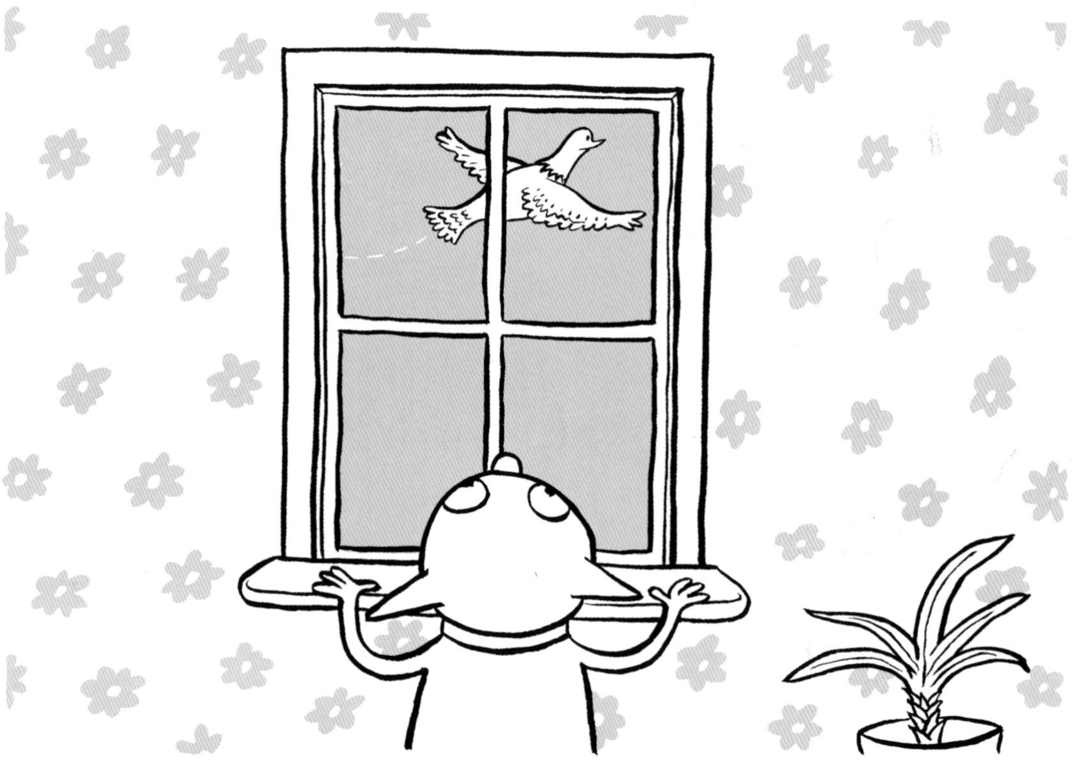

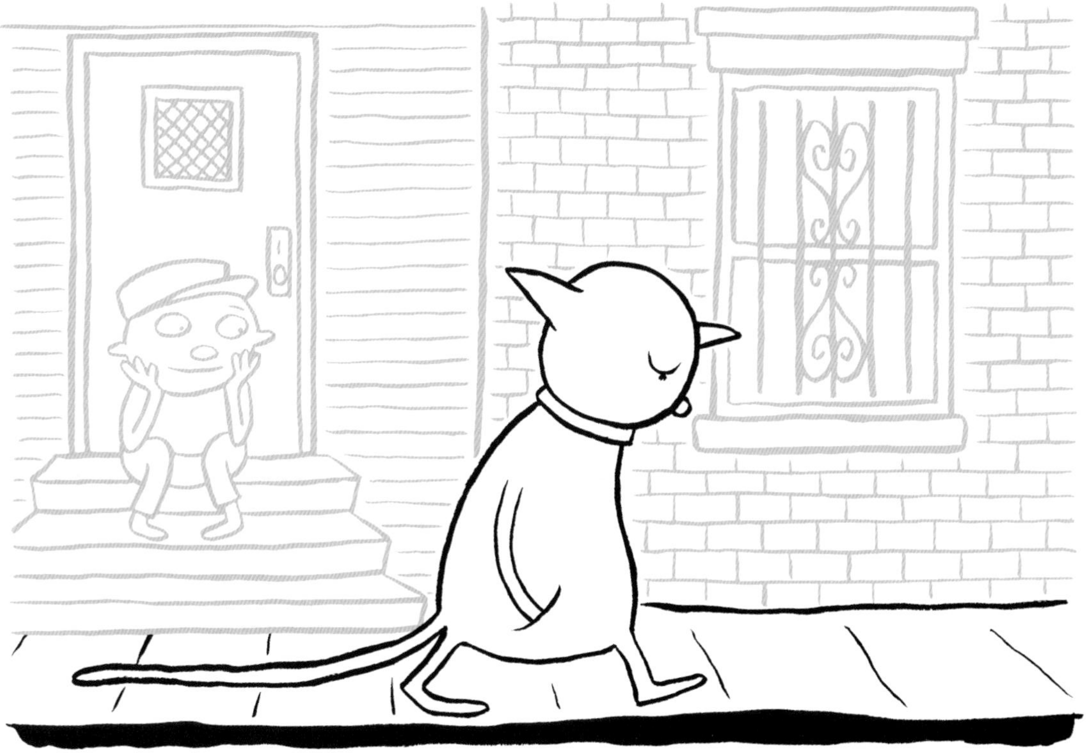

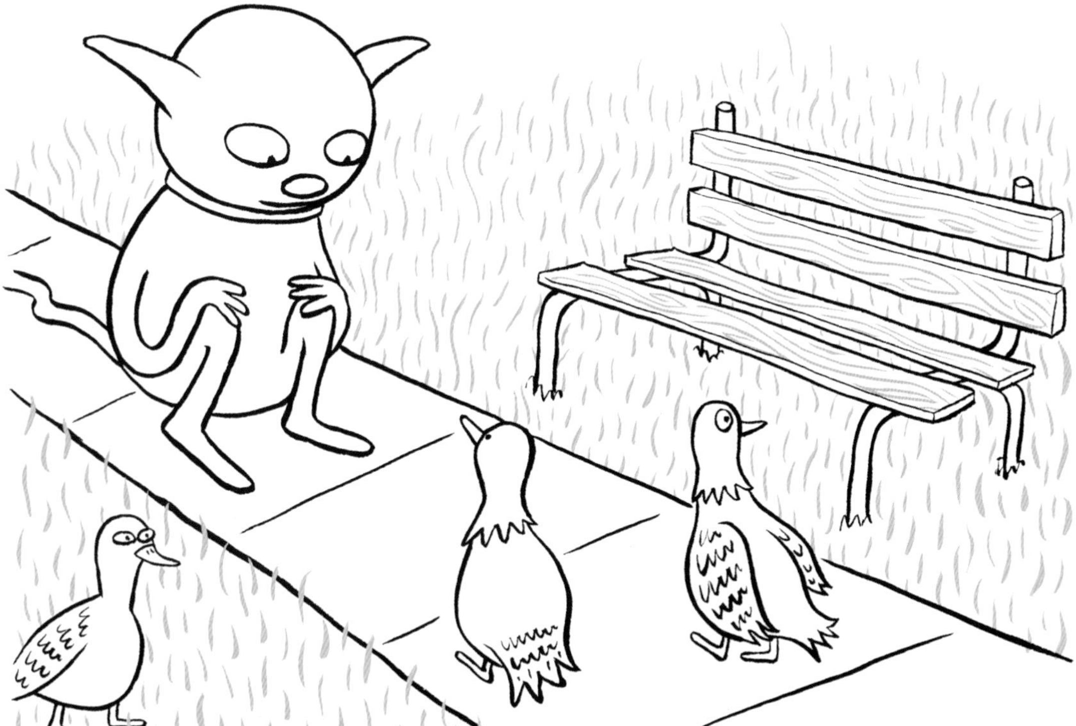

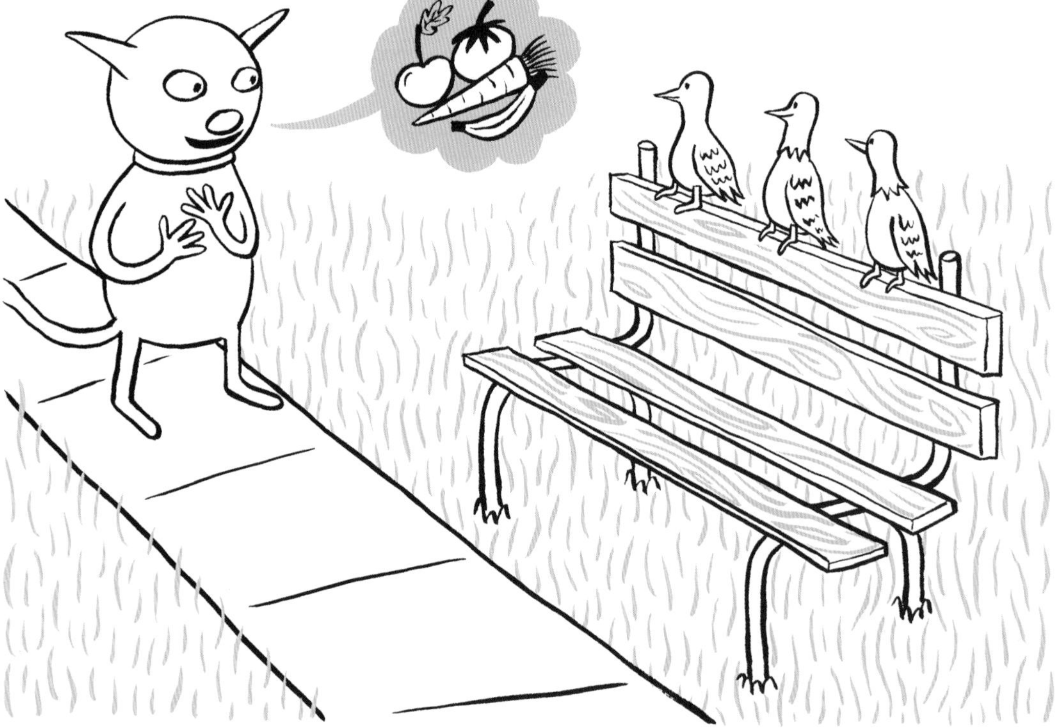

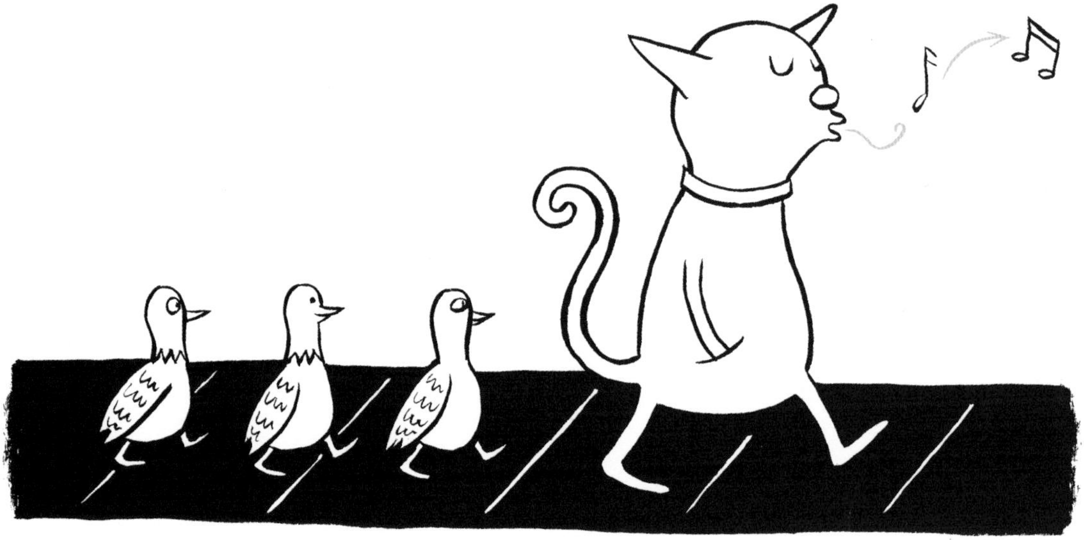

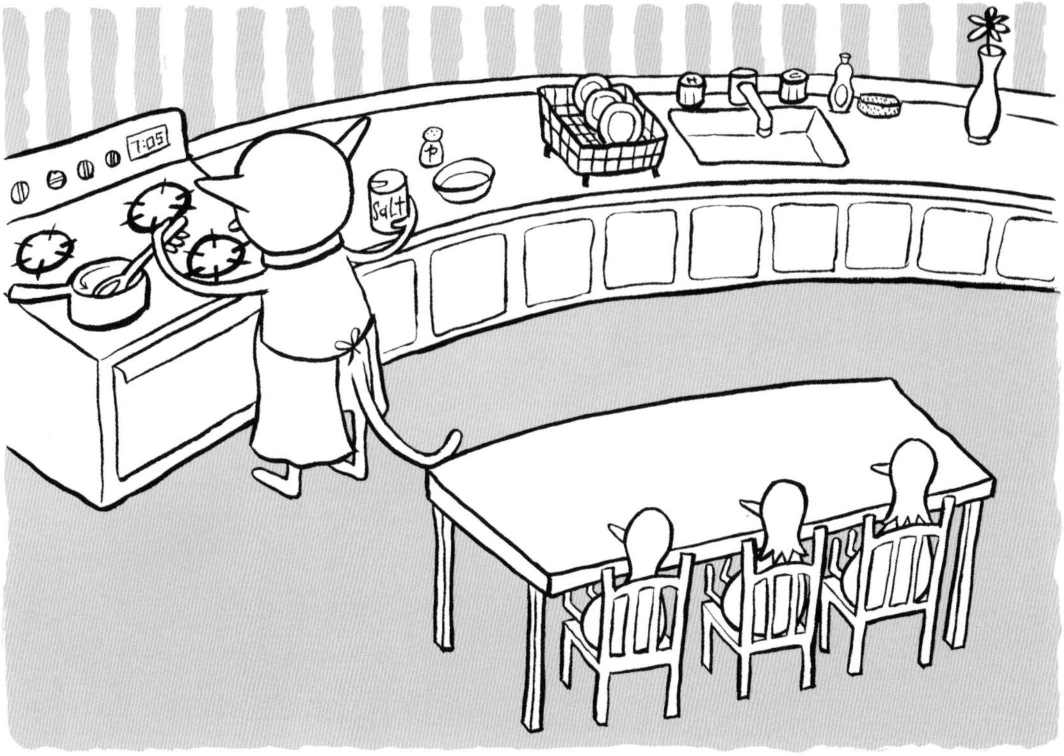
7:05
Salt

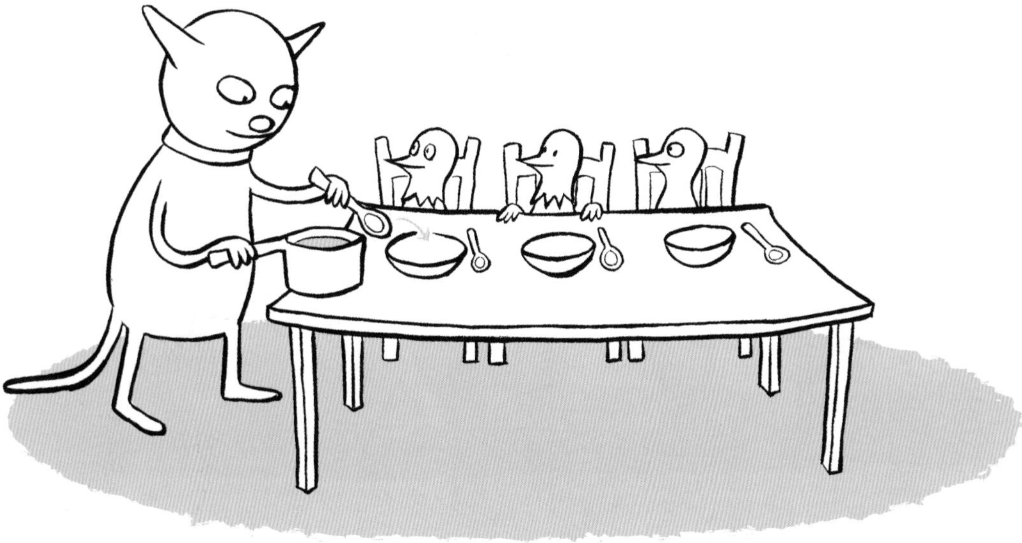

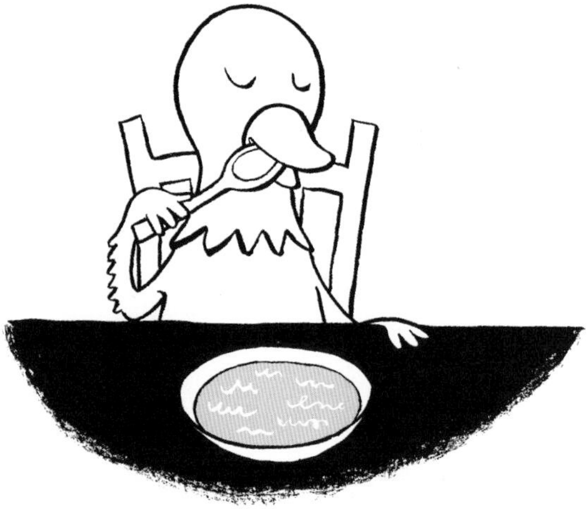

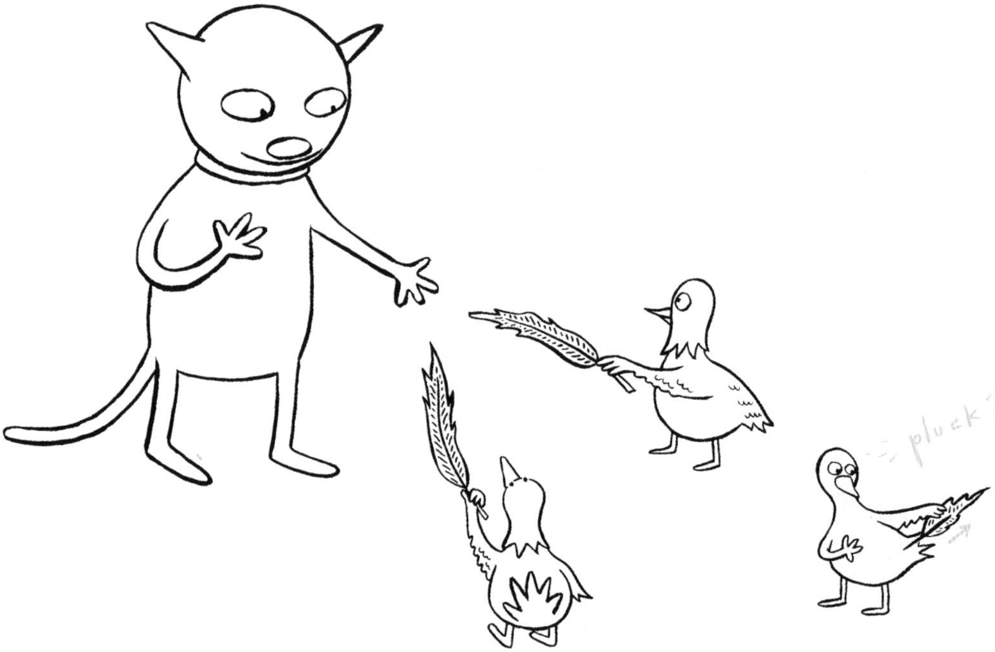
pluck

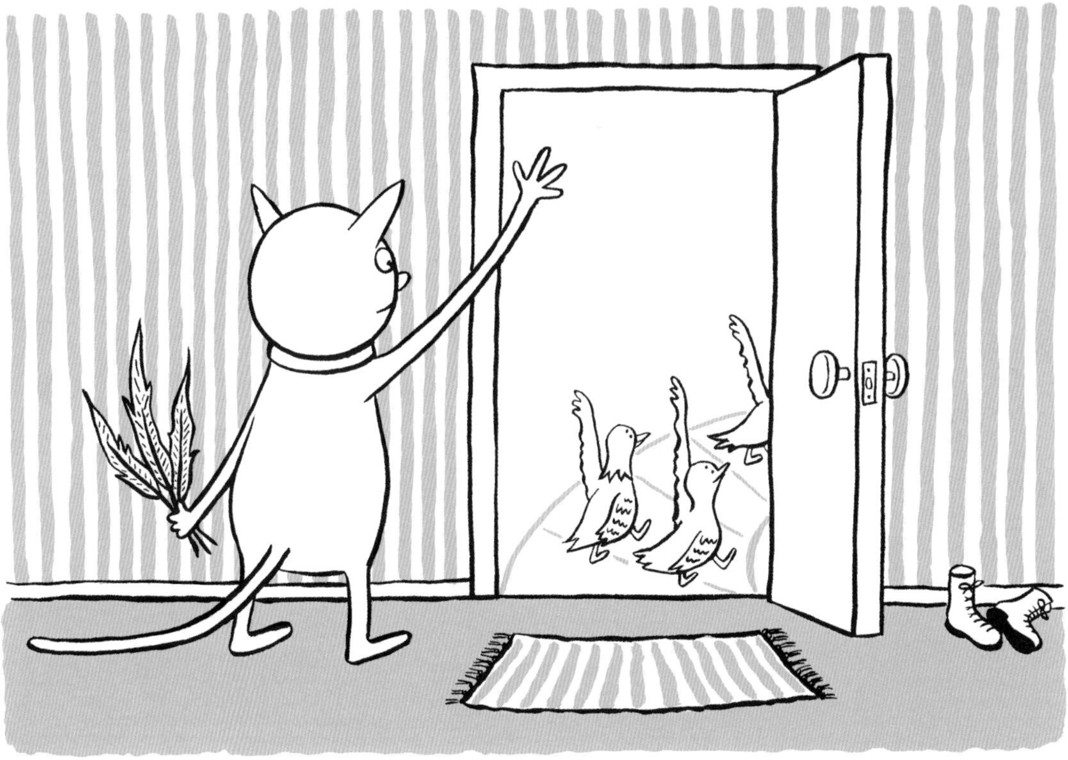

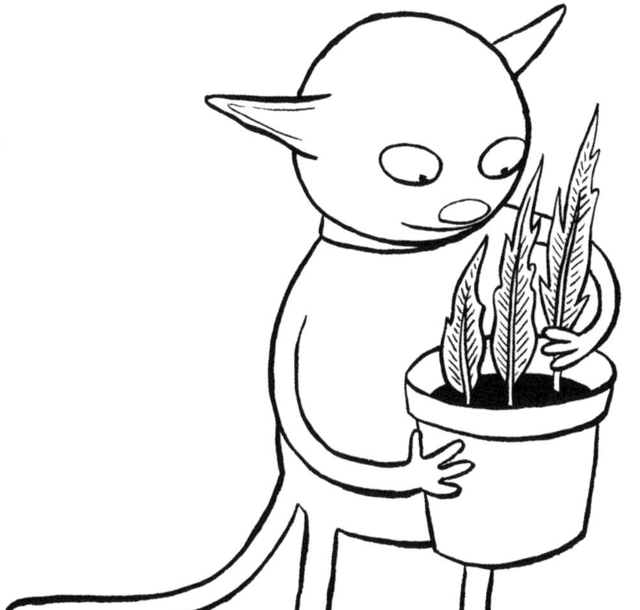

the Pie Eating Contest, October 2002

I did this one after going to the Annual Fourth of July Hot Dog Eating Contest at Coney Island. that year was kind of a turning point in the event. In previous years, the current record was 20-some hot dogs in 10 minutes. But the year I went, a skinny Japanese guy came and ate 50 hot dogs, beating the other contestants by a mile. It was a media sensation. He was suddenly a big star, and competitive eating seemed really popular.

I also remember wanting to draw a pawnshop, so I figured out how to string a (pretty random) story together featuring a pawnshop and a pie eating contest. I had no idea what a pawnshop actually looked like inside, so I picked a place on the Lower East Side to visit. I guess I was drawing all these places because I'd just moved to New York in late 2000 from Chicago, so it was all new and exciting.

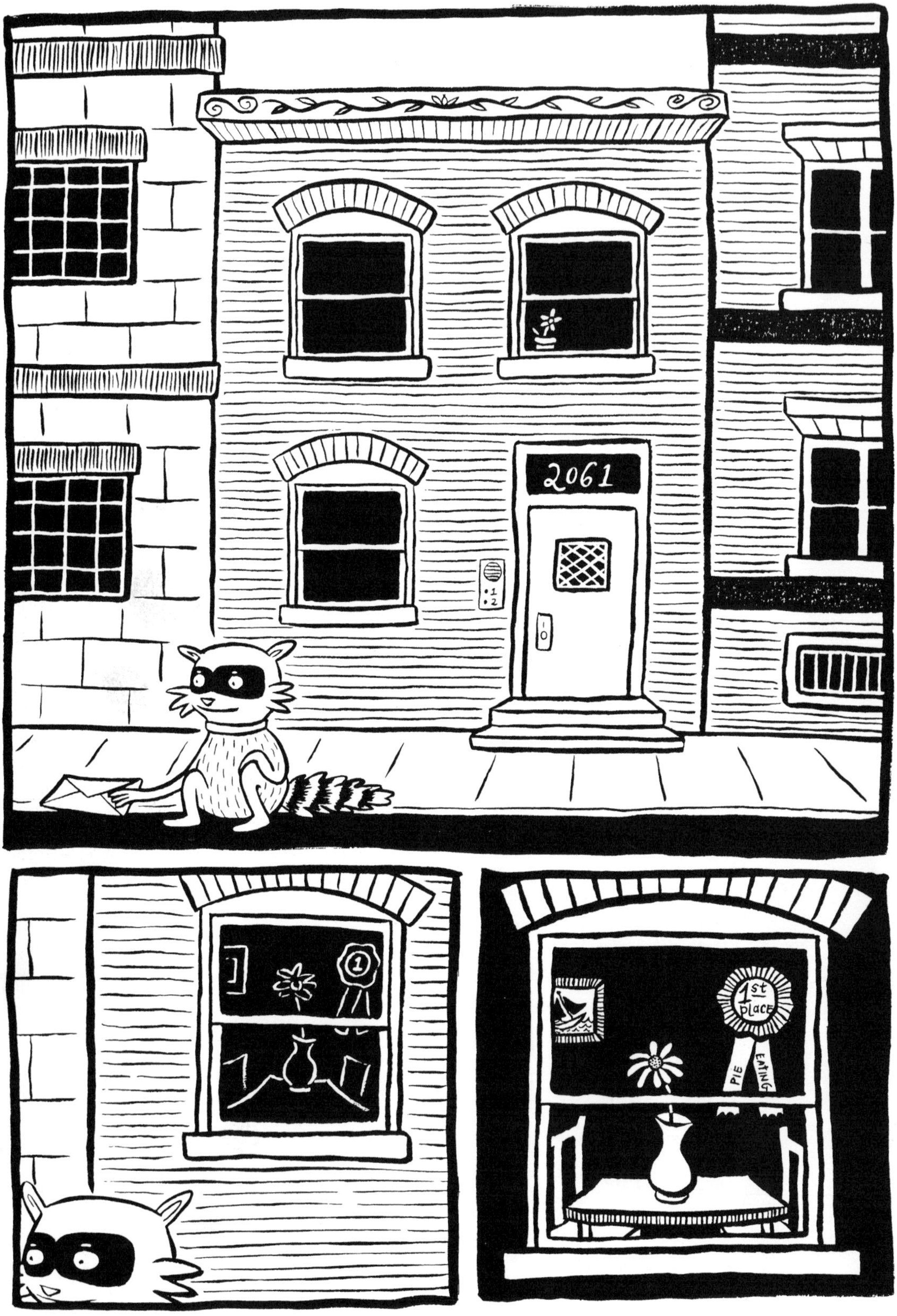
2061
1st place
PIE EATING

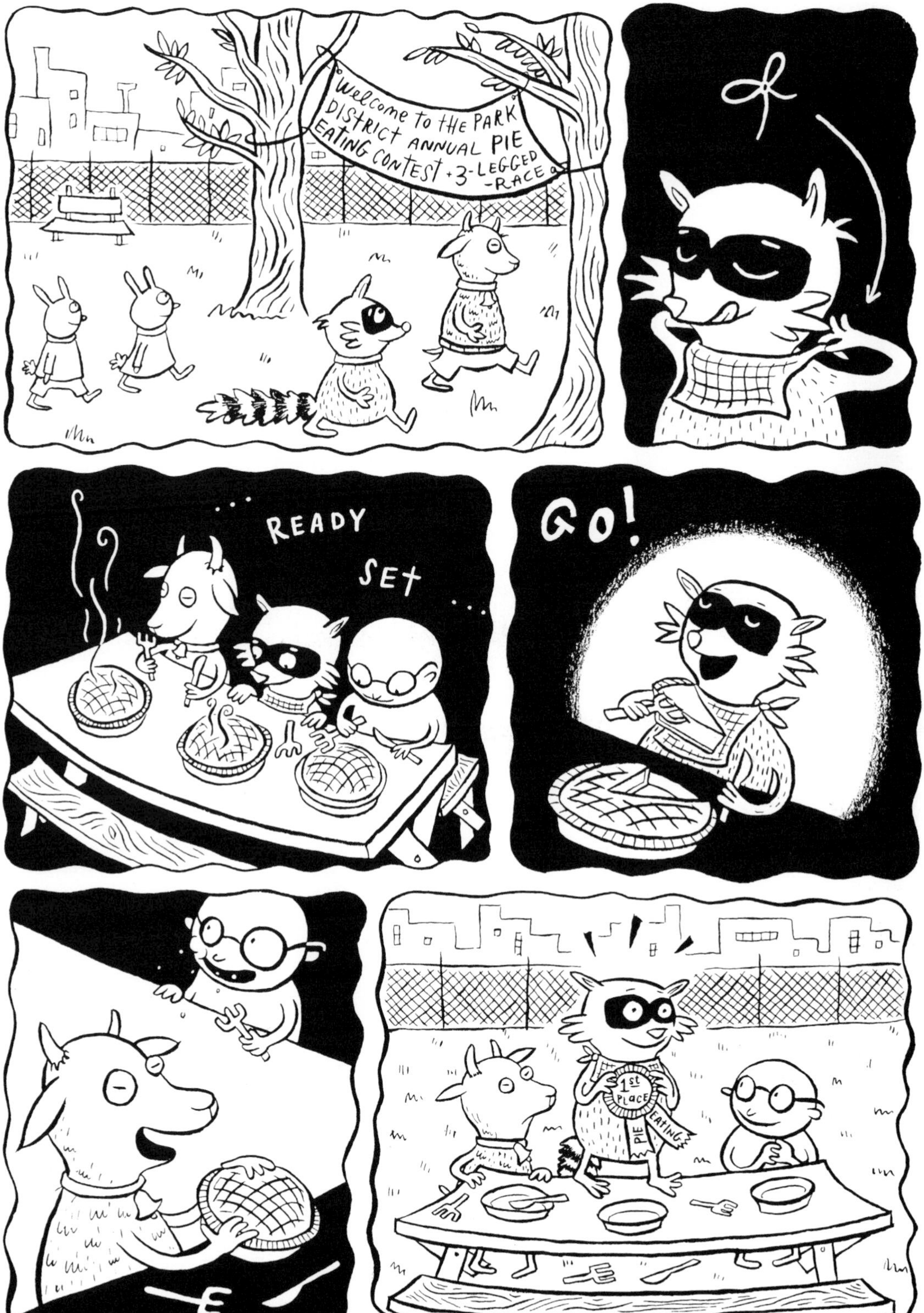
Welcome to the PARK DISTRICT ANNUAL PIE EATING CONTEST + 3-LEGGED -RACE
... READY
SET ...
GO!
1st PLACE
PIE EATING

THUNK
2061
•1
•2
2061
•1
•2
Rent (june)

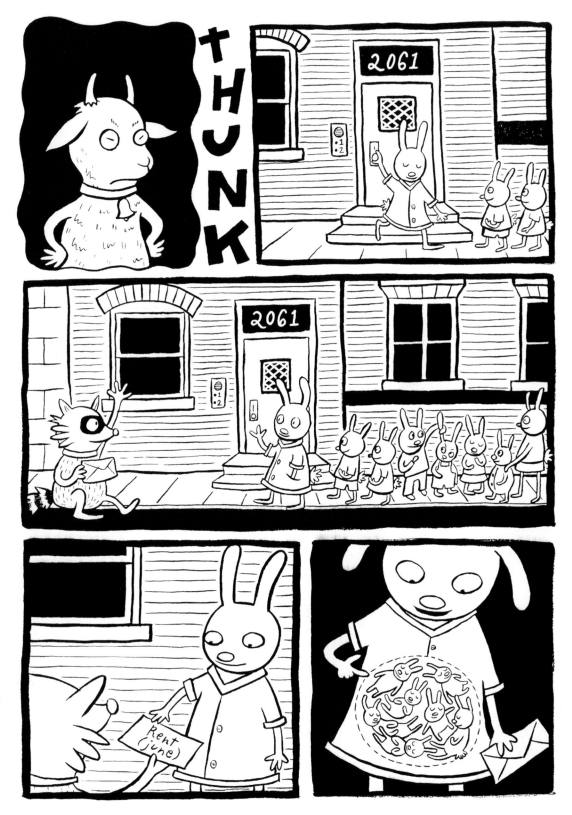

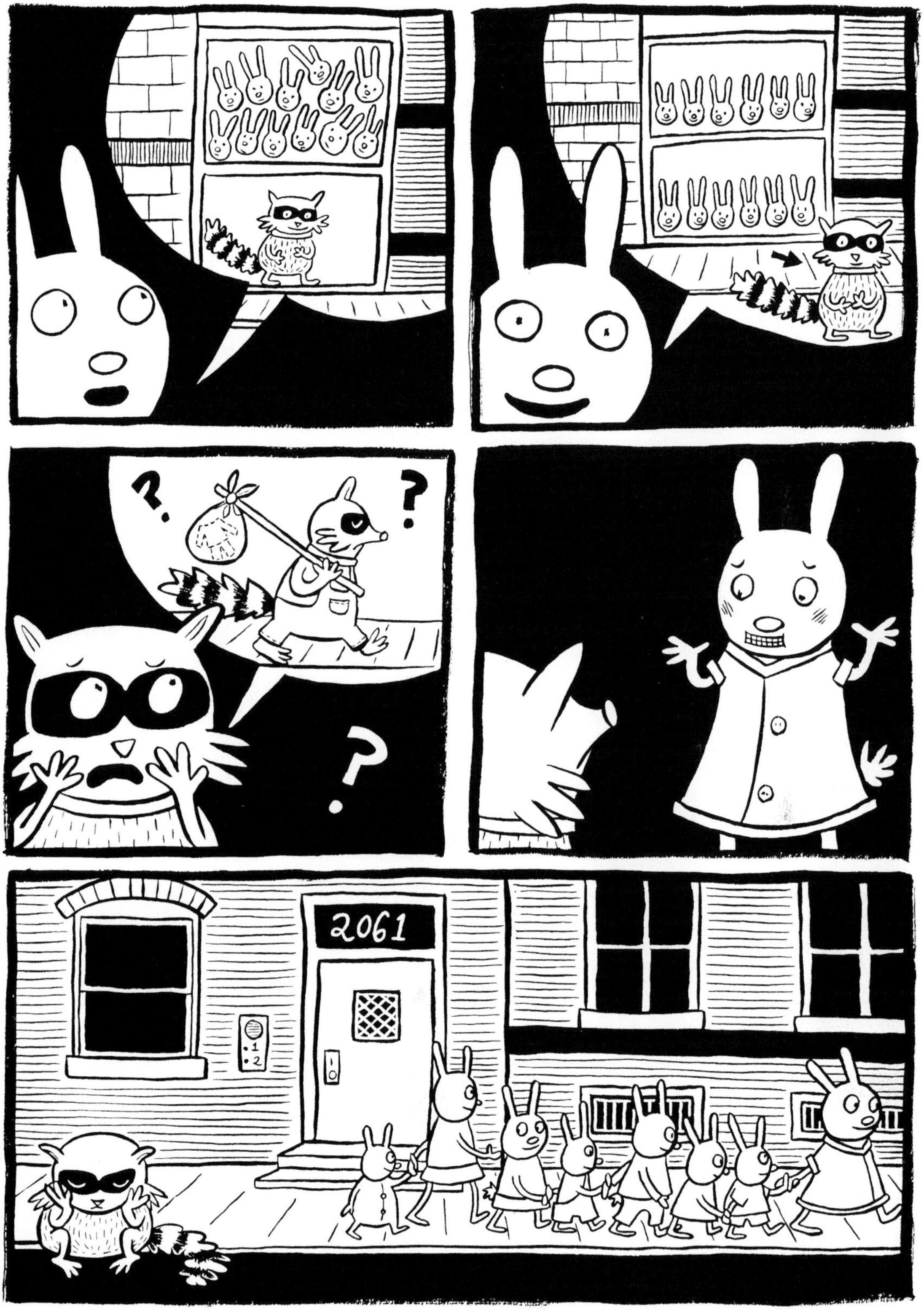
2061

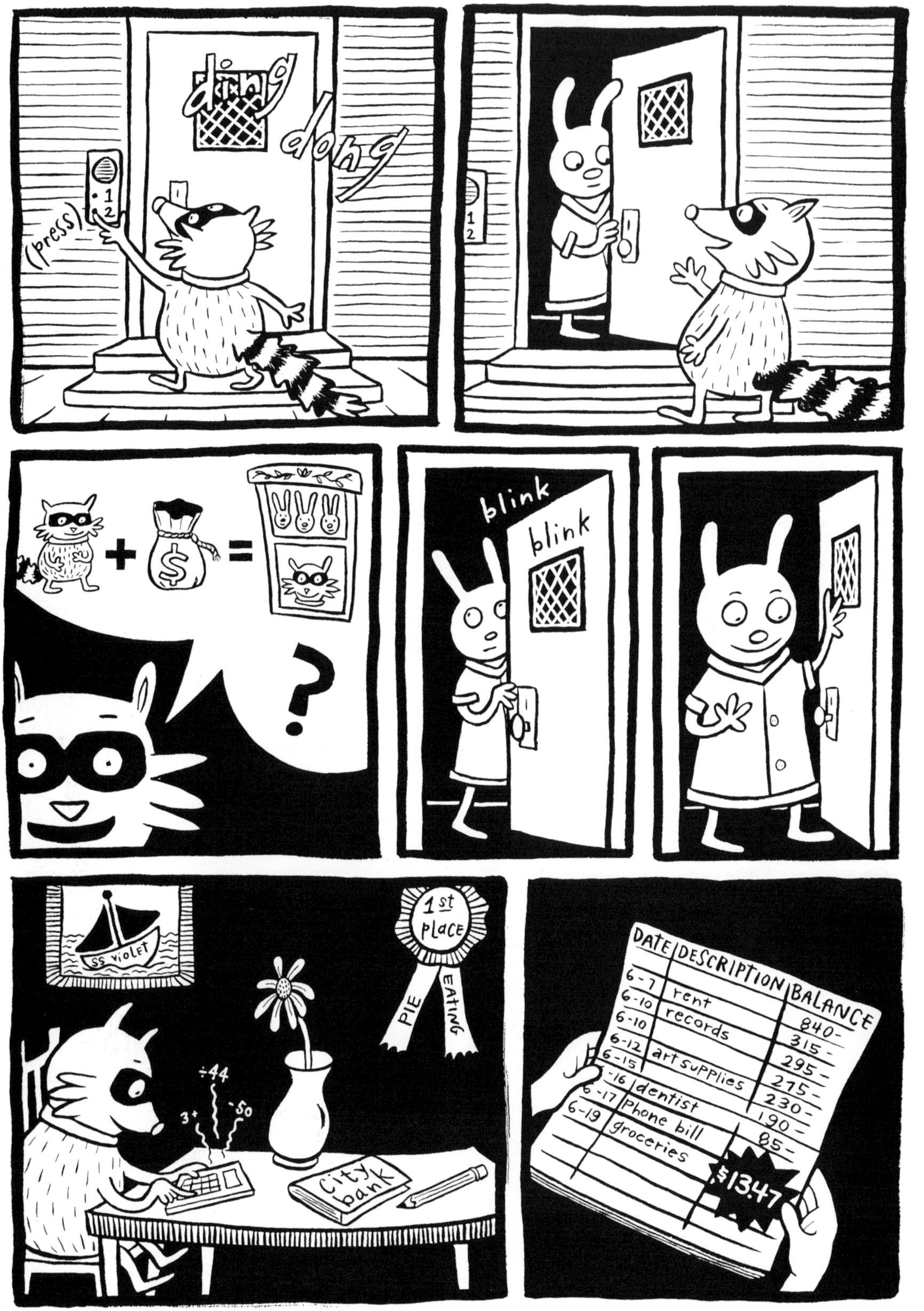

ding
dong
1
2
(press)
1
2
?
blink
blink
SS VIOLET
1st PLACE
PIE
EATING
÷44
3+
-50
city bank
DATE
DESCRIPTION
BALANCE
6-7 rent
6-10 records
6-10
6-12 art supplies
6-15
6-16 dentist
6-17 Phone bill
6-19 groceries
840-
315-
295-
275-
230-
190-
85-
$13.47

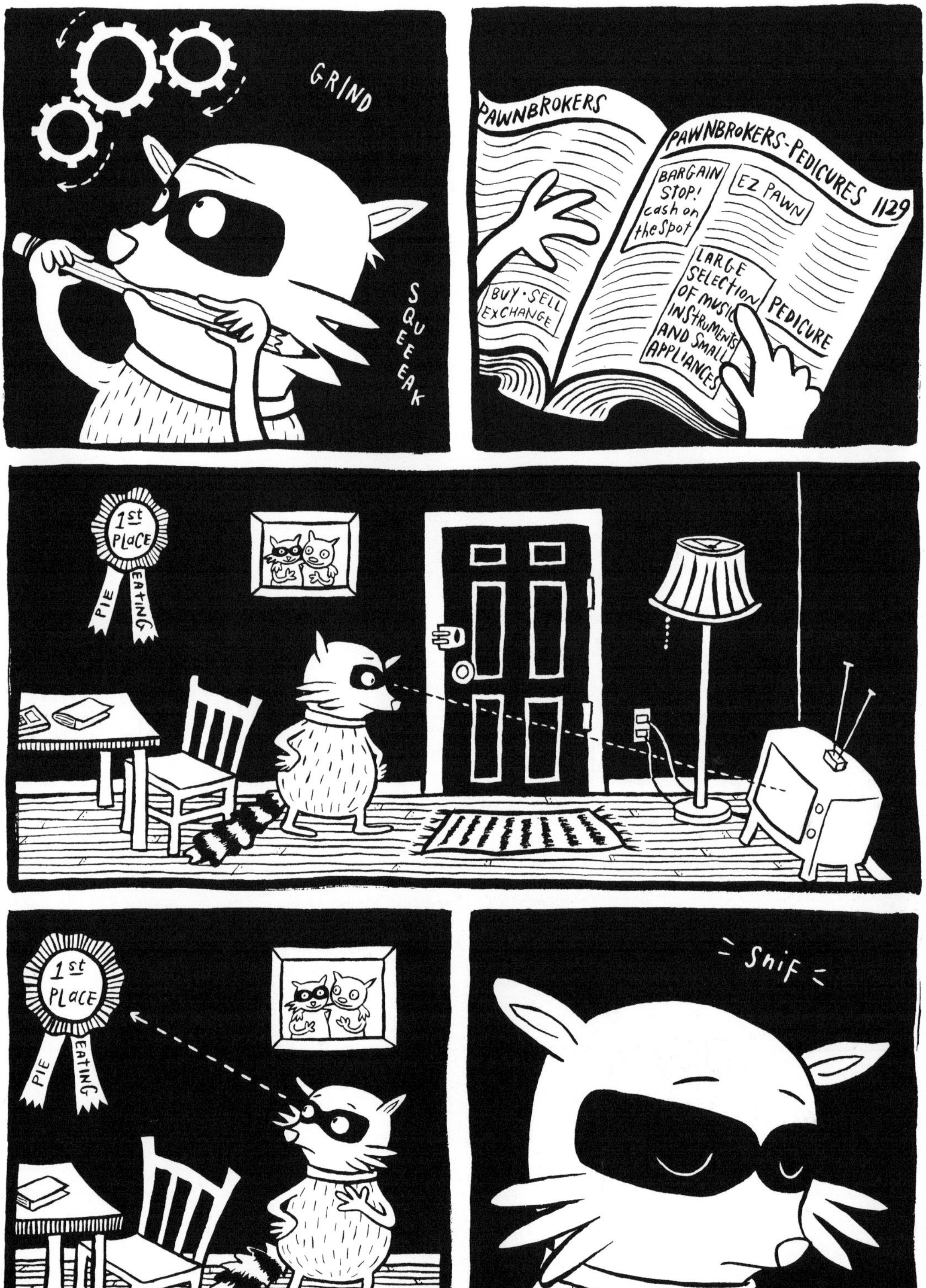
GRIND
SQUEEEEAK
PAWNBROKERS
PAWNBROKERS-PEDICURES 1129
BARGAIN STOP! cash on the Spot
EZ PAWN
BUY · SELL EXCHANGE
LARGE SELECTION OF MUSIC INSTRUMENTS AND SMALL APPLIANCES
PEDICURE
1st PLACE
PIE EATING
1st PLACE
PIE EATING
Snif

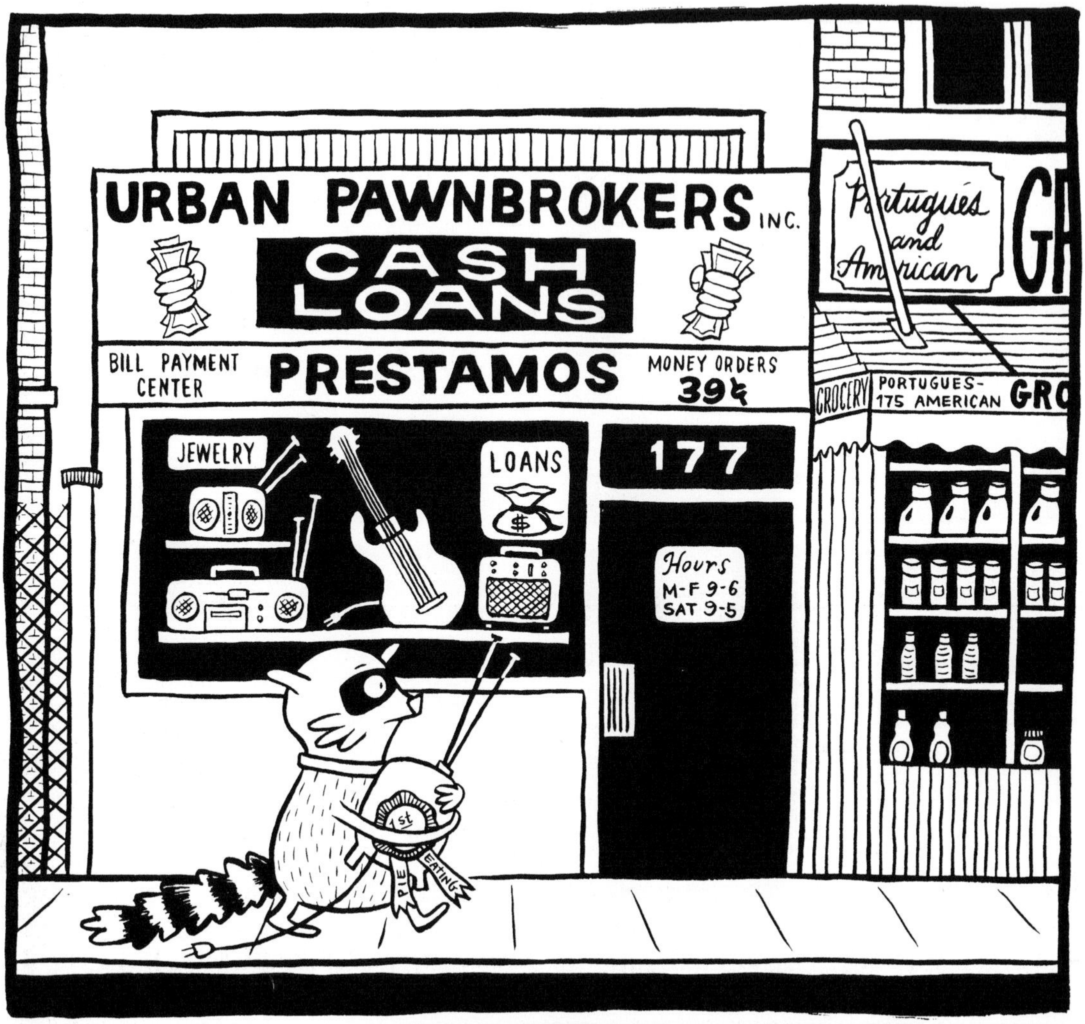
URBAN PAWNBROKERS INC.
CASH LOANS
BILL PAYMENT CENTER
PRESTAMOS
MONEY ORDERS 39¢
JEWELRY
LOANS
$
177
Hours M-F 9-6 SAT 9-5
Portugués and American
GROCERY
PORTUGUES-175 AMERICAN GRO
1st
PIE EATING

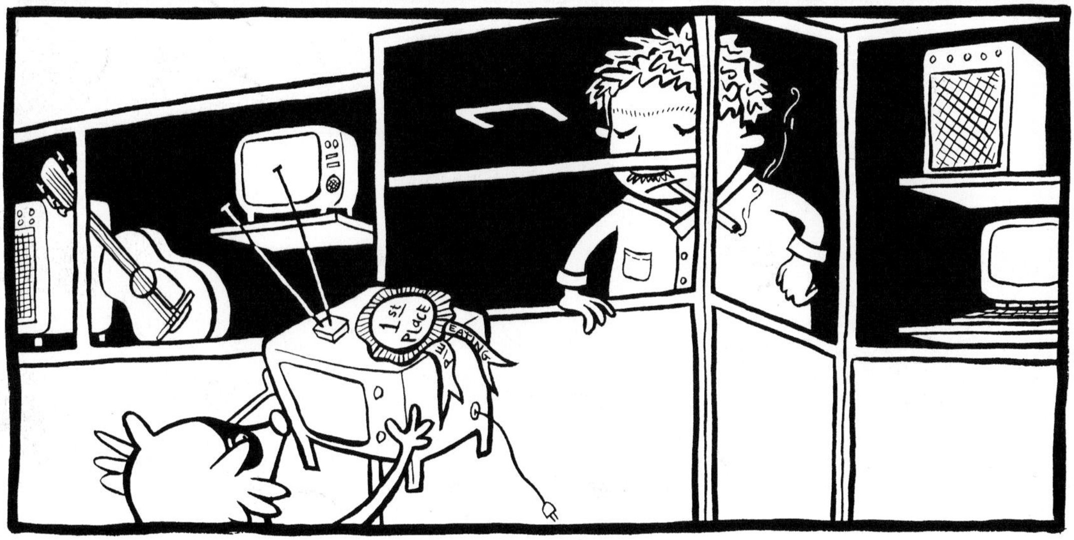
1st PLACE
PIE EATING

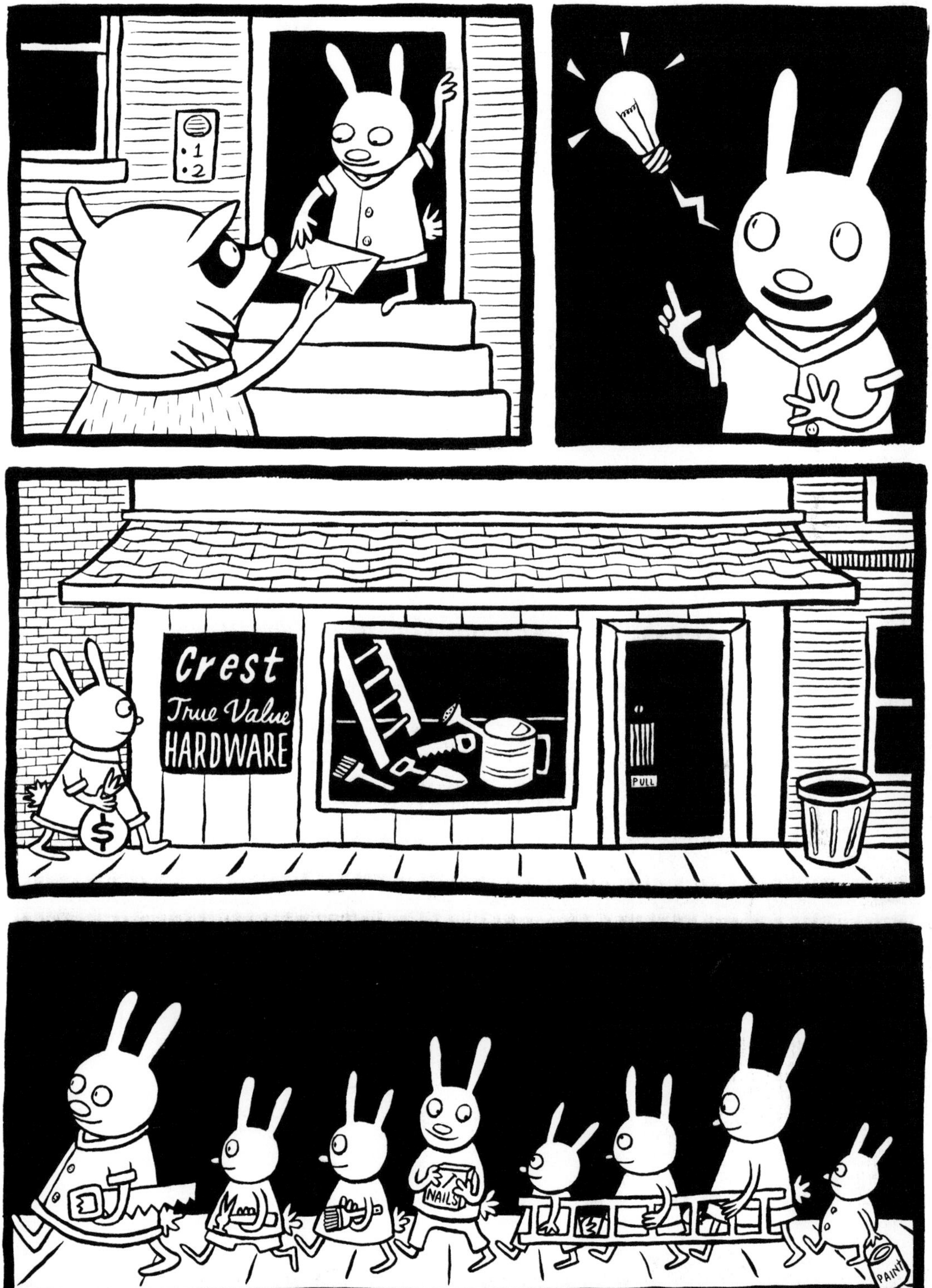
1
2
Crest
True Value
HARDWARE
PULL
NAILS
PAINT

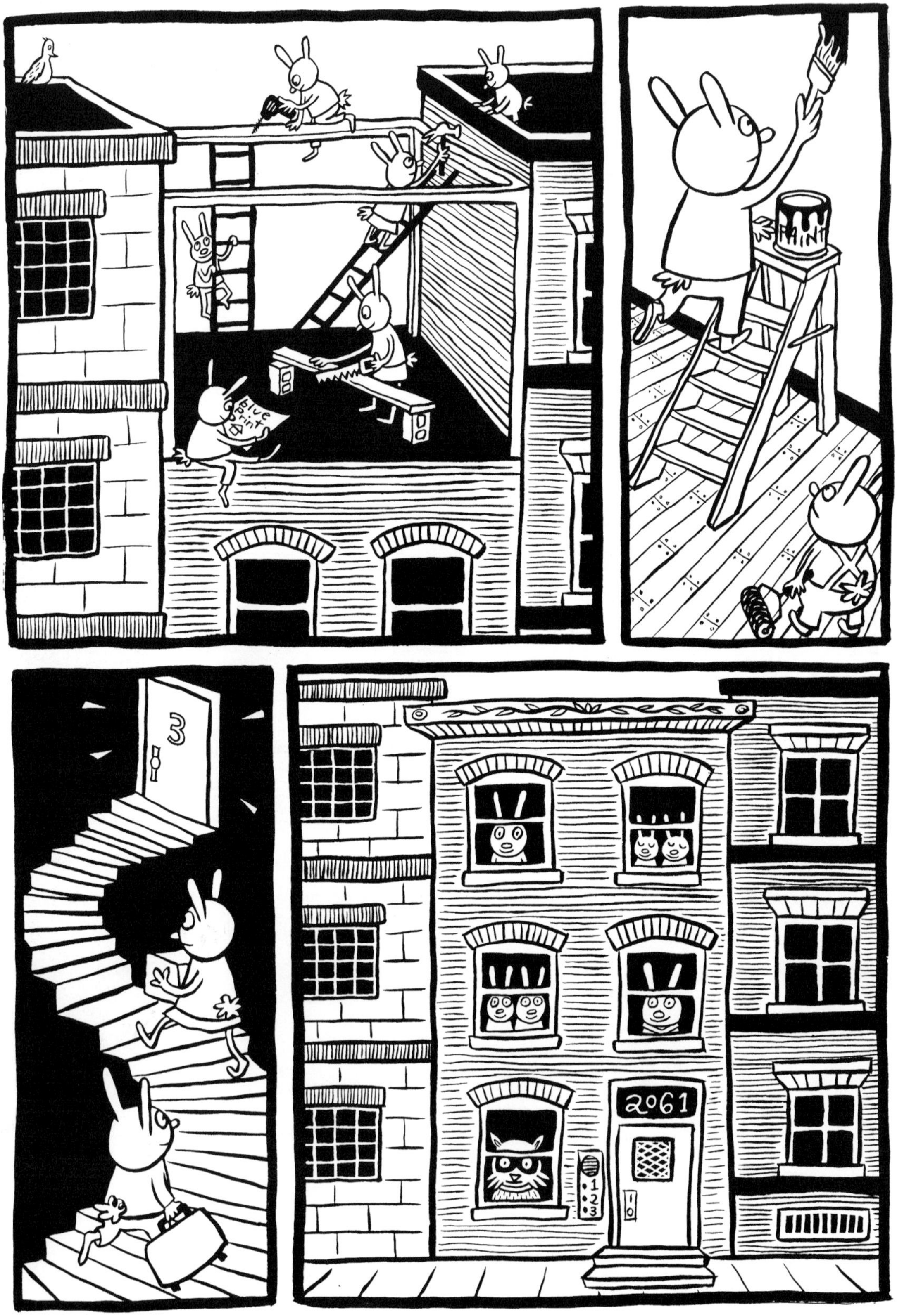
Blue Print
PAINT
3
2061
1
2
3

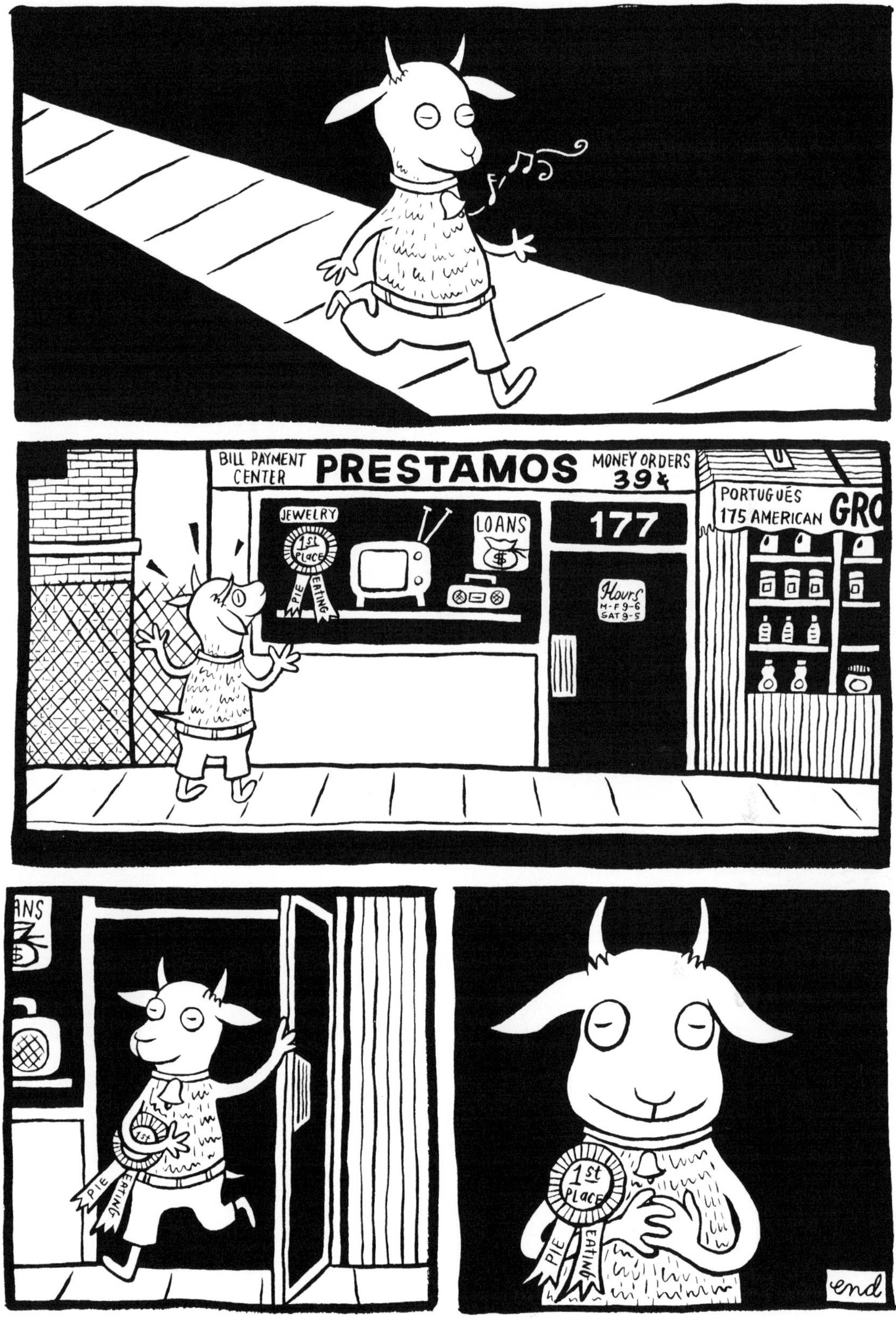
BILL PAYMENT CENTER
PRESTAMOS
MONEY ORDERS 39¢
JEWELRY
1st PLACE
PIE EATING
LOANS
177
Hours M-F 9-6 SAT 9-5
PORTUGUÉS
175 AMERICAN
GRO
1st
PIE EATING
1st PLACE
PIE EATING
end

The Pool, March 2002
    I can't even guess where this came from, although I vaguely recall a page from an old Japanese comic in which the top panel was a scene above the water and the bottom was the same scene underwater. That definitely inspired the page where, in the top panel, the Sheep is sitting on the pier with a fishing line, and, in the bottom panel, the sea creatures are looking at his flyer on the end of the hook. It may have sparked the whole story.

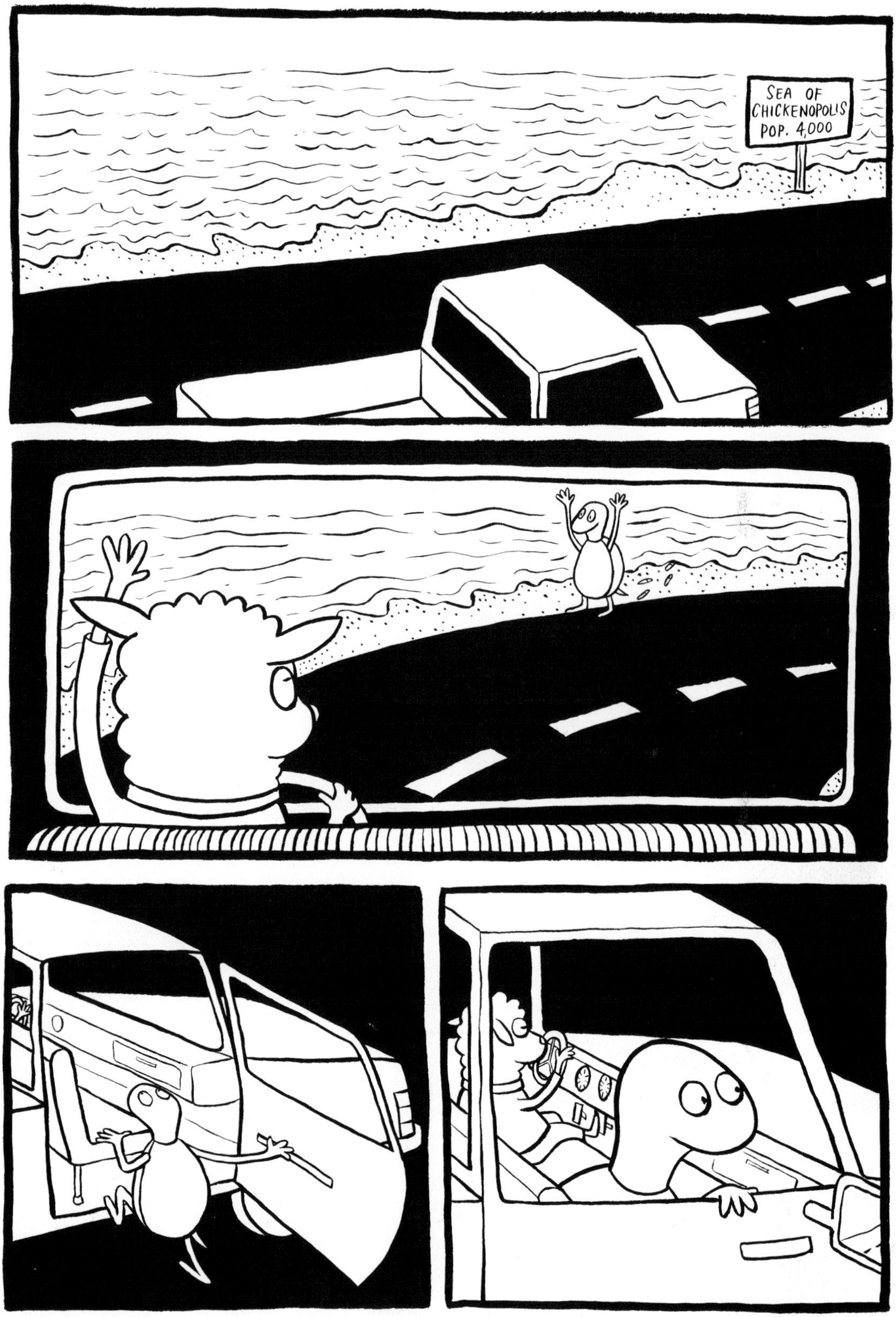
SEA OF CHICKENOPOLIS POP. 4,000

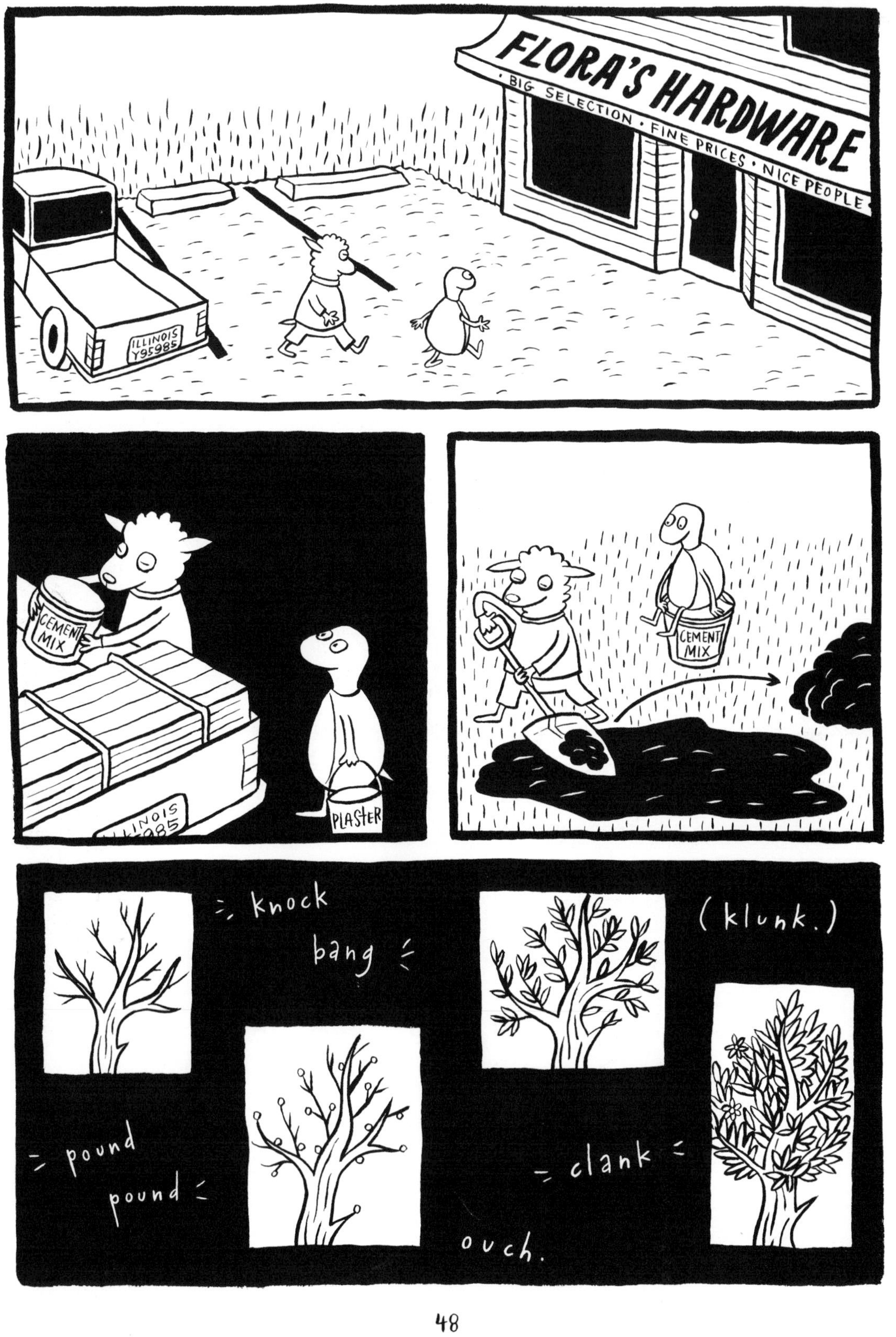
FLORA'S HARDWARE
• BIG SELECTION • FINE PRICES • NICE PEOPLE •
ILLINOIS Y95985
CEMENT MIX
PLASTER
CEMENT MIX
knock
bang
(klunk.)
pound
pound
clank
ouch.

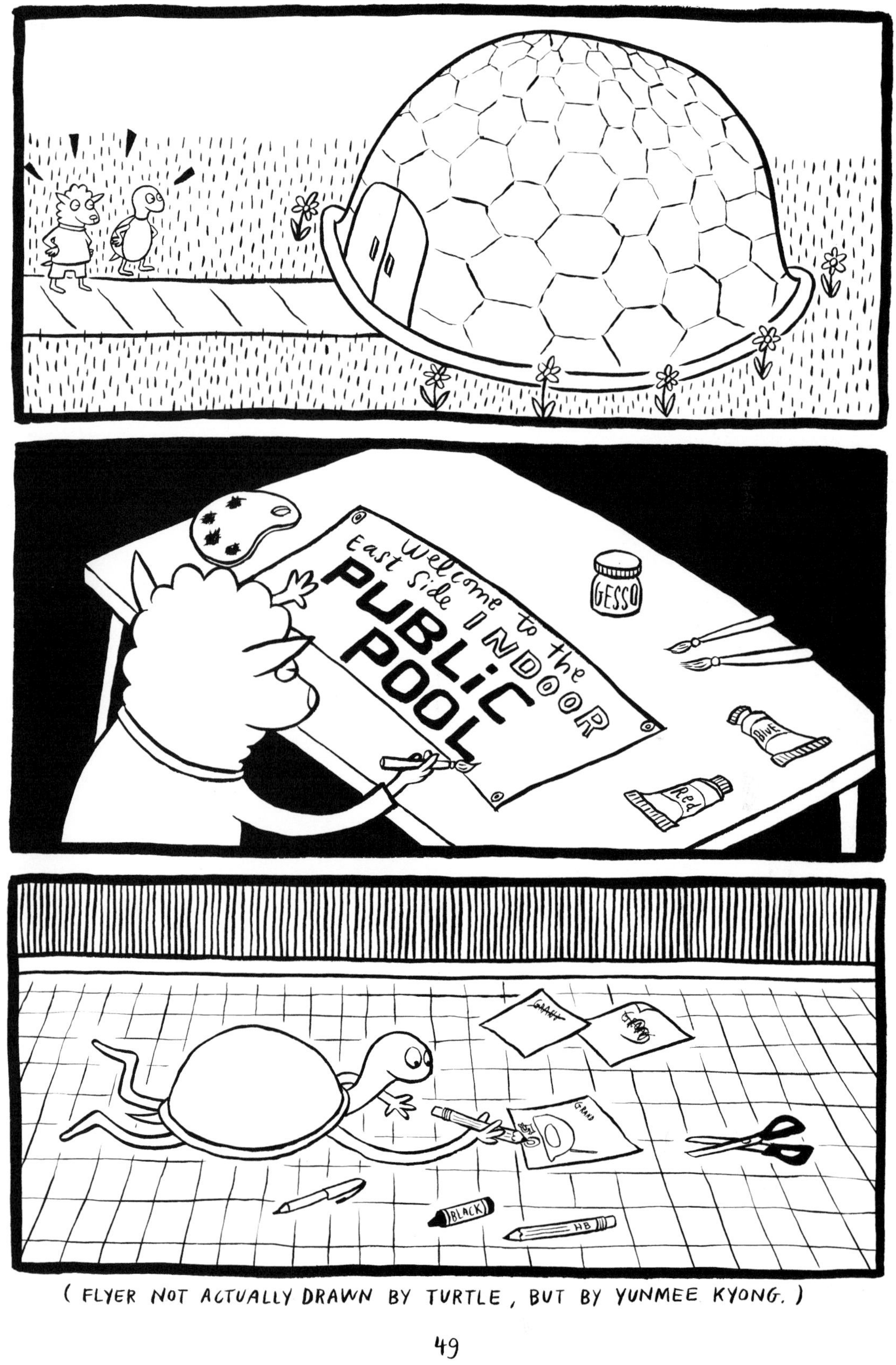
Welcome to the
East Side INDOOR
PUBLIC
POOL
GESSO
BLUE
Red
BLACK
HB

(FLYER NOT ACTUALLY DRAWN BY TURTLE, BUT BY YUNMEE KYONG.)

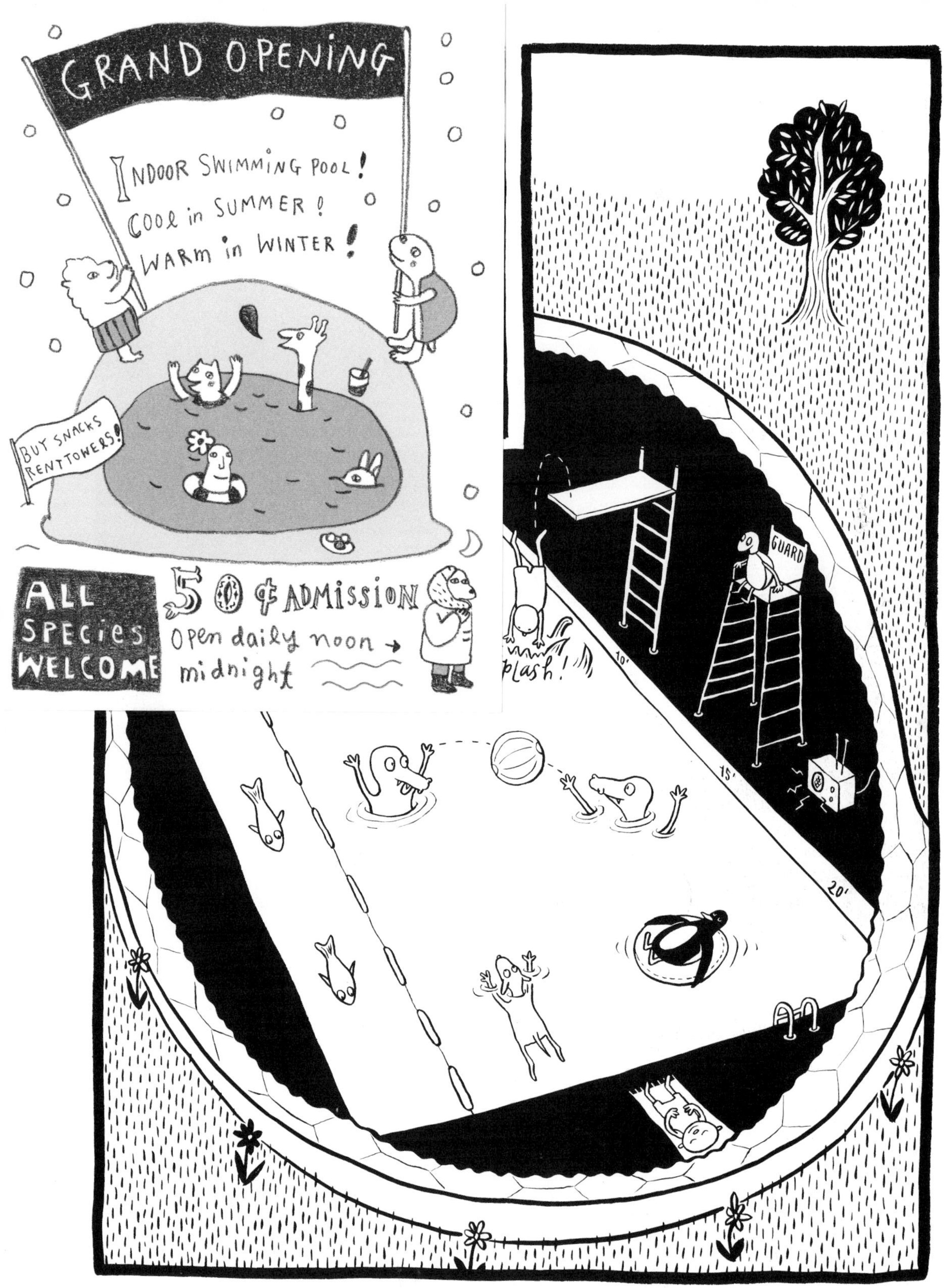
GRAND OPENING
INDOOR SWIMMING POOL!
COOL in SUMMER!
WARM in WINTER!
BUY SNACKS RENTTOWERS!
ALL SPECIES WELCOME
50¢ ADMISSION
Open daily noon → midnight
plash!
10'
GUARD
15'
20'

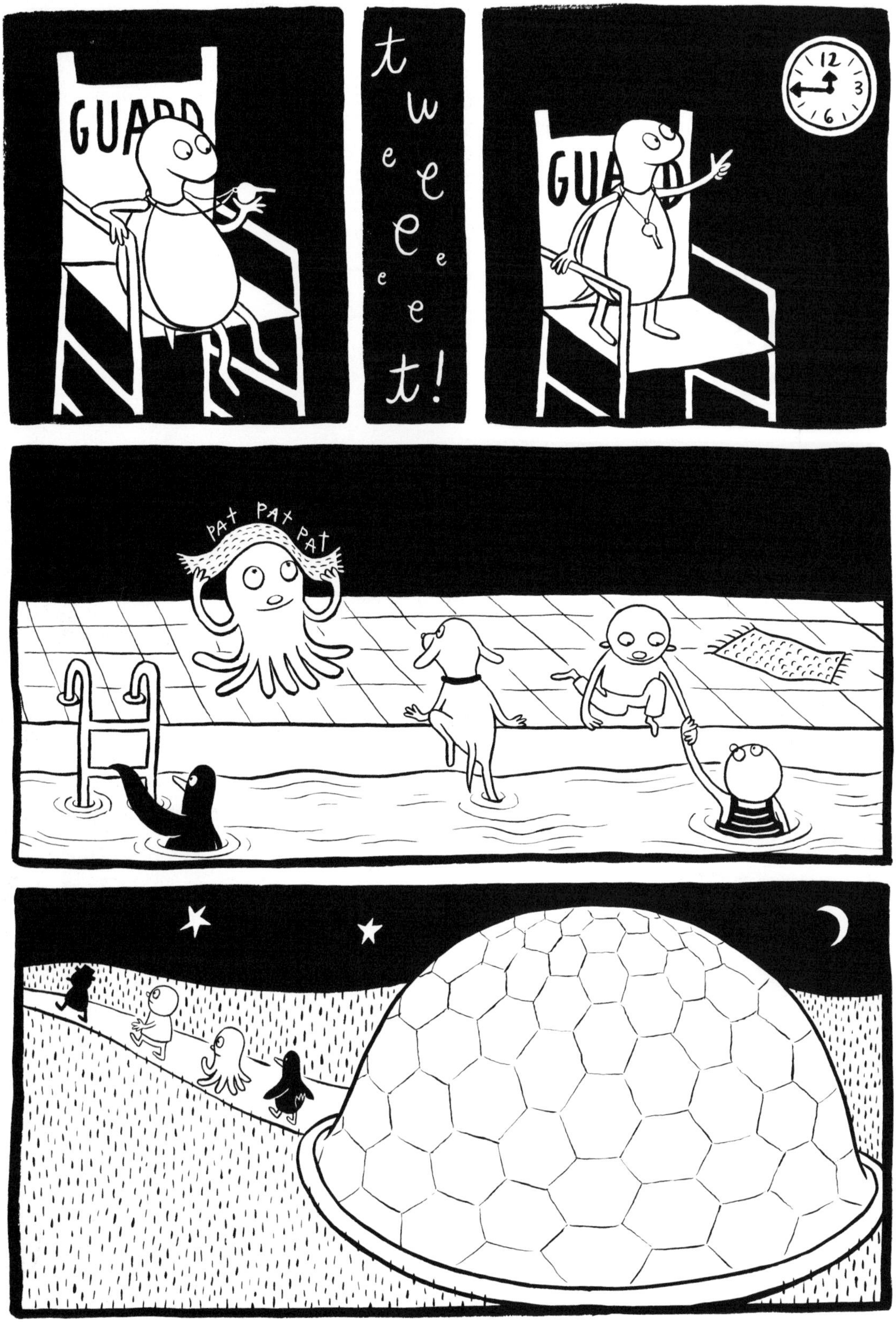
GUARD
tweeeeeet!
GUARD
12
3
6
PAT PAT PAT

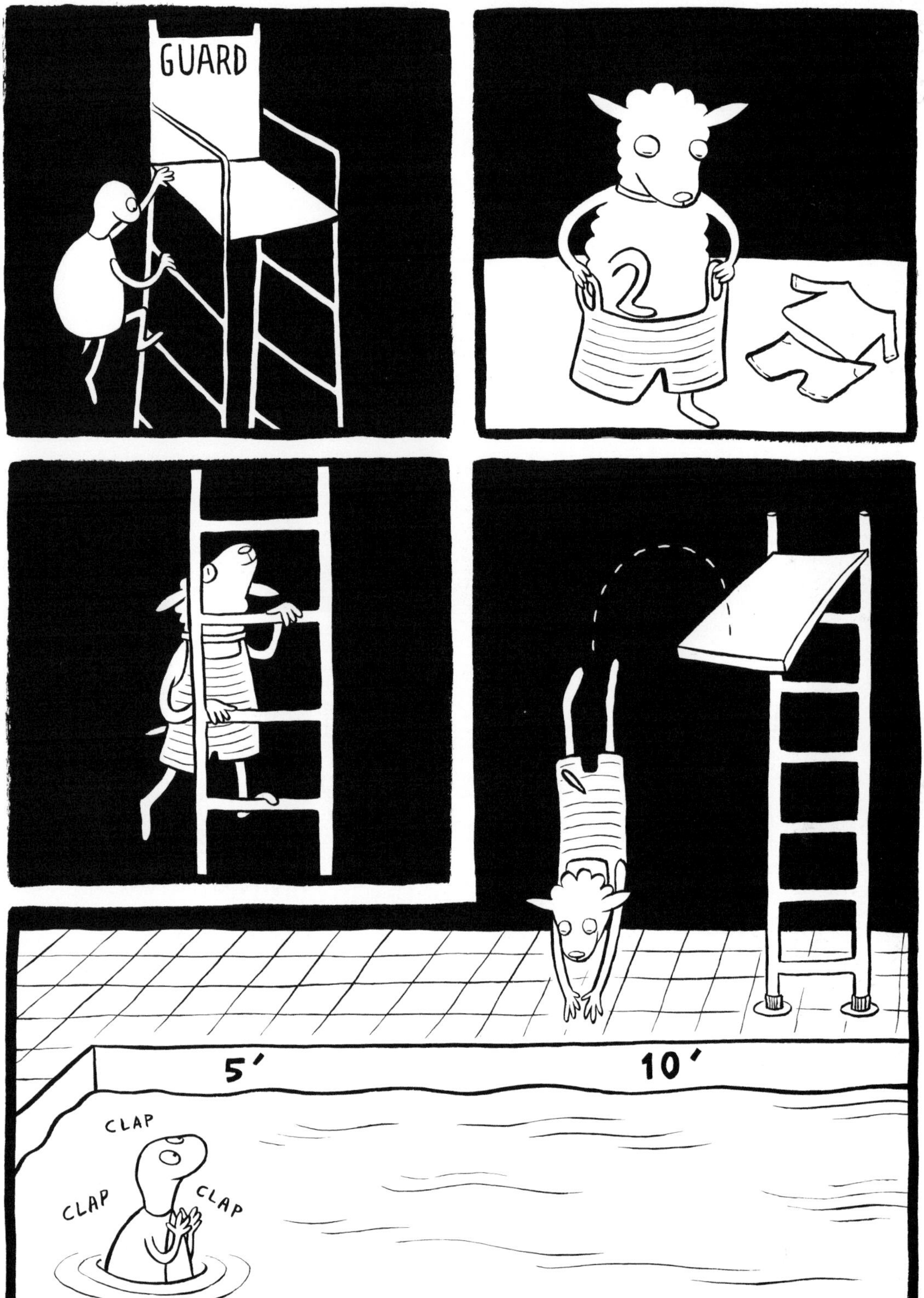
GUARD
2
5'
10'
CLAP
CLAP
CLAP

Bee Comic, July 2002

I guess I'd been in New York for about two years by now. It was so much more crowded and packed with people than Chicago. I became interested in how people also cram livestock into these super-urban settings. The livestock that I mainly saw were rooftop pigeons, and I became really fixated on these rooftop coops. I did see the occasional runaway rooster in my first neighborhood, but I think they were for cockfights, which I didn't want to know about. So I interviewed a friend of a friend about beekeeping. He was in Chicago, but it seemed all part of a whole, since bees are another kind of livestock that people keep in urban settings.

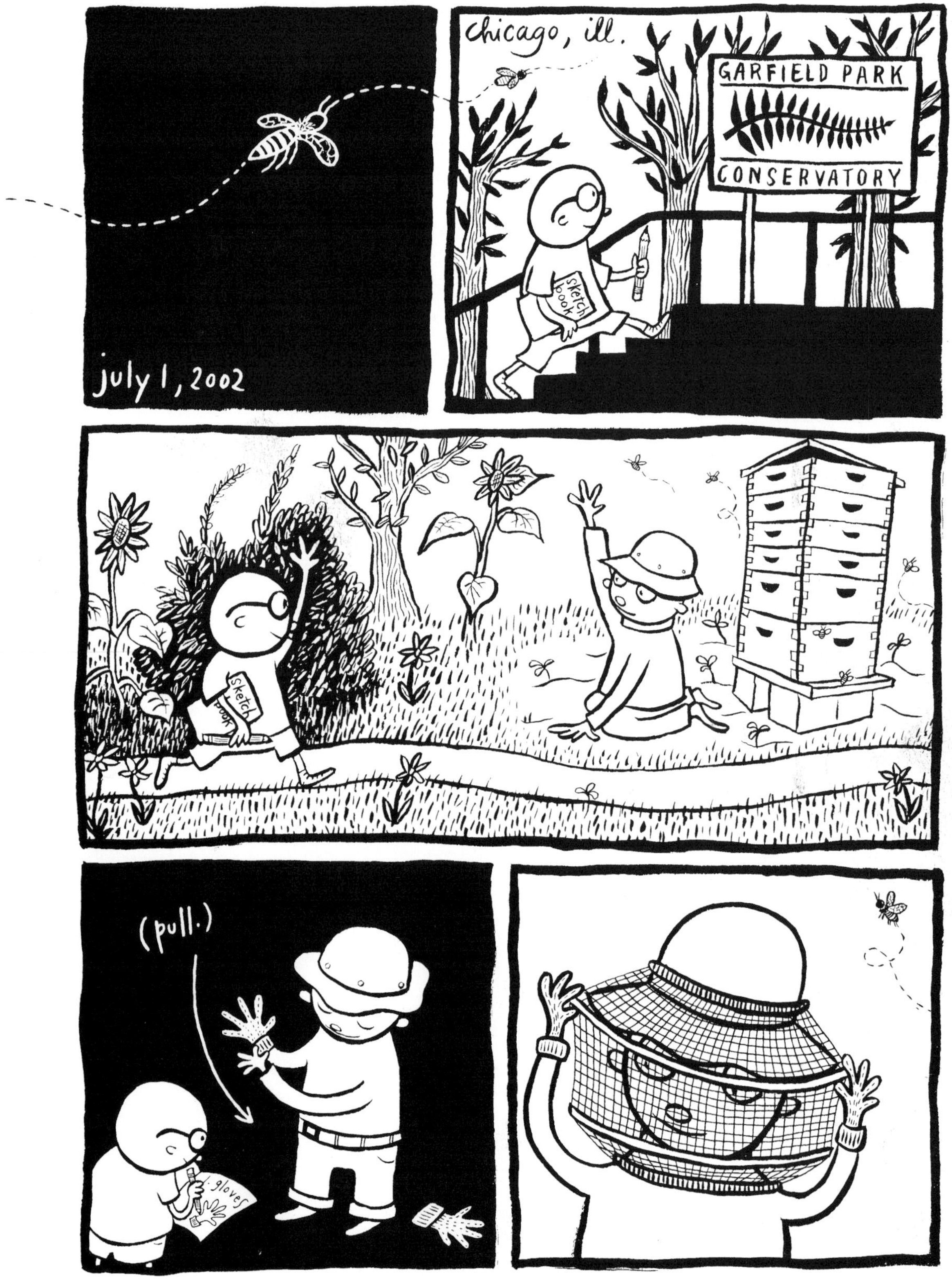
july 1, 2002
chicago, ill.
GARFIELD PARK
CONSERVATORY
sketch book
sketch book
(pull.)
gloves

GLOVES

plain cotton gloves will prevent beestings.

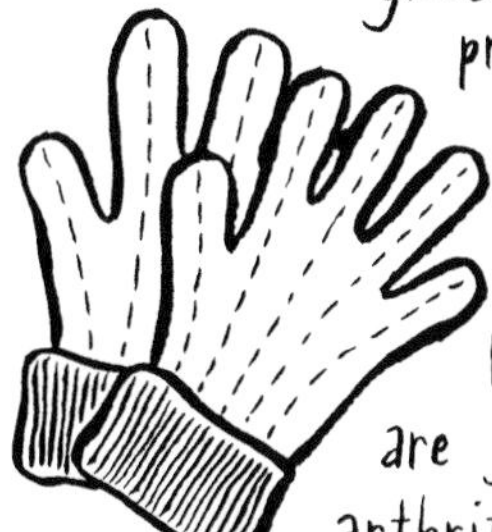

beestings are good for arthritis; some people want them. these people don't need gloves.

HAT

protective mesh fits over brim of hat.

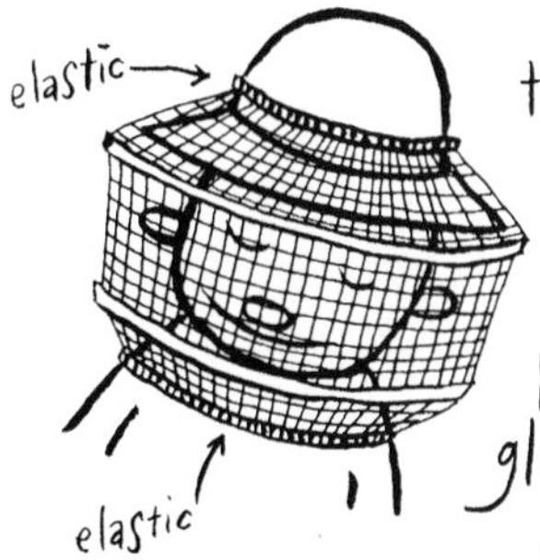
elastic
elastic

to keep your whole body covered, you will need long pants and shirt, gloves, hat, boots, and face mask.

HIVE TOOL

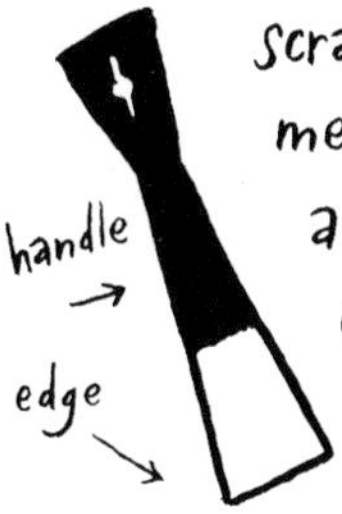
handle
edge

looks like a paint scraper and made of metal. super-handy, always keep it on you. the components of the beehive are sticky with propolis – it is used to pry things apart.

WORKER BEES

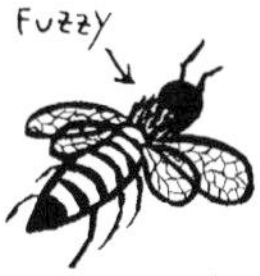
Fuzzy

Almost all bees in the hive are workers, and all workers are ladies. workers can live as short as 6 weeks, after which they die from exhaustion.

DRONES

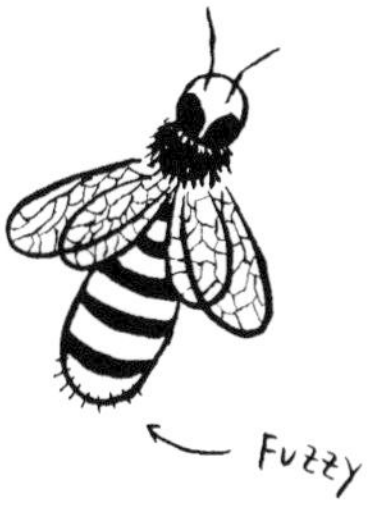
Fuzzy

Drones are male bees. There are not very many in the hive, but they are easily spotted on account of their large size. Their purpose is reproduction, and mostly they hang out and eat. Drones do not sting.

SMOKER

Smoke calms bees by causing them to feed involuntarily on honey. Before the hive is disassembled, smoke can be infused into the hive to distract the bees from the work of the beekeeper.

1. put dried leaves or paper inside smoker.

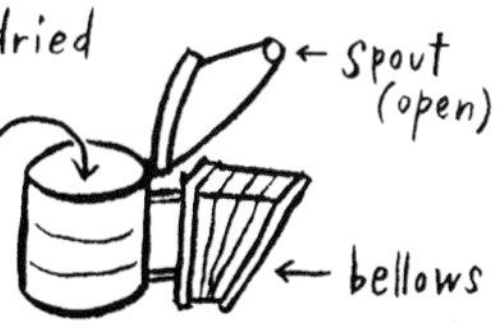
spout (open)
bellows

2. set fire to dried leaves or paper and close top.
3. squeeze bellows to cause smoke to come out of spout.

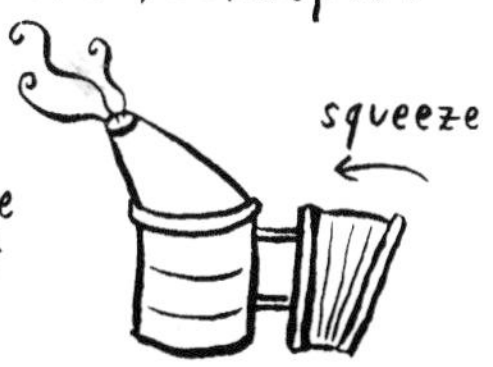
squeeze

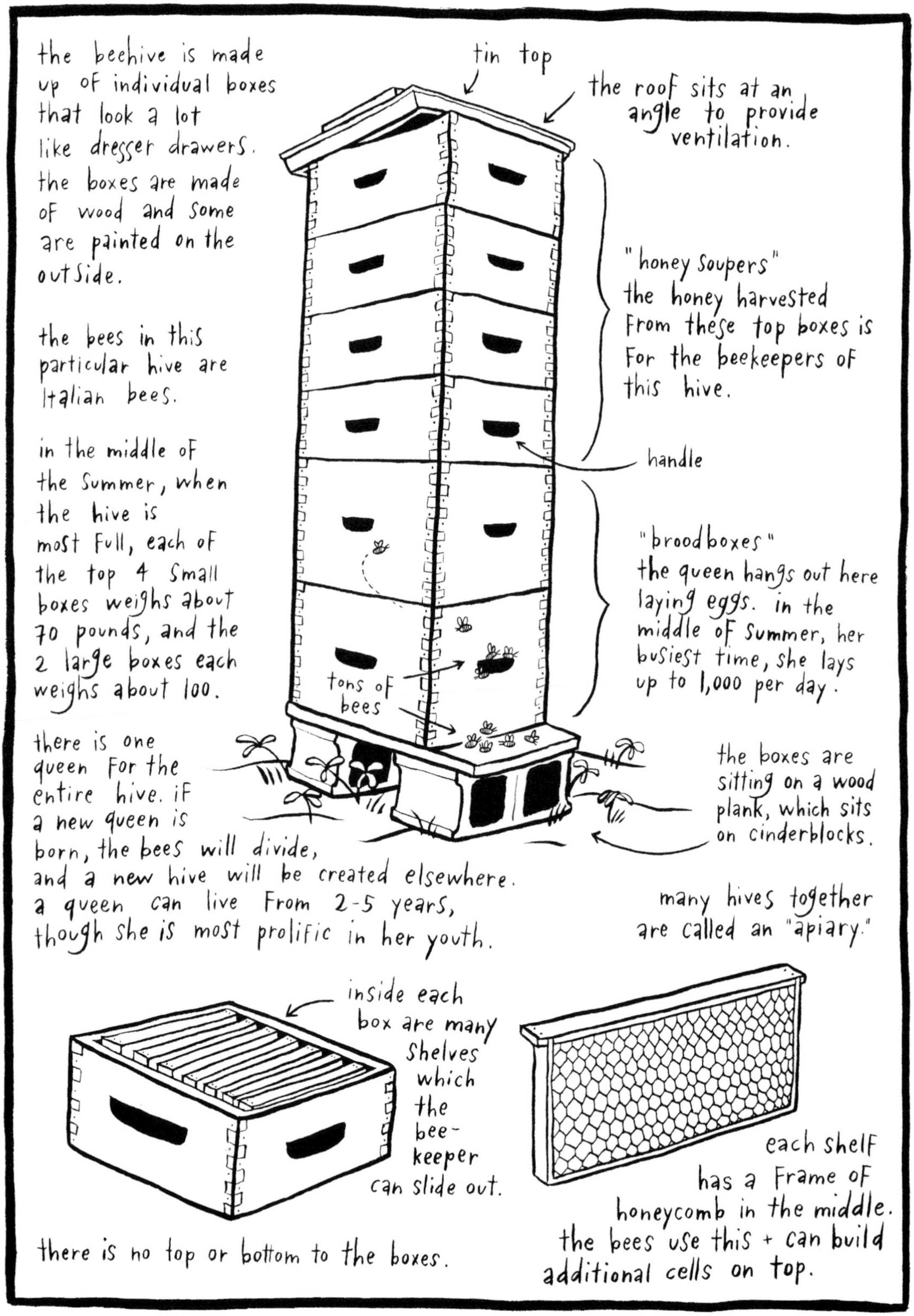

the beehive is made up of individual boxes that look a lot like dresser drawers. the boxes are made of wood and some are painted on the outside.
tin top
the roof sits at an angle to provide ventilation.
"honey soupers" the honey harvested from these top boxes is for the beekeepers of this hive.
the bees in this particular hive are Italian bees.
in the middle of the summer, when the hive is most full, each of the top 4 small boxes weighs about 70 pounds, and the 2 large boxes each weighs about 100.
handle
"broodboxes" the queen hangs out here laying eggs. in the middle of summer, her busiest time, she lays up to 1,000 per day.
tons of bees
there is one queen for the entire hive. if a new queen is born, the bees will divide, and a new hive will be created elsewhere. a queen can live from 2-5 years, though she is most prolific in her youth.
the boxes are sitting on a wood plank, which sits on cinderblocks.
many hives together are called an "apiary."
inside each box are many shelves which the bee-keeper can slide out.
each shelf has a frame of honeycomb in the middle. the bees use this + can build additional cells on top.
there is no top or bottom to the boxes.

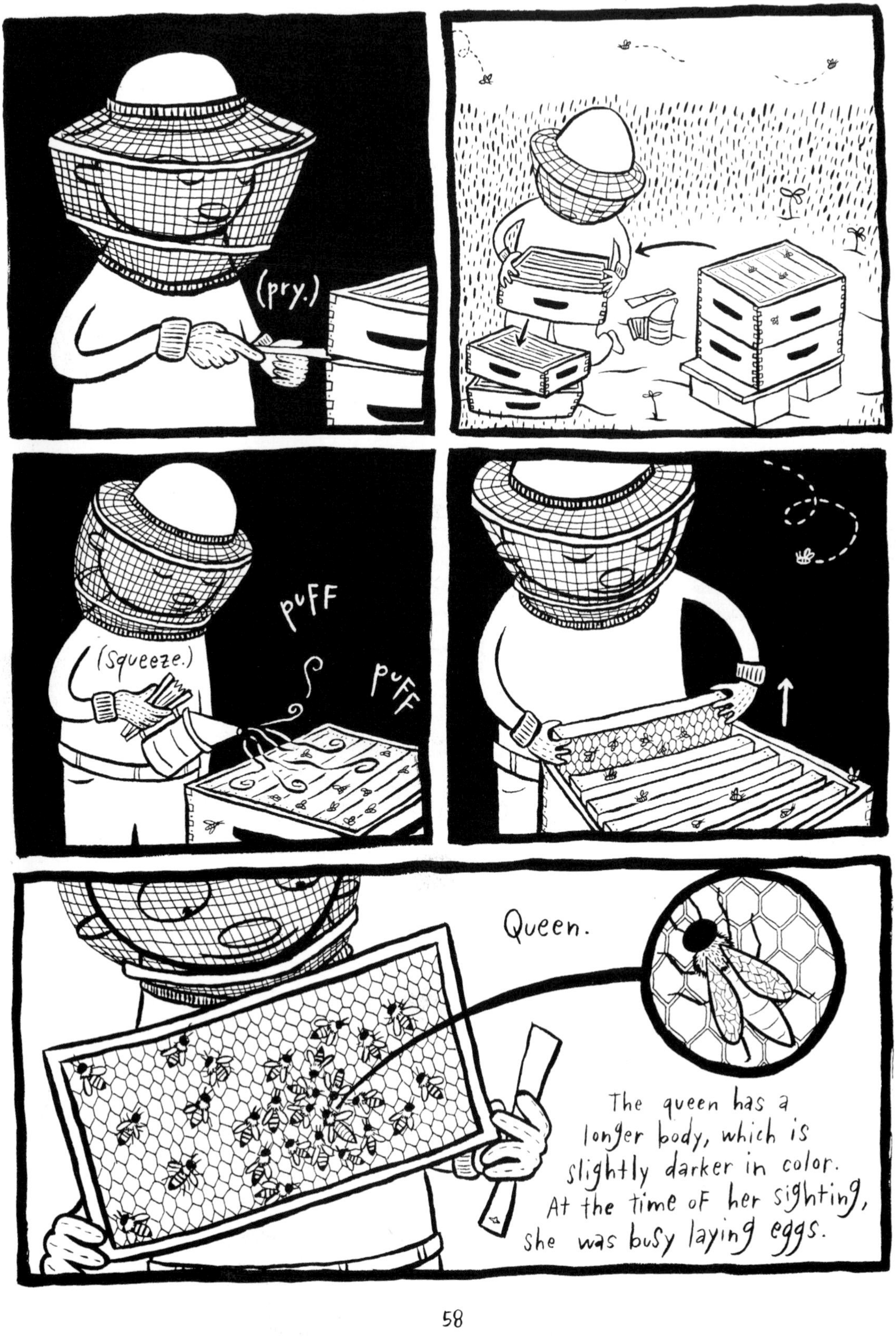
(pry.)
puFF
(squeeze.)
puFF
Queen.
The queen has a longer body, which is slightly darker in color. At the time of her sighting, she was busy laying eggs.

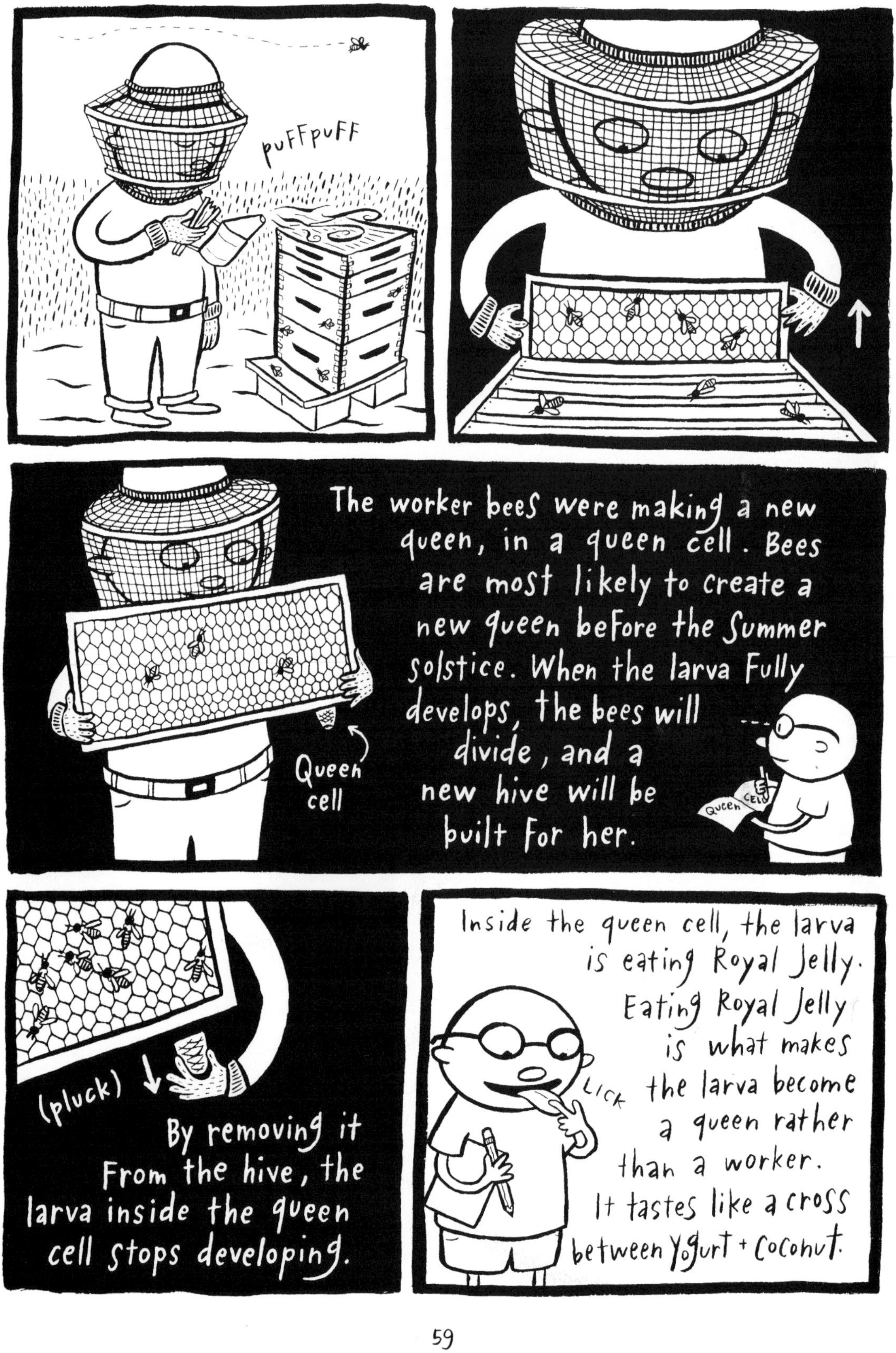

puffpuff
The worker bees were making a new queen, in a queen cell. Bees are most likely to create a new queen before the Summer solstice. When the larva fully develops, the bees will divide, and a new hive will be built for her.
Queen cell
Queen
(pluck)
By removing it from the hive, the larva inside the queen cell stops developing.
Inside the queen cell, the larva is eating Royal Jelly. Eating Royal Jelly is what makes the larva become a queen rather than a worker. It tastes like a cross between yogurt + coconut.
LICK

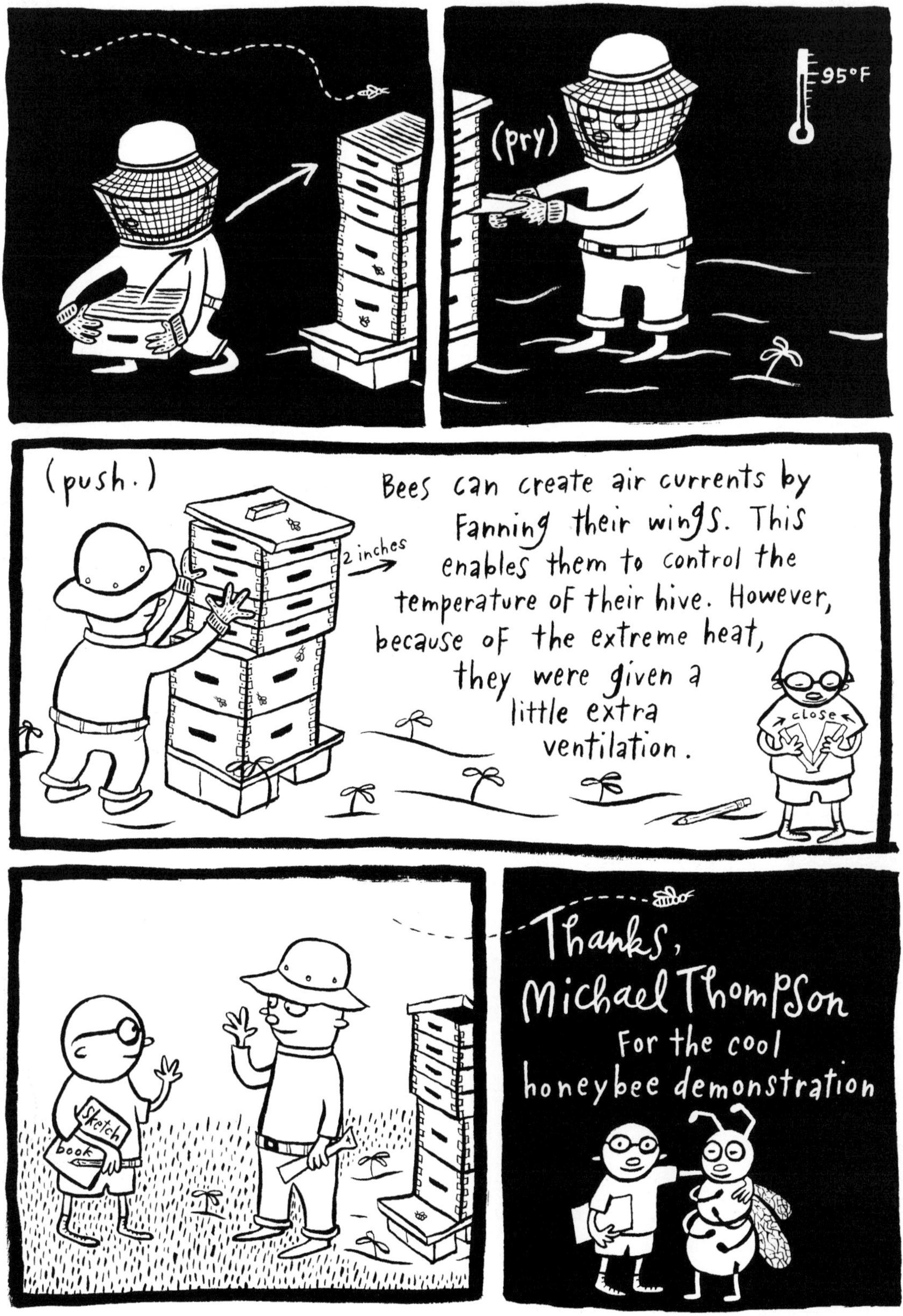
(pry)
95°F
(push.)
2 inches
Bees can create air currents by fanning their wings. This enables them to control the temperature of their hive. However, because of the extreme heat, they were given a little extra ventilation.
close
Sketch book
Thanks, Michael Thompson
For the cool honeybee demonstration

Paper Dolls! December 2002

All of these comics, up to this point, were done in the era before Google image search and before digital cameras were in wide use. So all research required me going to the place and doing location sketches. The other resource that folks used at the time for inspiration and reference was the New York Public Library Picture Collection at the mid-Manhattan branch. (It's still there but probably sees way less action.) For these paper dolls, I remember checking out several files full of paper dolls for inspiration. There were tons and most of them were very old.

paper dolls

SAILOR CAT · WINTER PERSON · BAKER DOG
· TRAVELING COMPANIONS ·

NOTE: IF you are borrowing this book from a library, school, or friend, or if you don't want to tear the pages out of your book, you can make a photocopy and assemble your paper dolls from your copies.

DIRECTIONS:

1 Cut along solid outer lines. Fold along dotted lines.

2 Fold bottom flaps of character outward (see Figure 1) to help character stand upright on its own.

FIGURE 1

3 After folding two halves of character together, lock in place using tabs along outer edges. To do this, use scissors or an X-Acto knife (if you're a kid, have a grownup help!) to cut along solid line in center of left tab. Fit small tab on right into this slot.

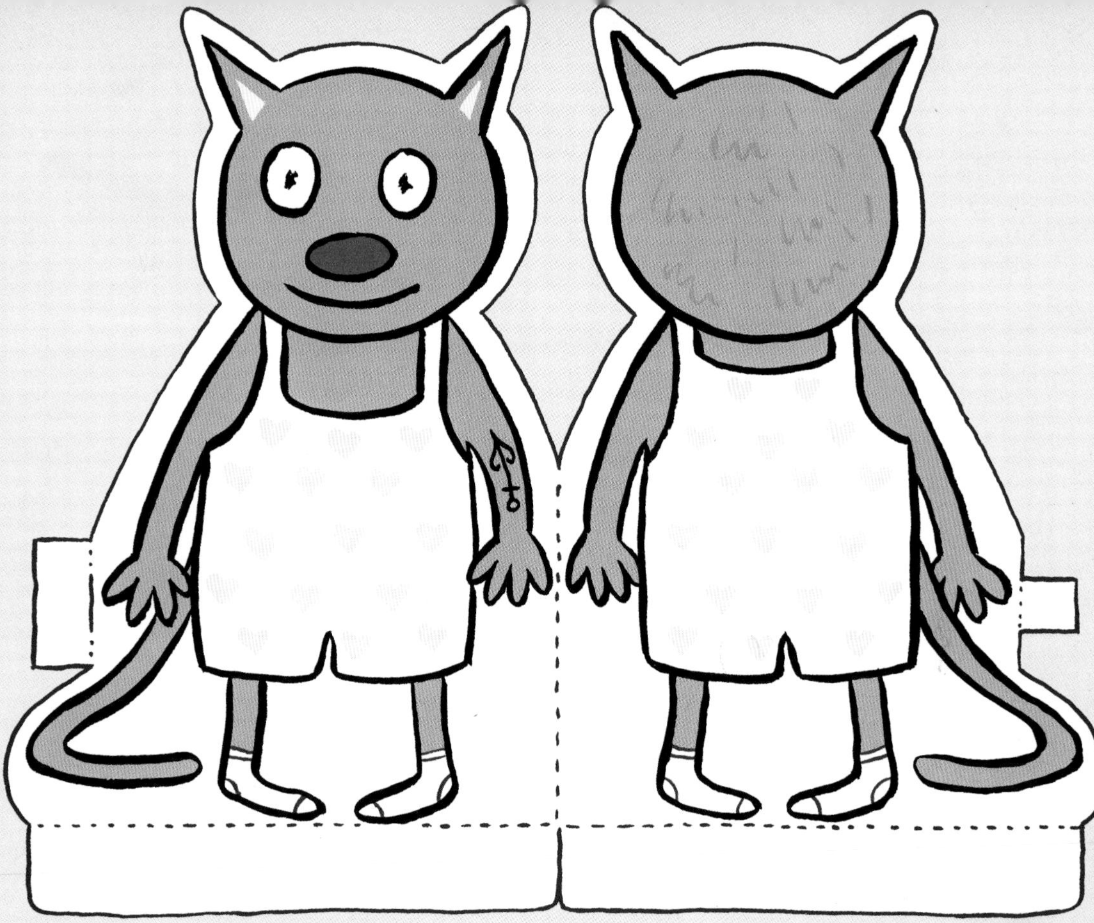

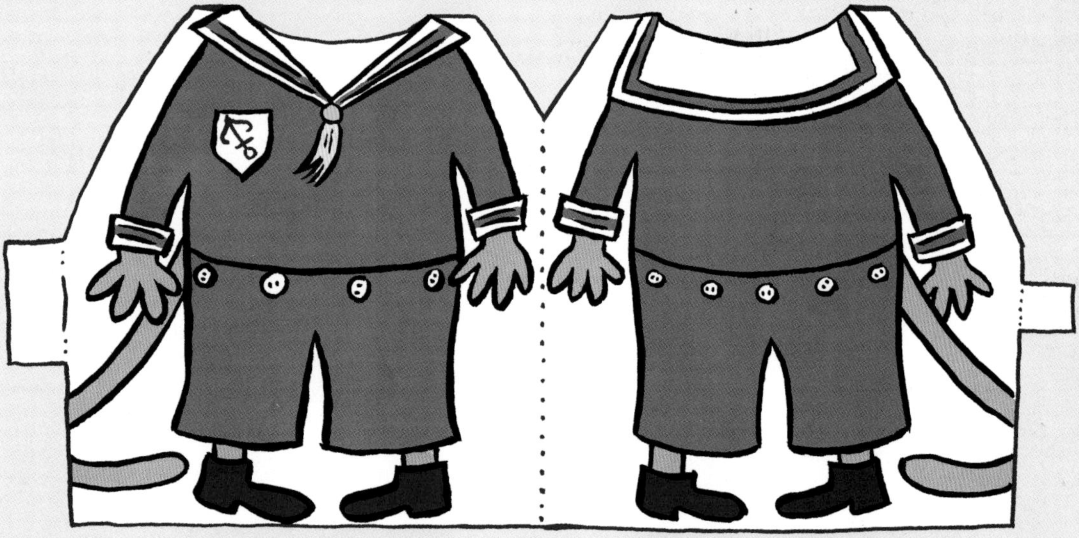

note : please refer to following page for sailor cap.

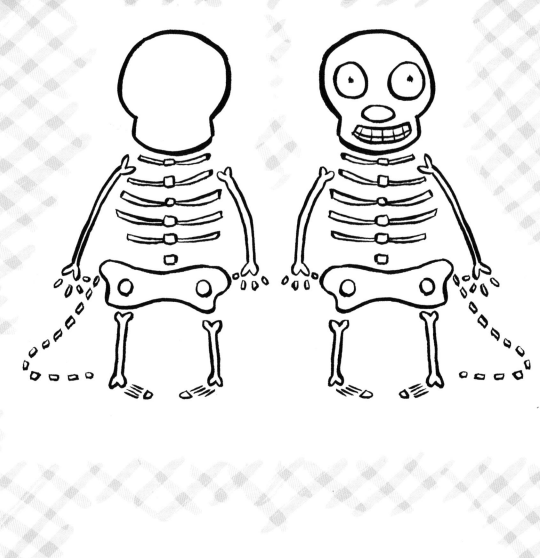

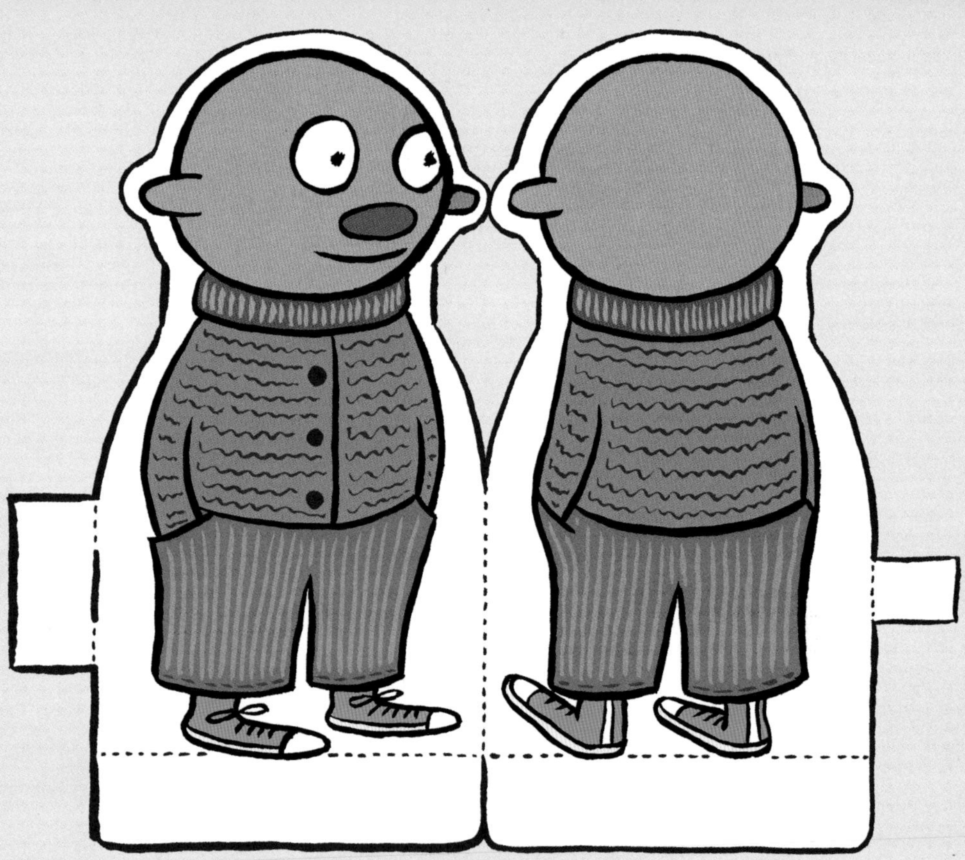

Scarf.

(place around neck before Fastening tab.)

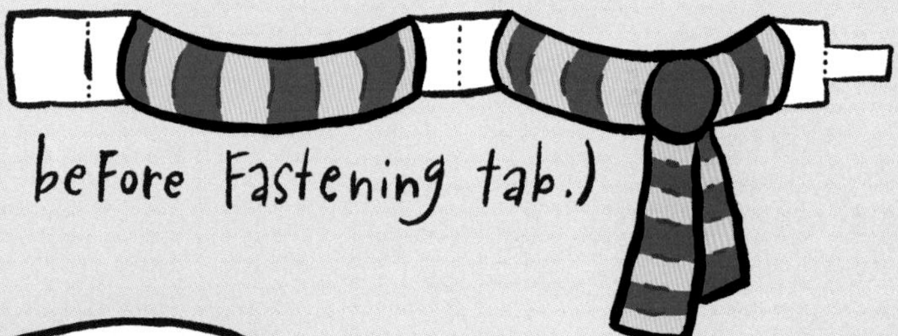

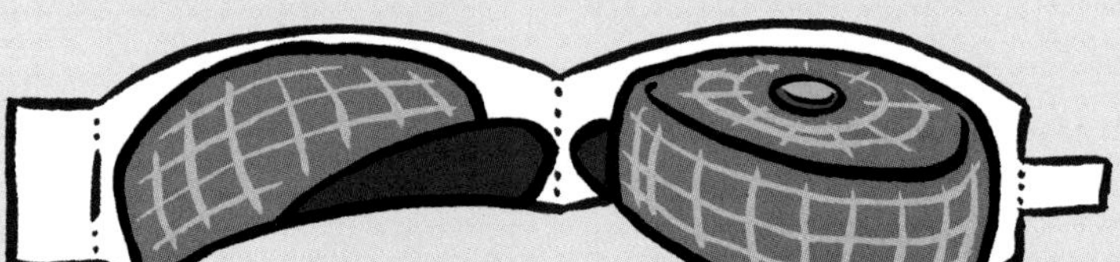

cap.

Sailor hat
For cat.

(see Preceding page.)

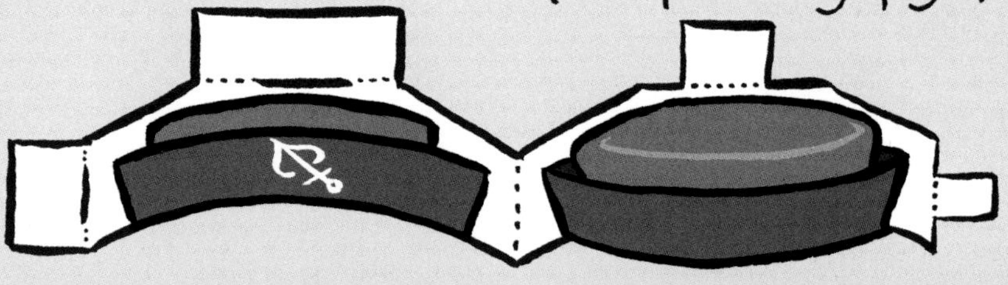

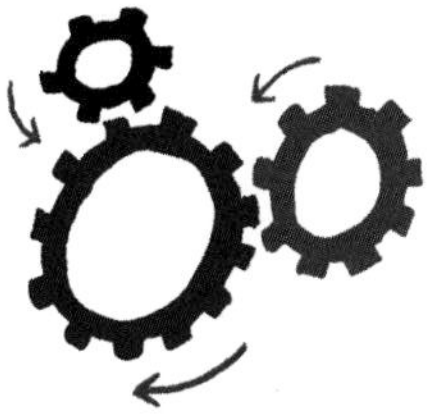

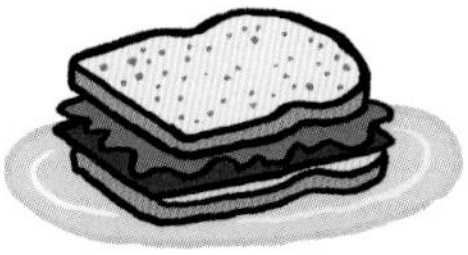

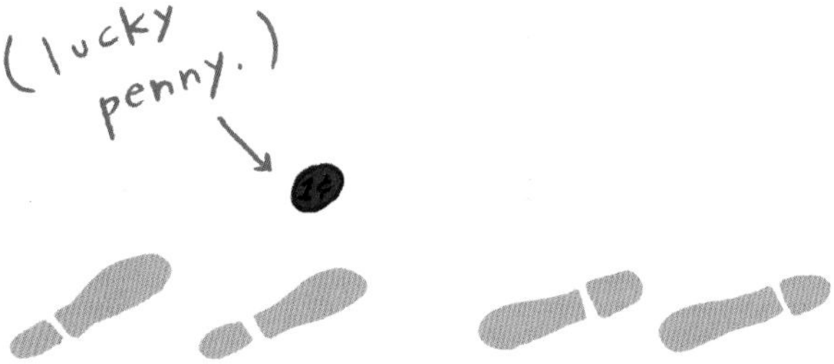
(lucky penny.)
1¢

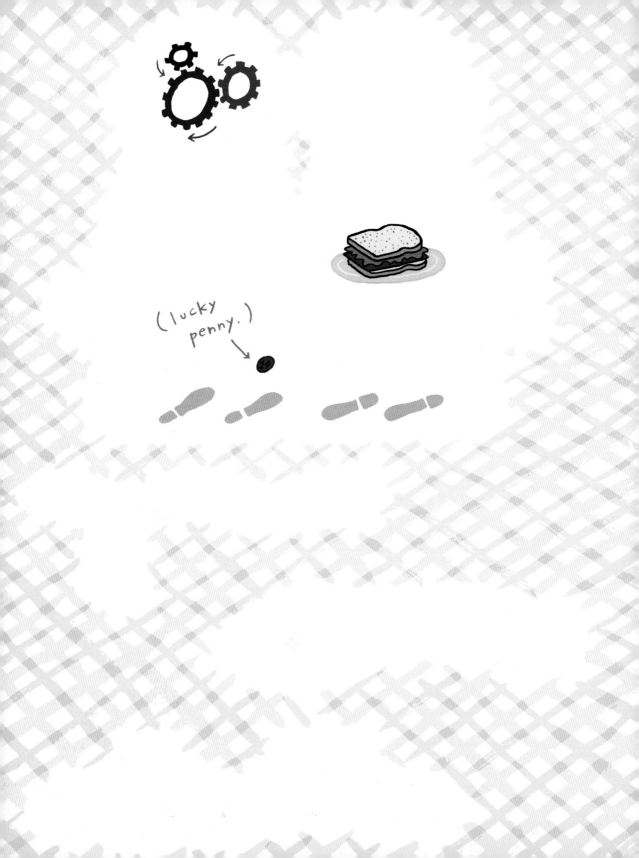

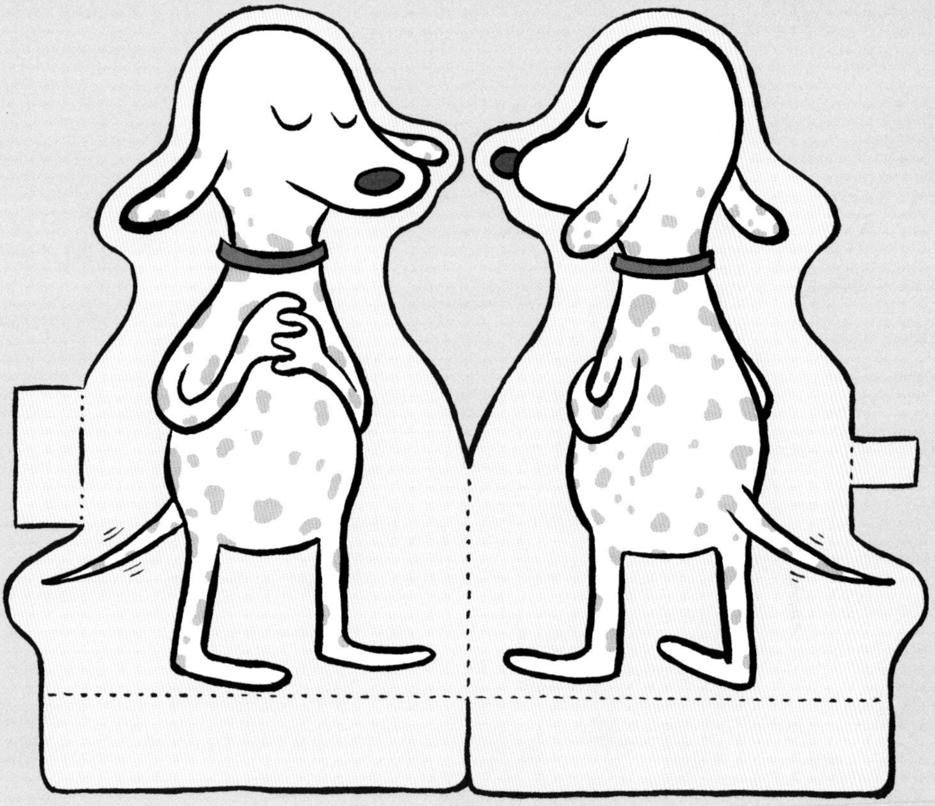

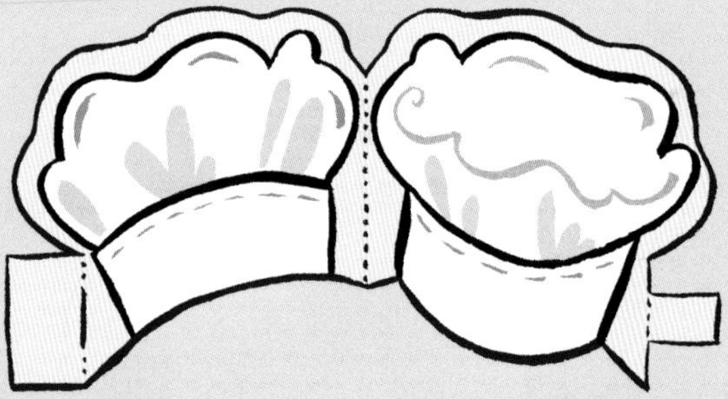

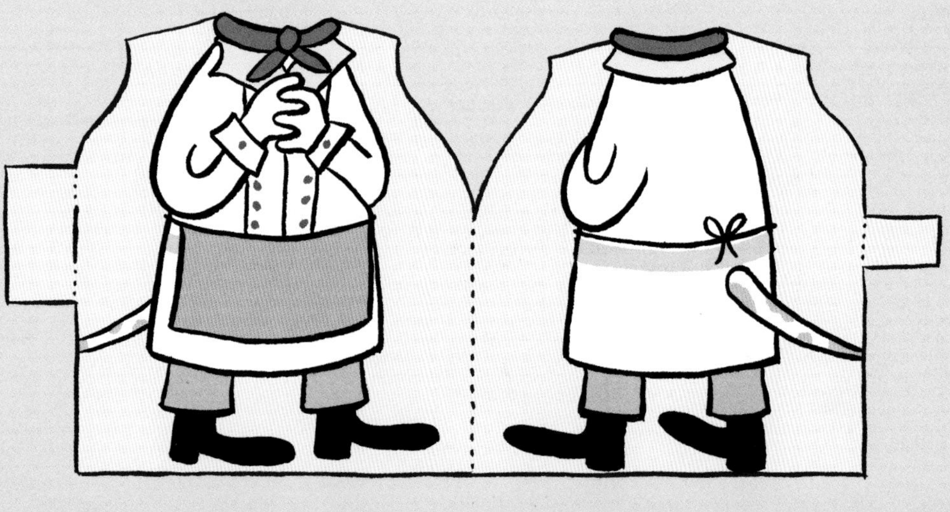

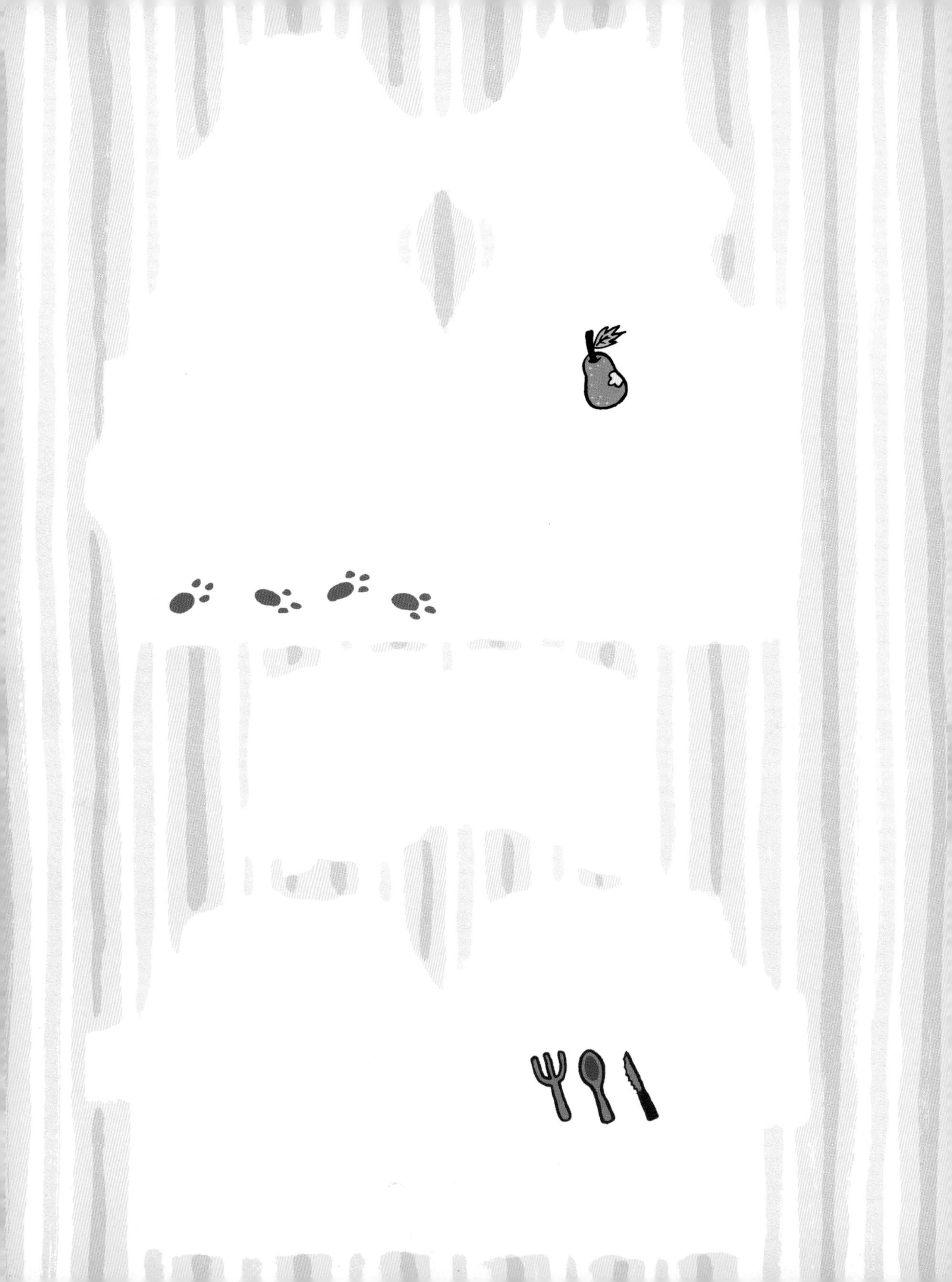

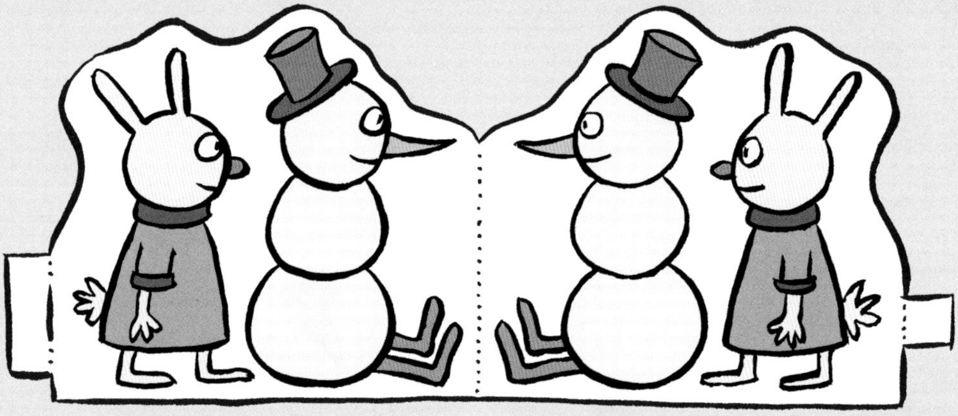

(characters fit inside vehicles.)

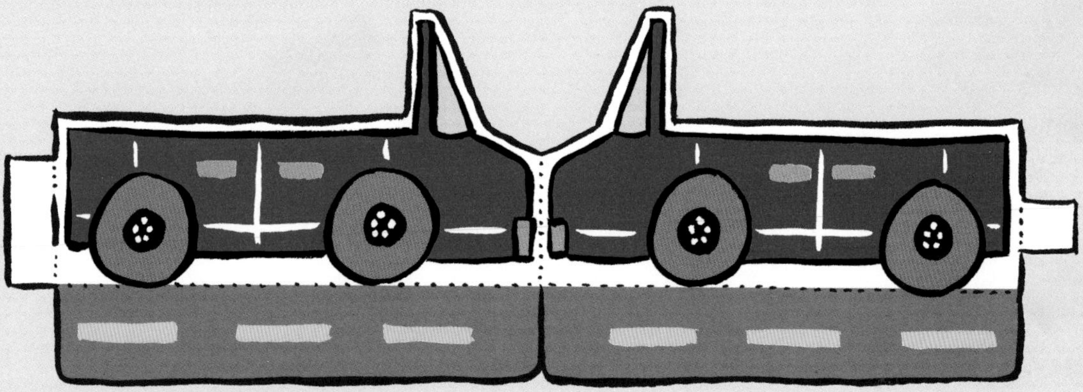

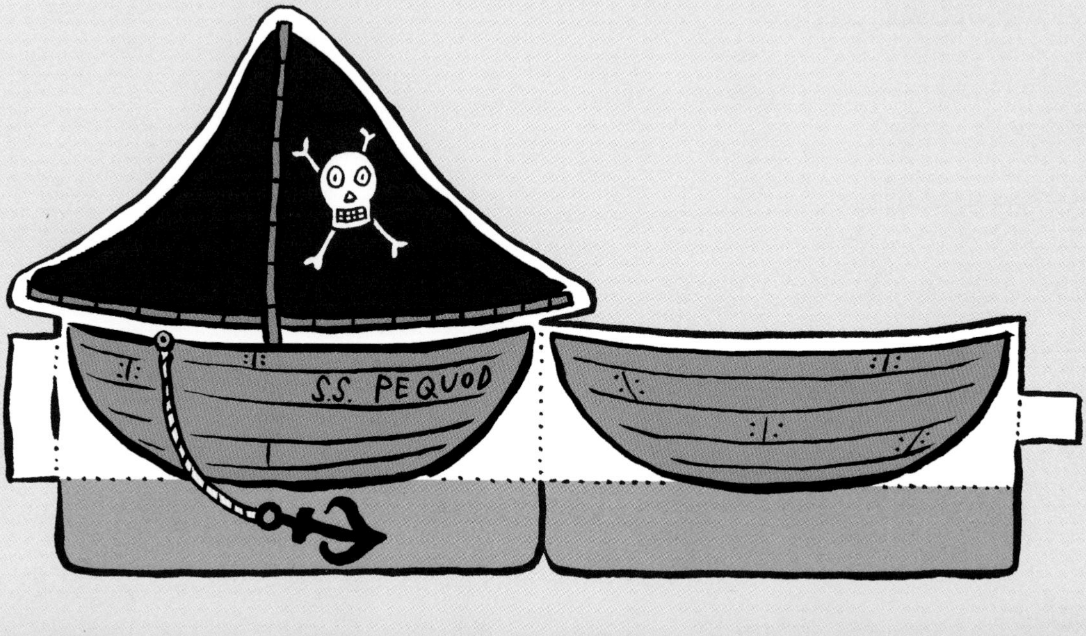
S.S. PEQUOD

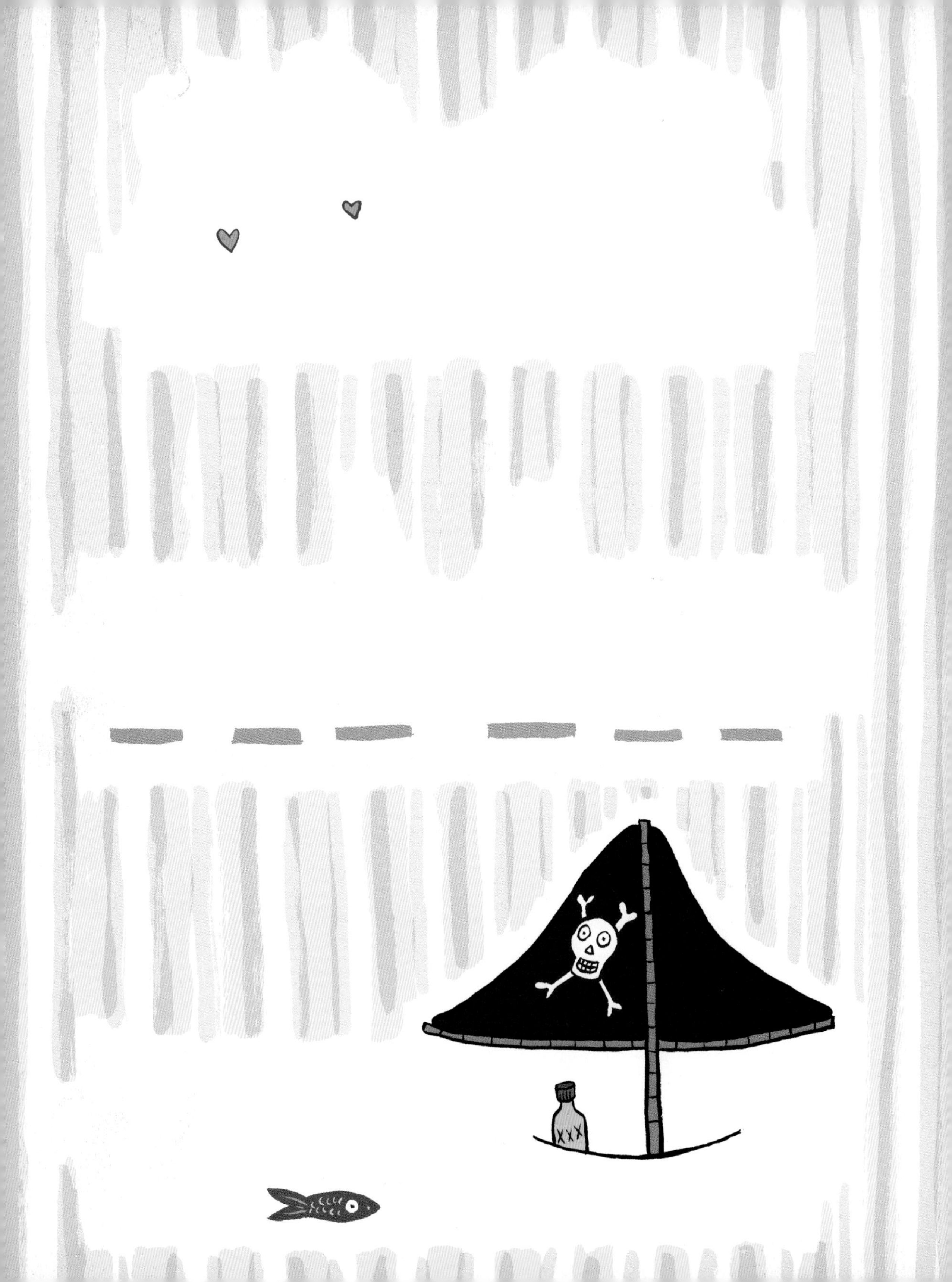

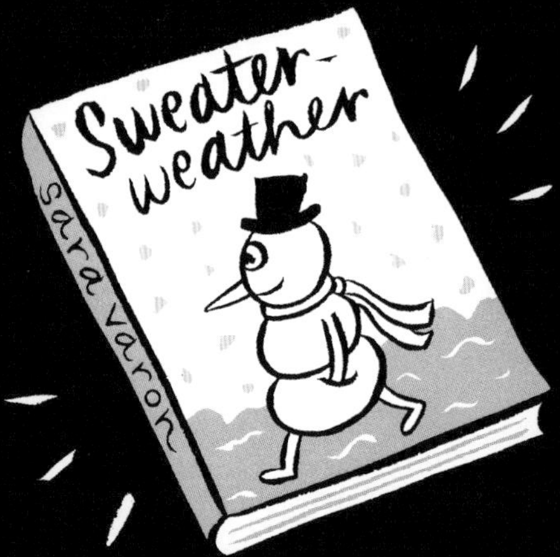
Sweater-
weather
Sara Varon

"Sweaterweather" Wraparound Cover, 2003

The wraparound image that made the cover of the original "Sweaterweather" is the view from a window inside MoMA PS1 (the contemporary art center) in Queens. It was taken on an especially snowy day looking out the back toward the 11101 post office building.

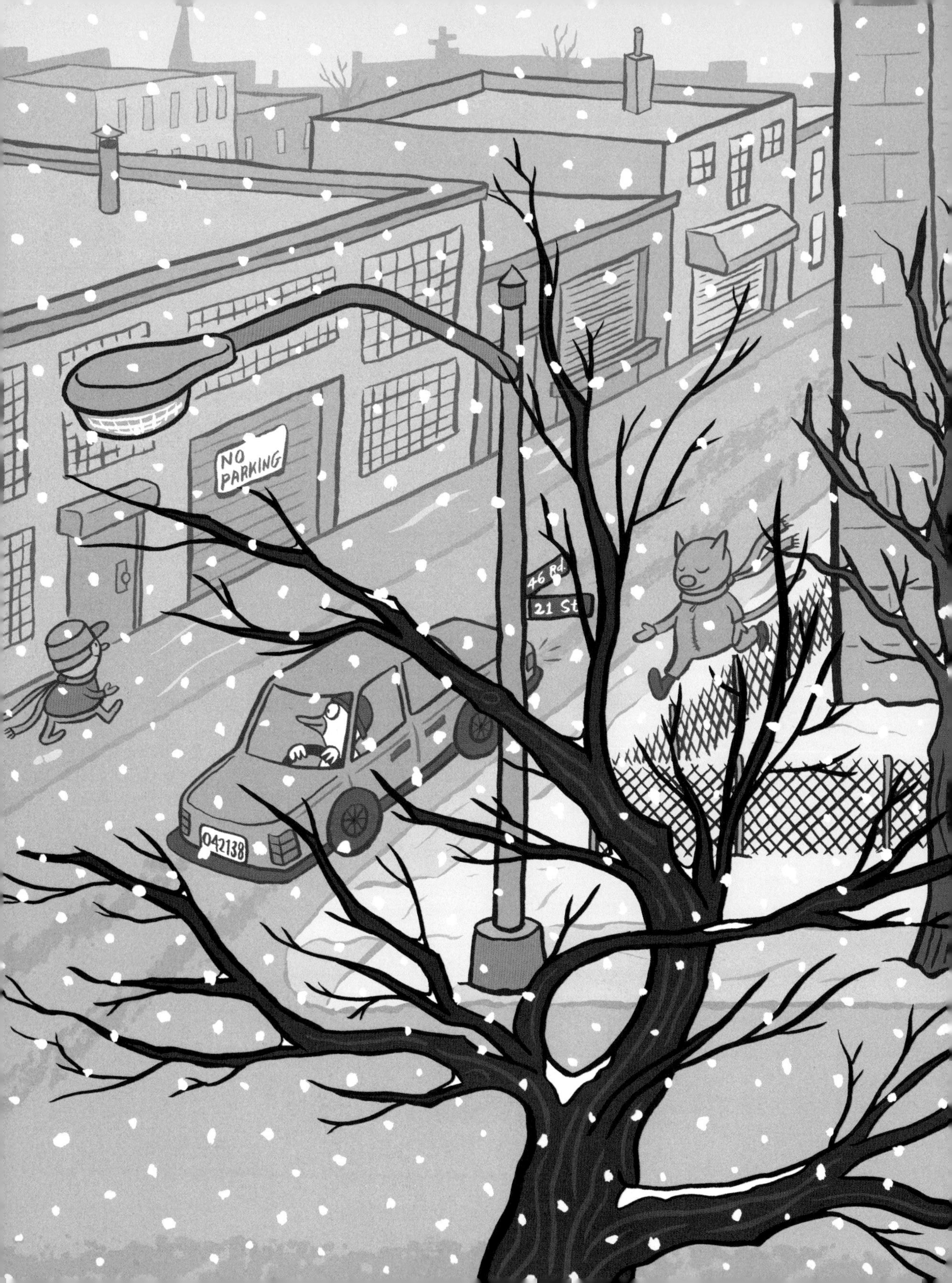
NO PARKING
46 Rd.
21 St
042138

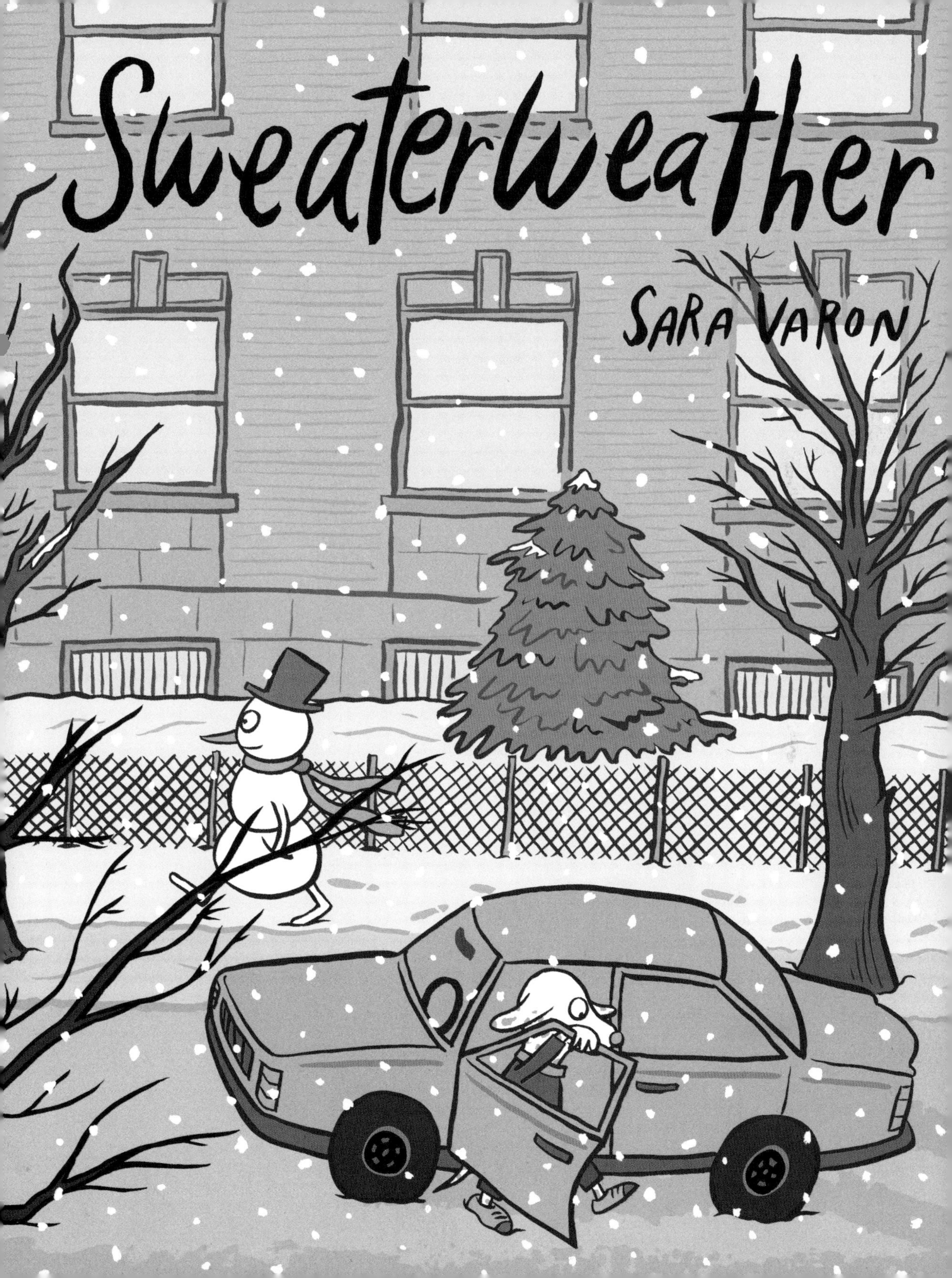
Sweaterweather
SARA VARON

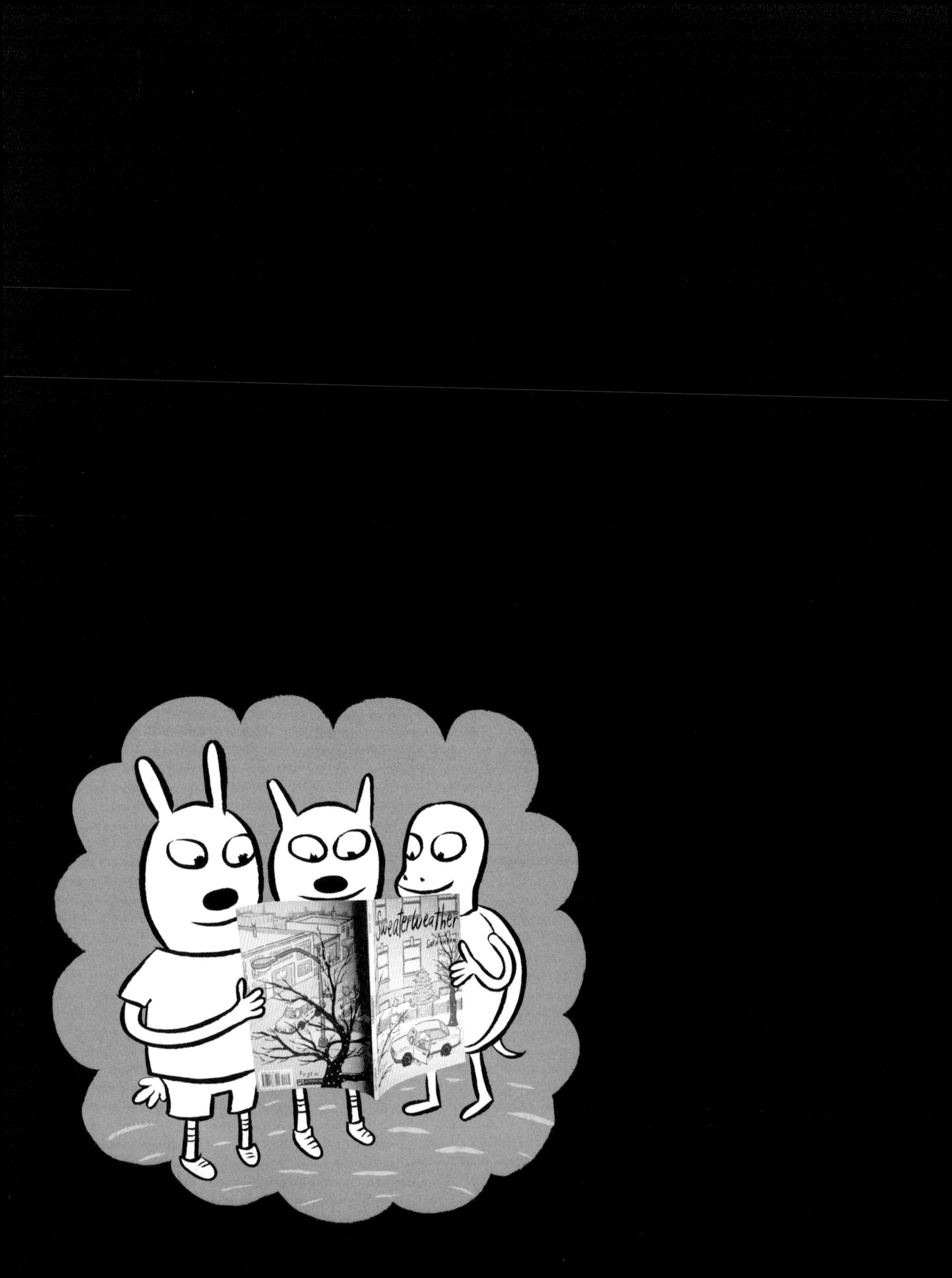
Sweaterweather
Sara Varon

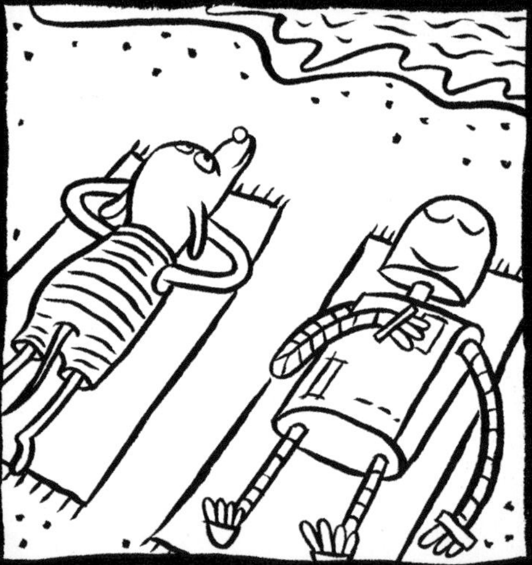

Dog and Robot Comic, July 2003

This comic was supposed to be part of Chris Pitzer's robot-themed anthology, "Project Telstar." I missed the deadline but made the comic anyway because I thought it'd be a good exercise. (My repertoire of characters at that point contained only animals.) Since my comics all had happy endings, I decided to switch it up and go with the theme of betrayal. Not a malicious betrayal, but a friend who betrays another friend by accident, certainly without bad intentions. Though I didn't connect it at the time, I'd recently put my dog Violet to sleep, which is probably the source of the theme. This would make me the dog in the story and Violet the robot.

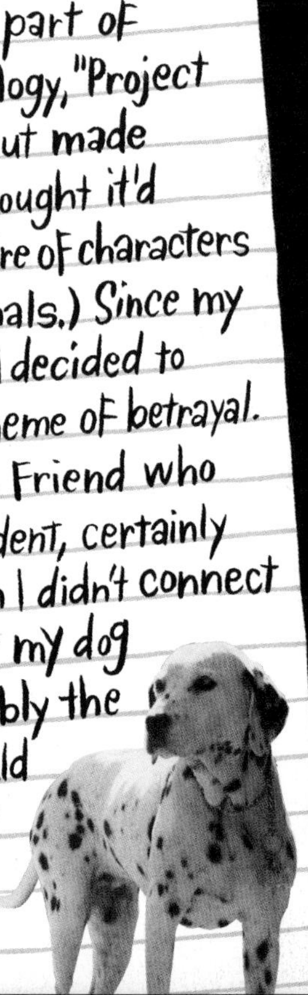

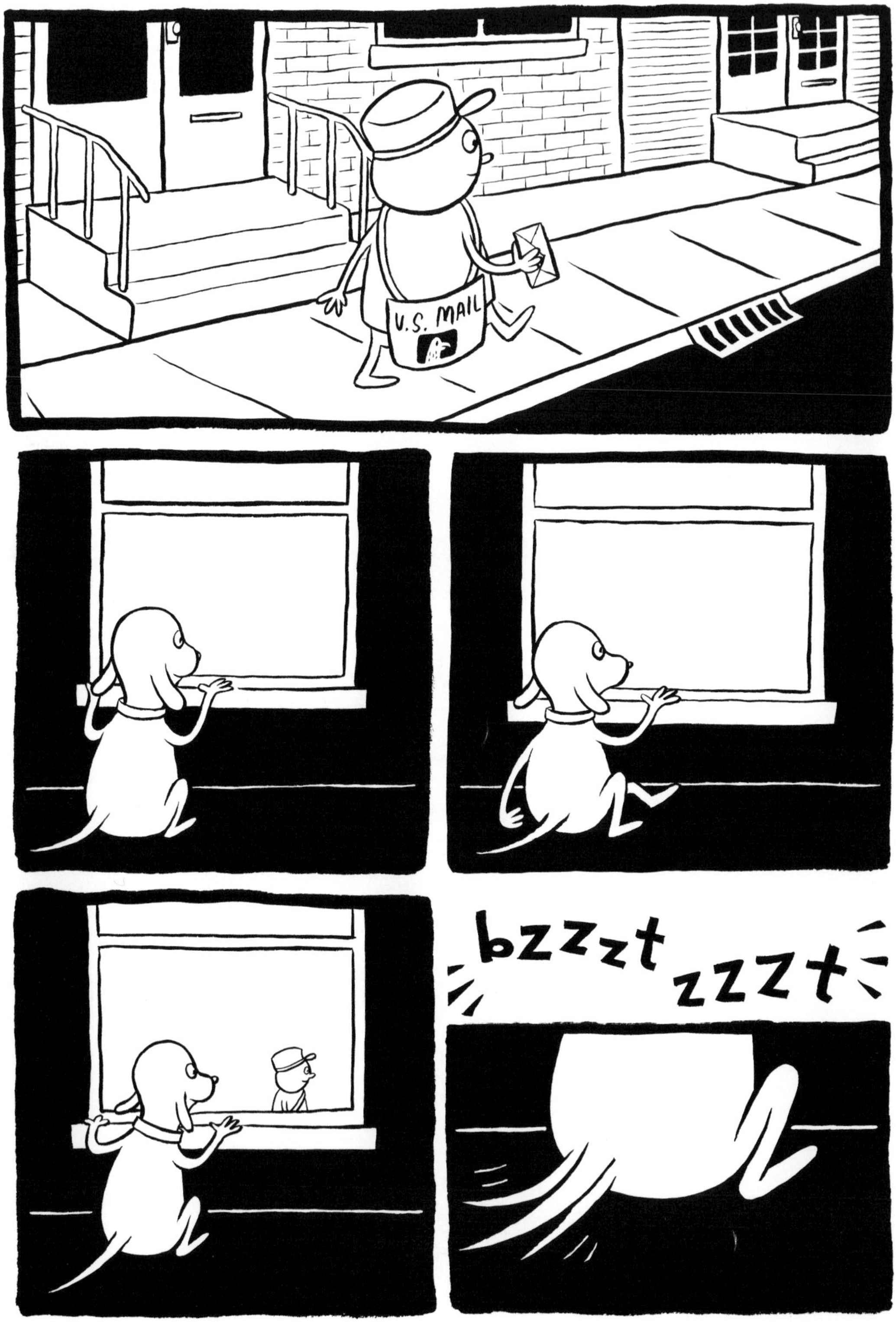
U.S. MAIL
bzzzt
zzzt

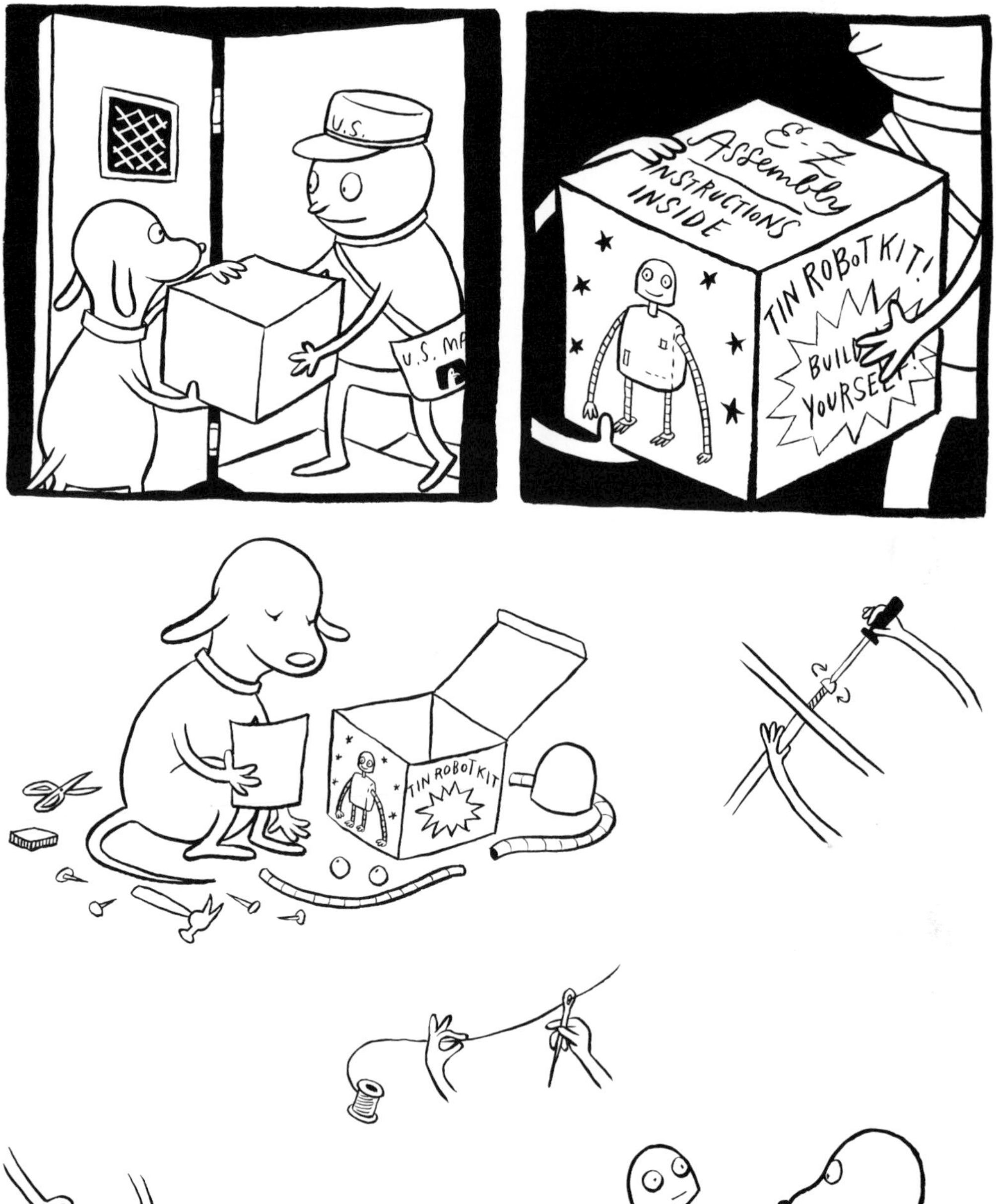

U.S.
U.S. MA
E-Z Assembly
INSTRUCTIONS INSIDE
TIN RoBoT KIT!
BUIL
YOURSE
TIN RoBoT KIT
GLUE
FINAL STEP: Attach Arms and Legs.

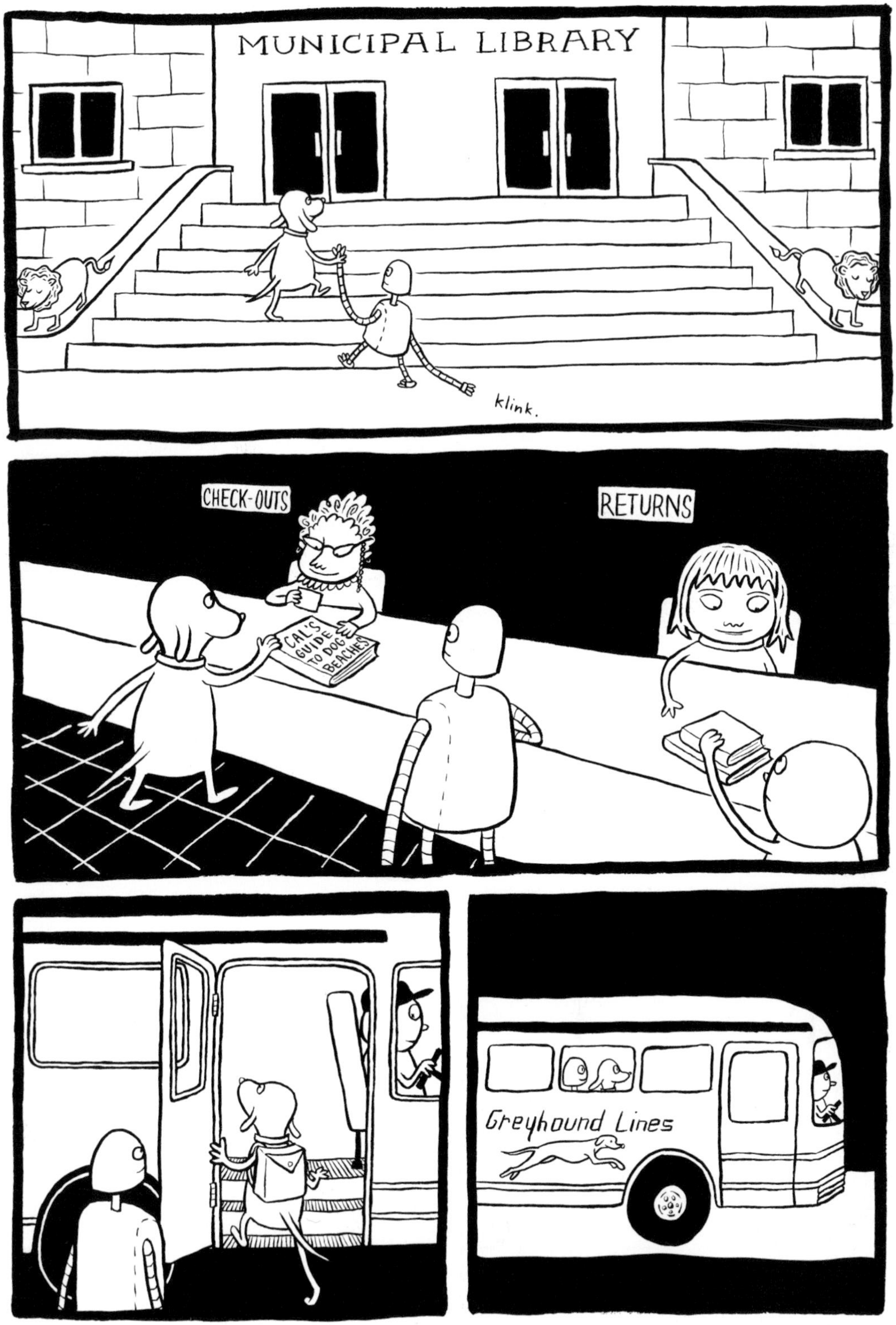
MUNICIPAL LIBRARY
klink.
CHECK-OUTS
RETURNS
CAL'S GUIDE TO DOG BEACHES
Greyhound Lines

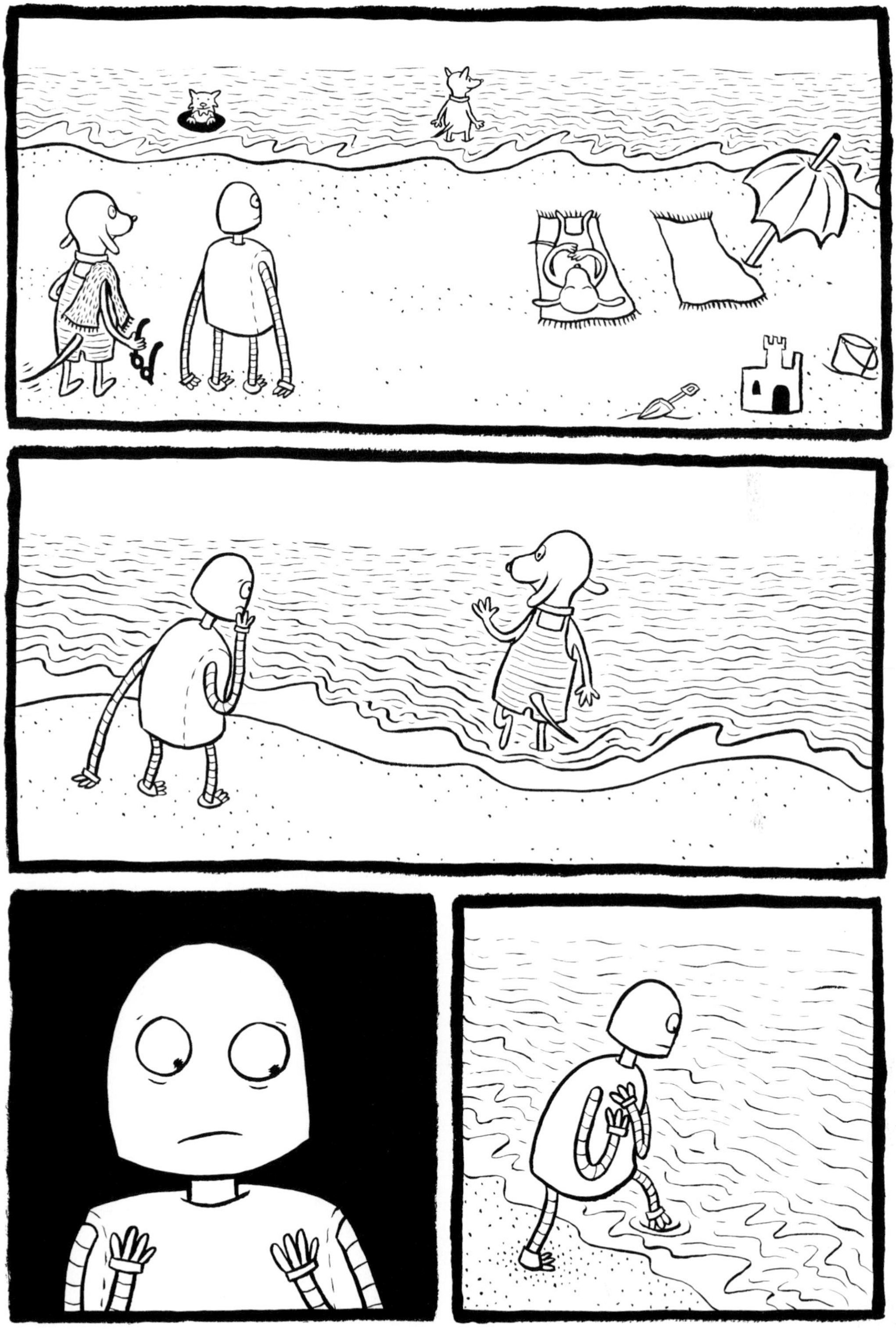

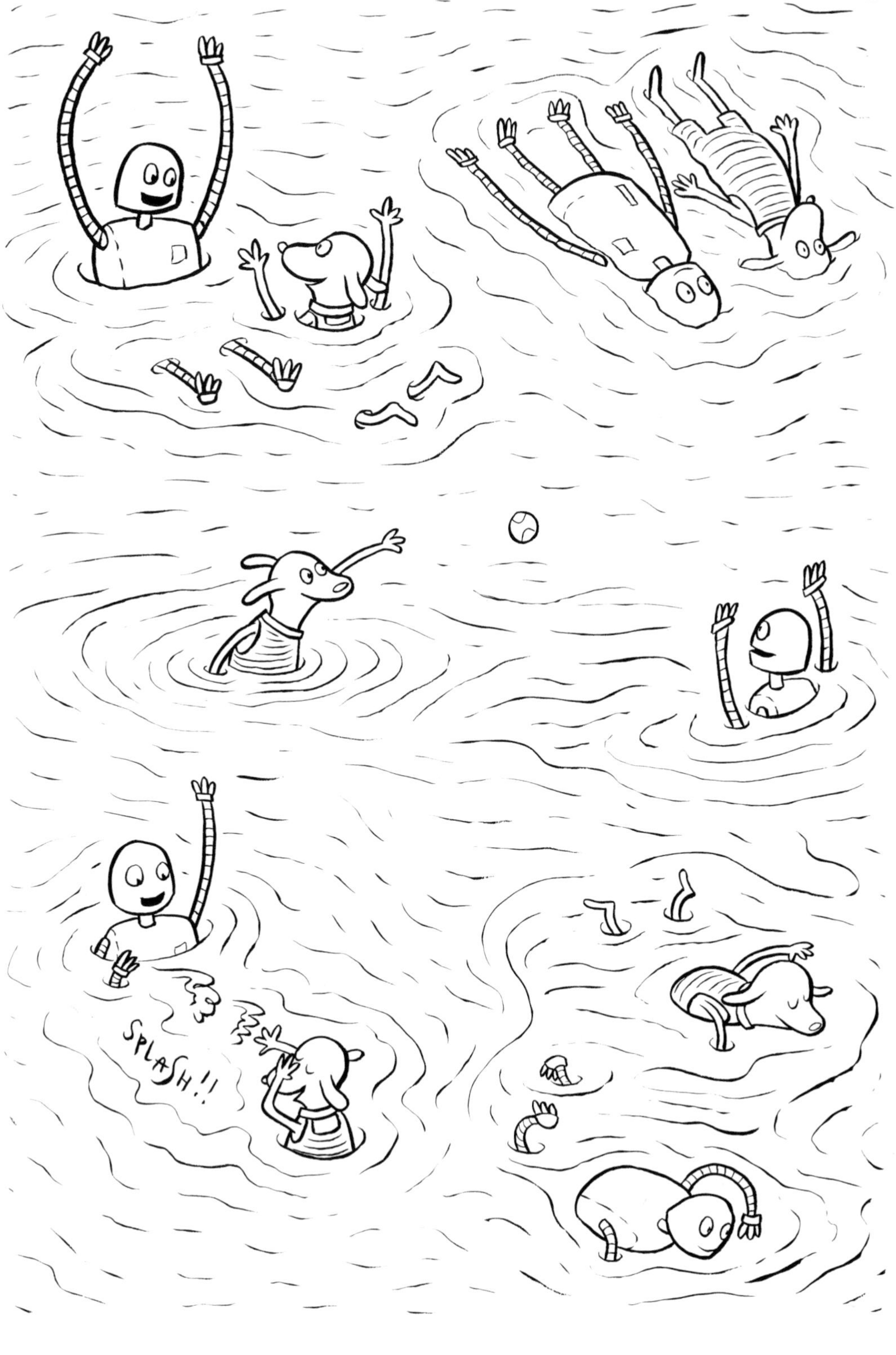
SPLASH!!

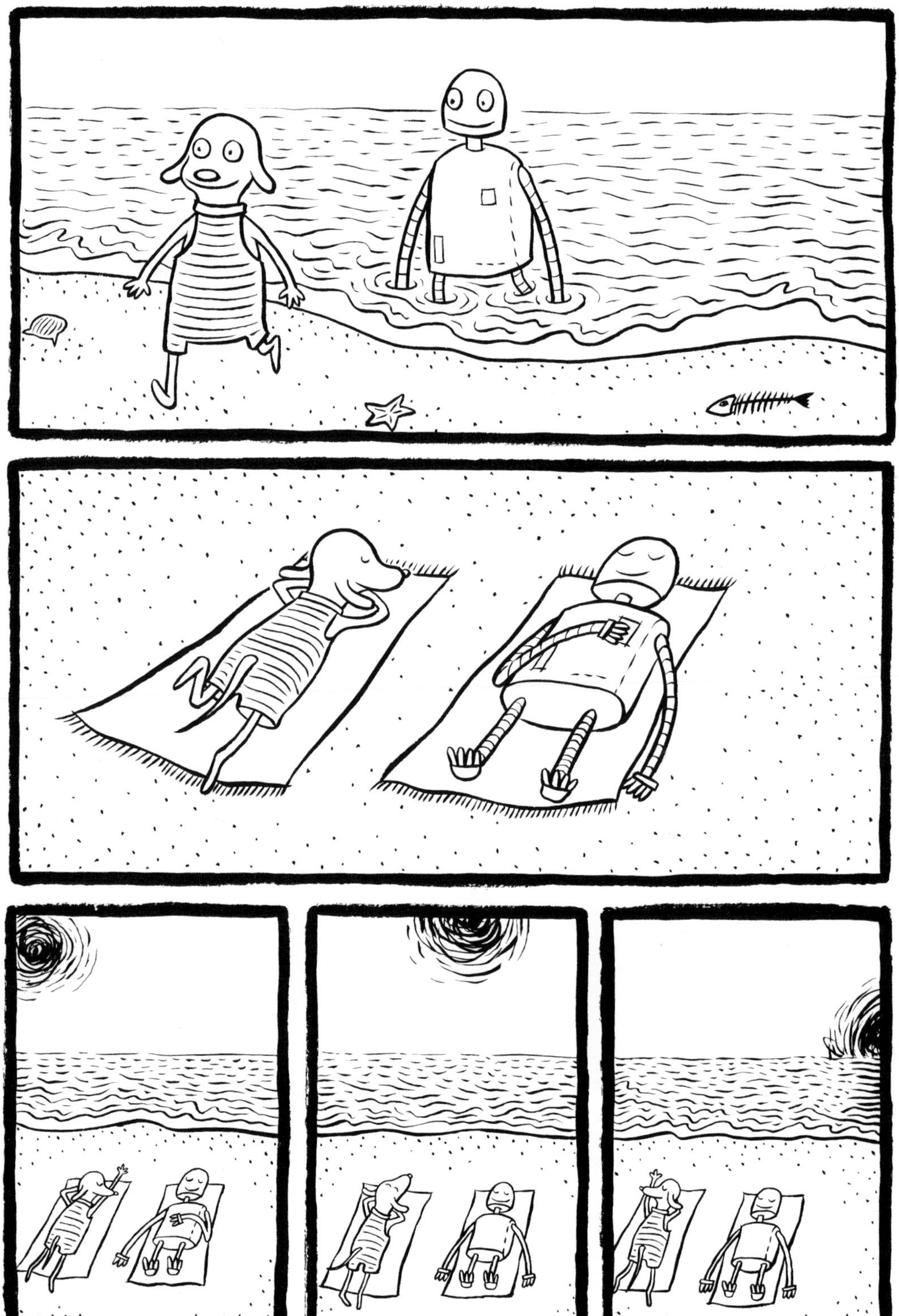

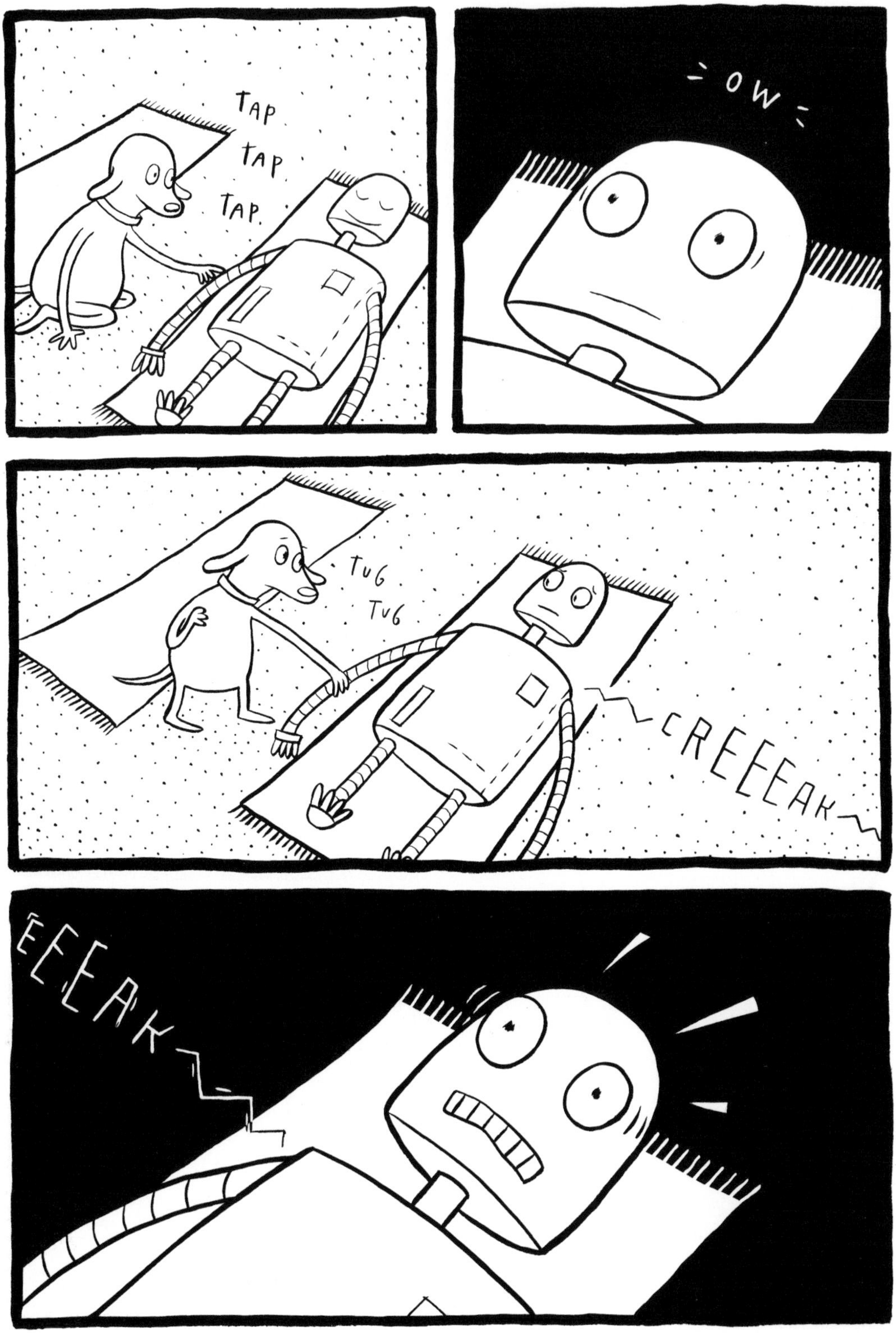
TAP
TAP
TAP
OW
TUG
TUG
CREEEAK
EEEAK

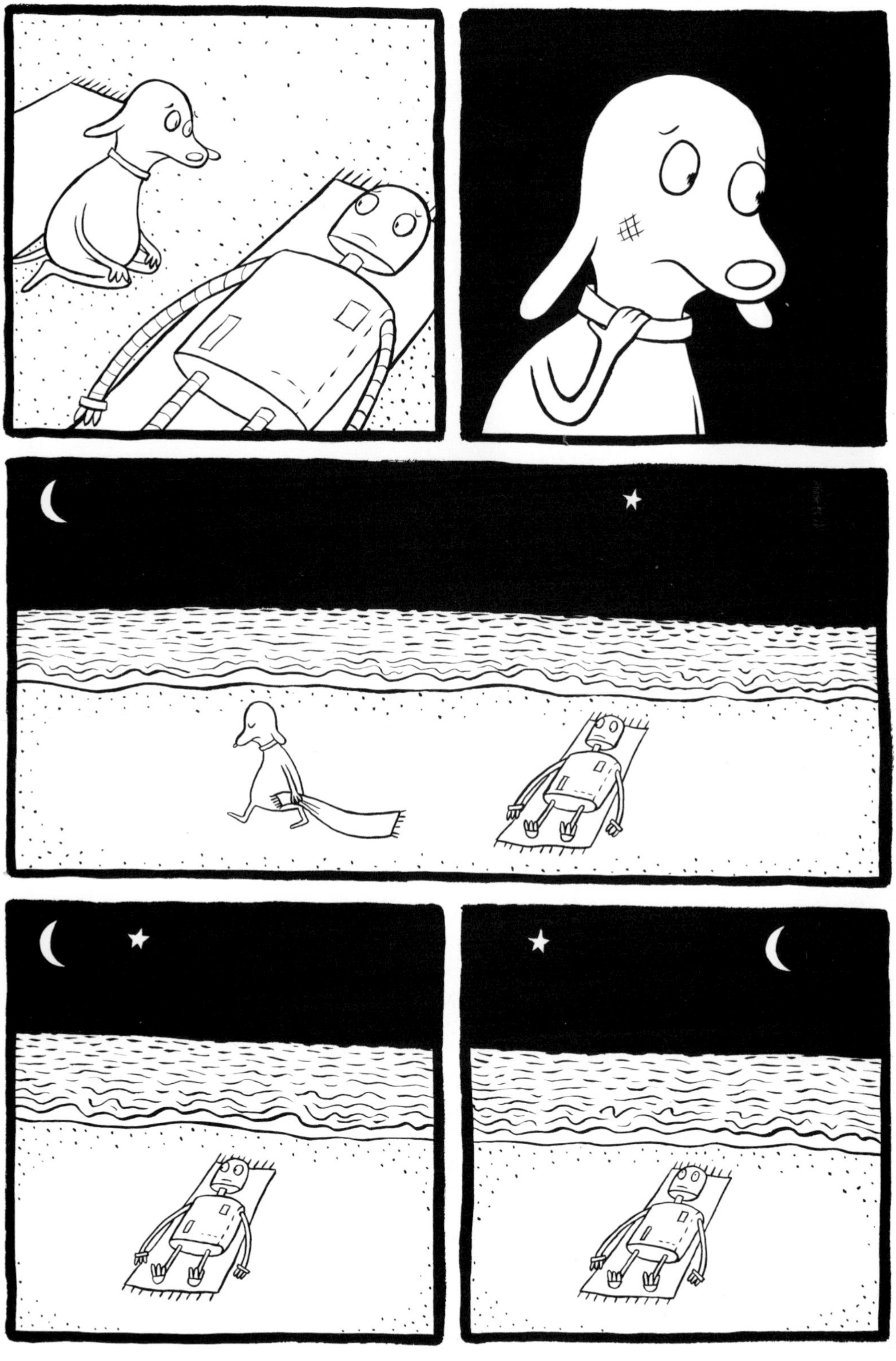

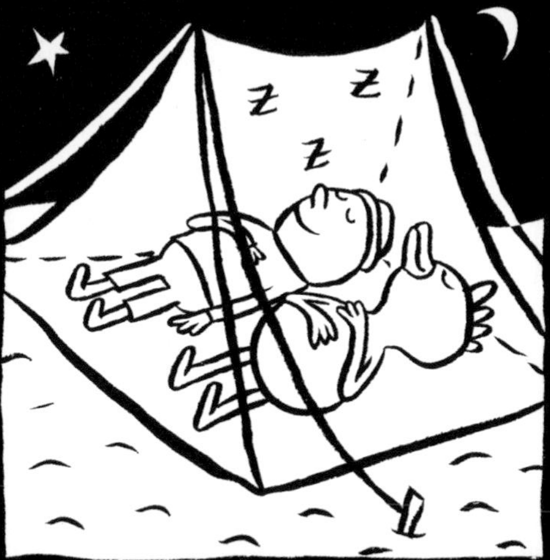
Z Z
Z

Camping Comic, December 2003

This one was for a comics contest and the theme that year was camping. For several years, scenes of camping showed up a lot in my work. I'm not a huge camper or anything, but I did miss nature a lot when I first moved to New York. Also, I took a really awesome camping trip in 2000 with my friend Cindy, who is an expert camper and had all the gear. We went to the White Mountains in Vermont and took Violet. I don't think Violet had ever been to the forest before and for these couple of days she was in dog heaven. They were probably the best days of her life. Oh, yeah, and I won the comics competition and got a trip to Fumetto in Lucerne, Switzerland.

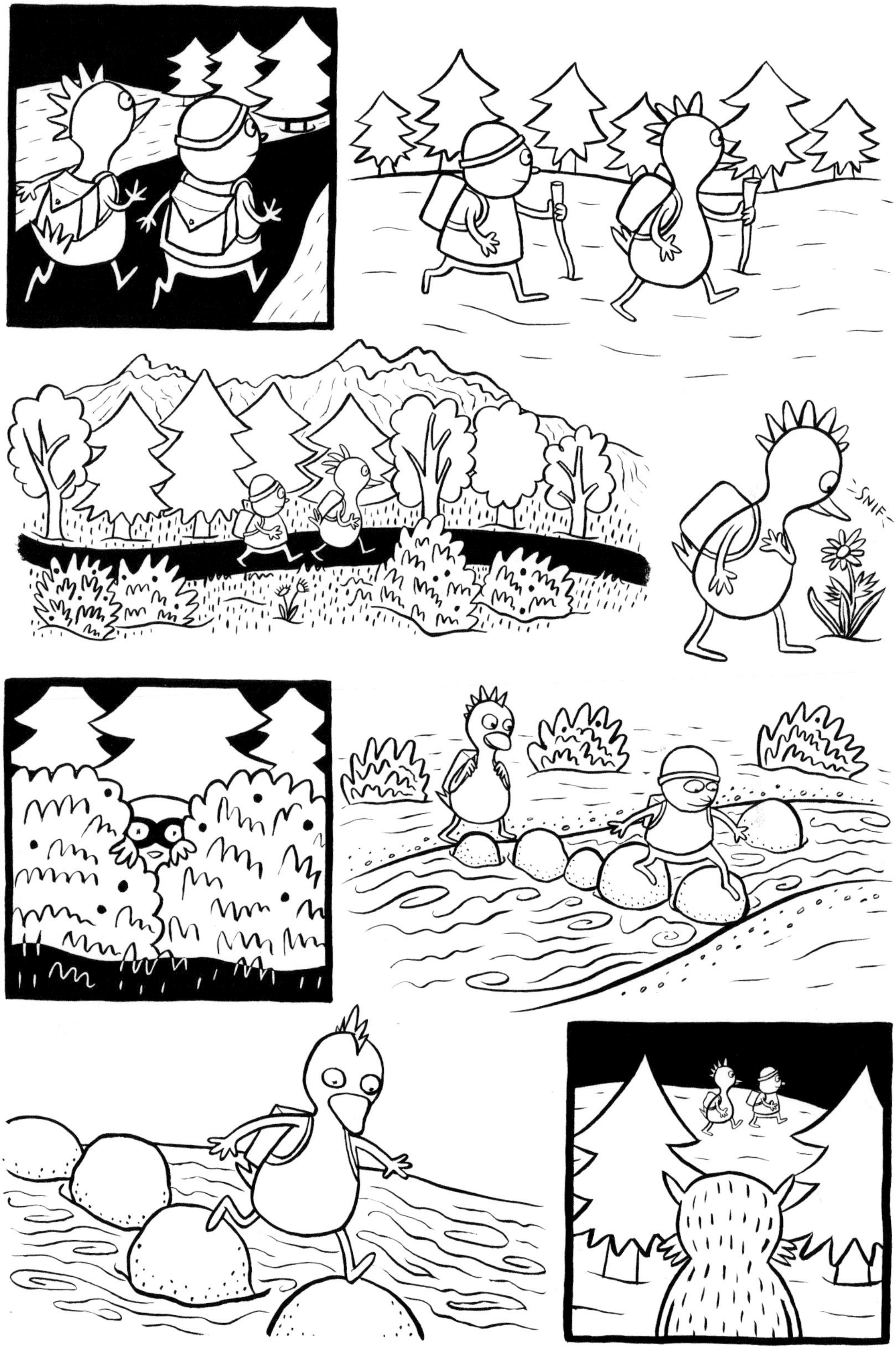
SNIF

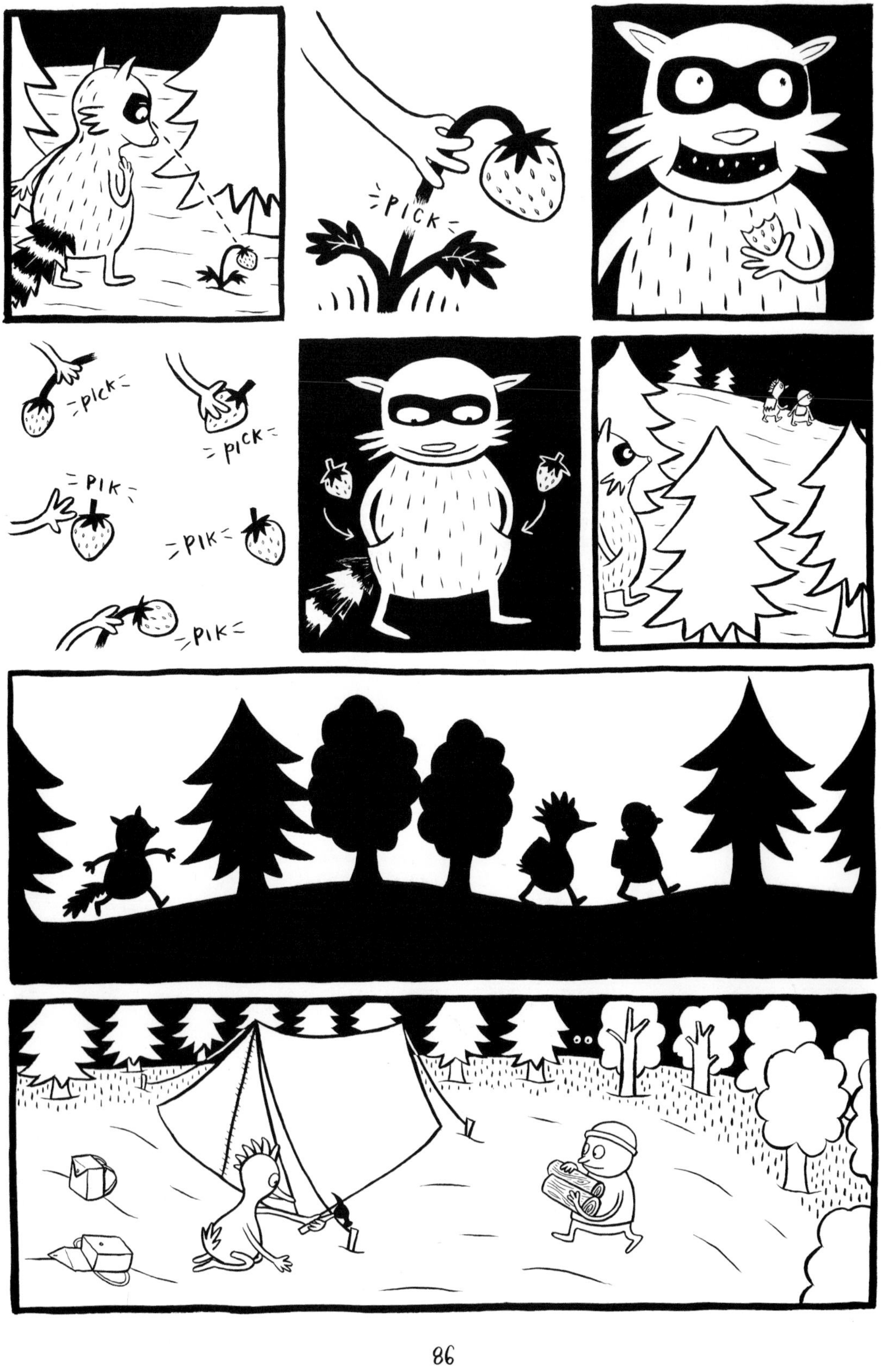
PICK
PICK
PICK
PIK
PIK
PIK

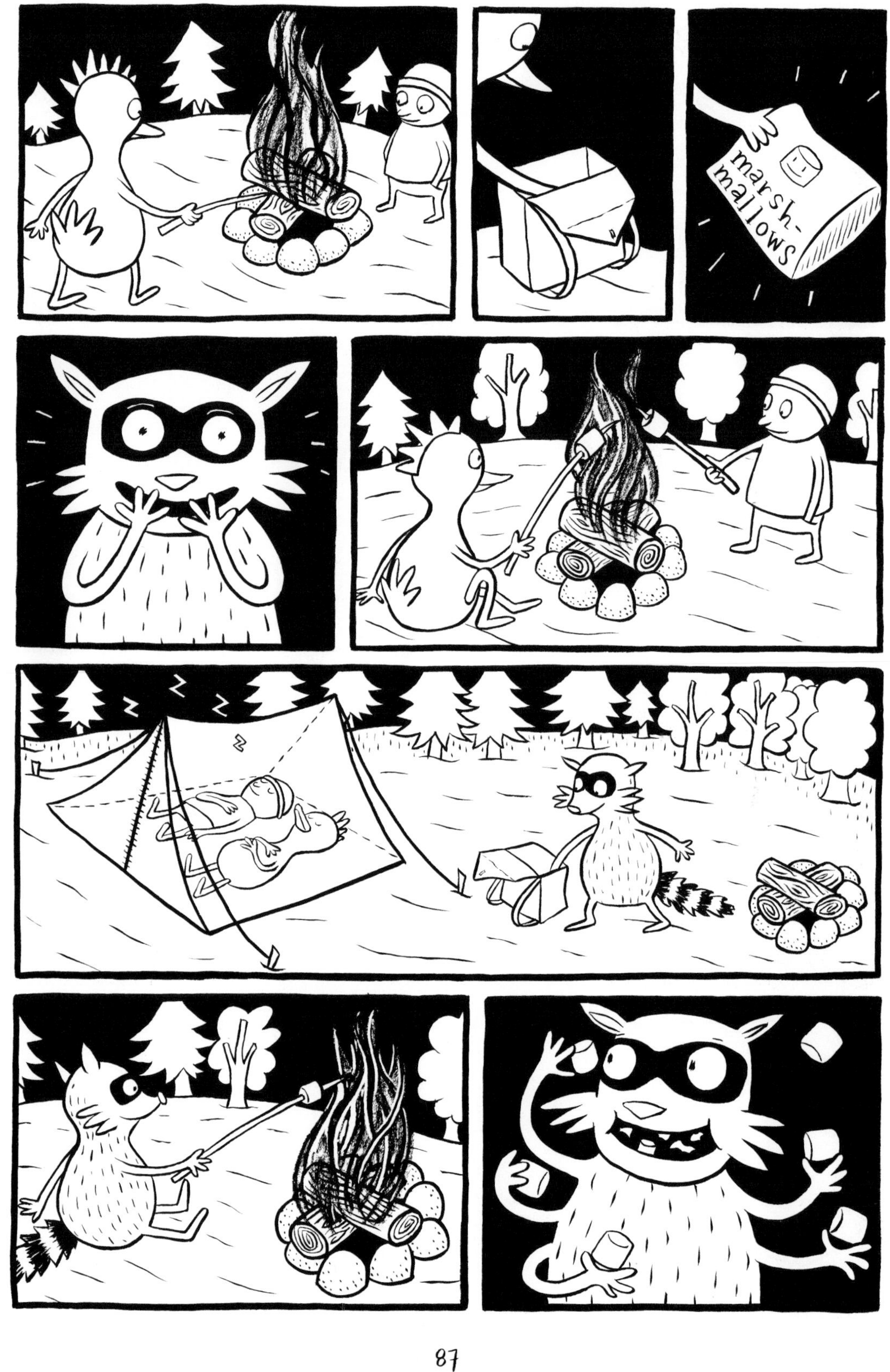
marsh-
mallows

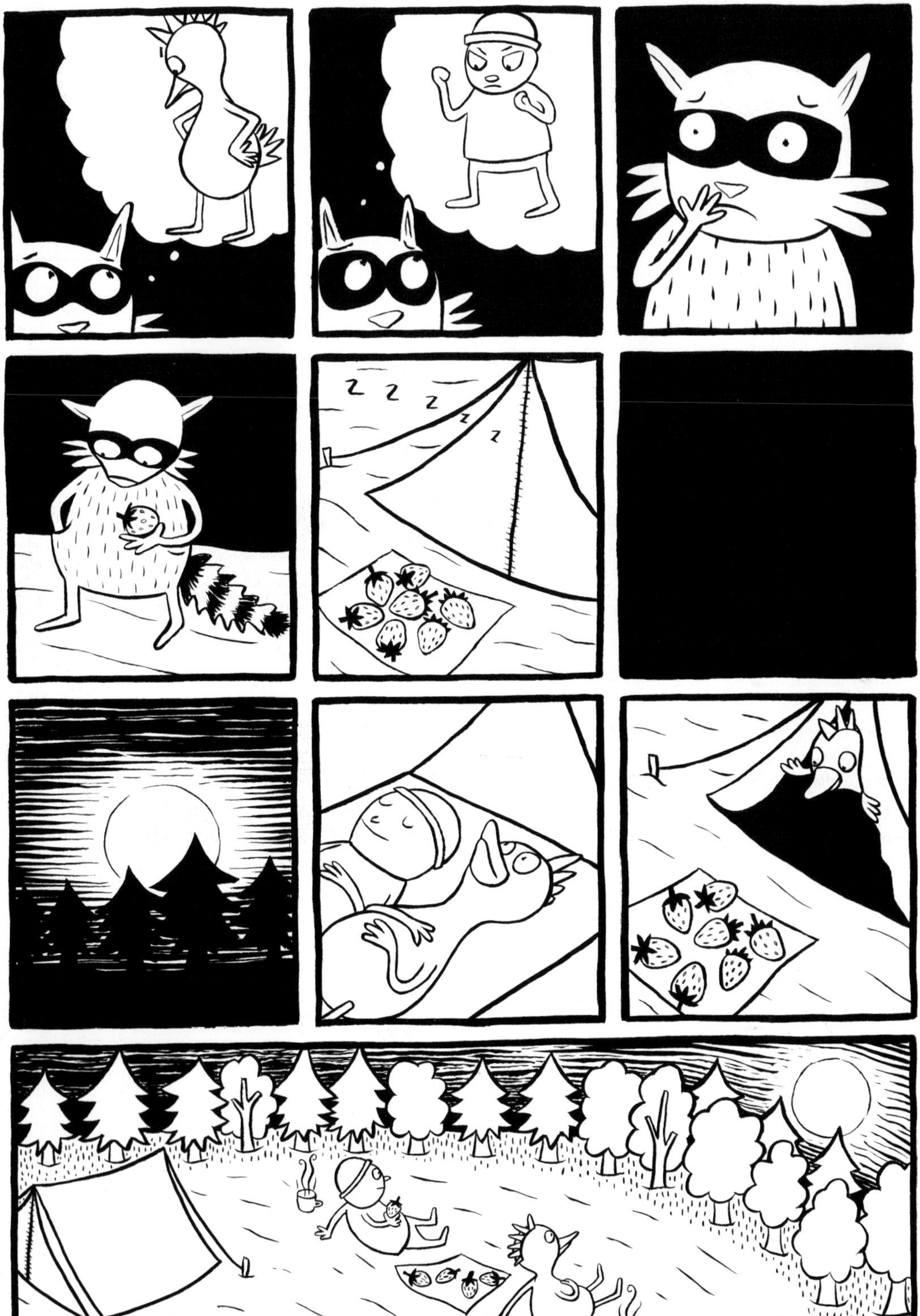
Z Z Z Z Z
end

Boxing Comic, May 2005
    I started boxing at the beginning of 2004
and continued for about 10 years. It was kind
of a big part of my life — I even worked for
a boxing tournament for several years. (An
extremely fun job.) I didn't have a lot of
opportunities to fit boxing into my work. So
this was my big chance to get it all out! In the
story, I made my characters friends because I
felt a little bad about them hurting each other.
I guess I wanted to make it clear that there
were no sour feelings between them.

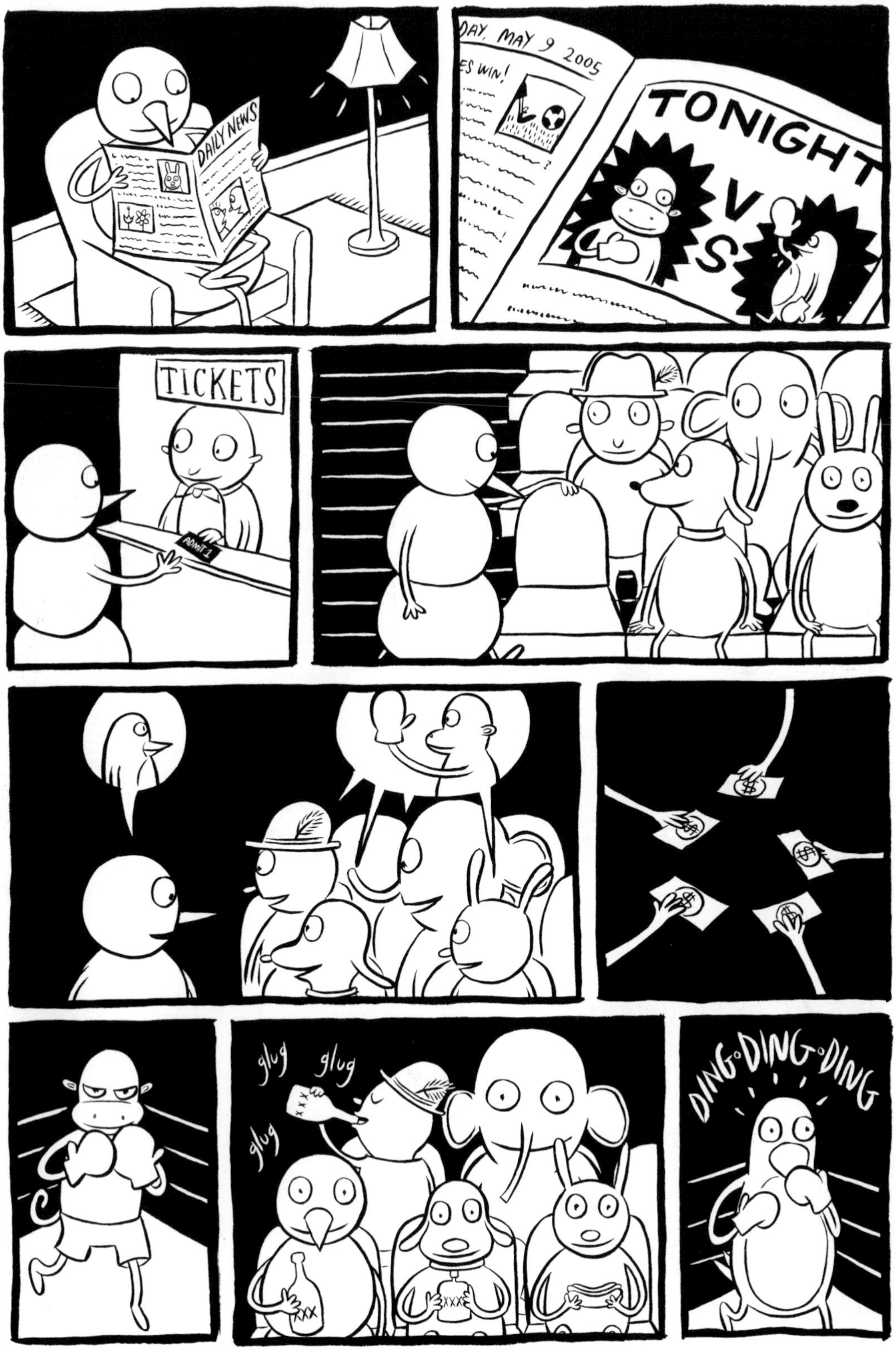
DAILY NEWS
DAY, MAY 9 2005
ES WIN!
TONIGHT
VS
TICKETS
ADMIT 1
glug glug
glug
DING DING DING

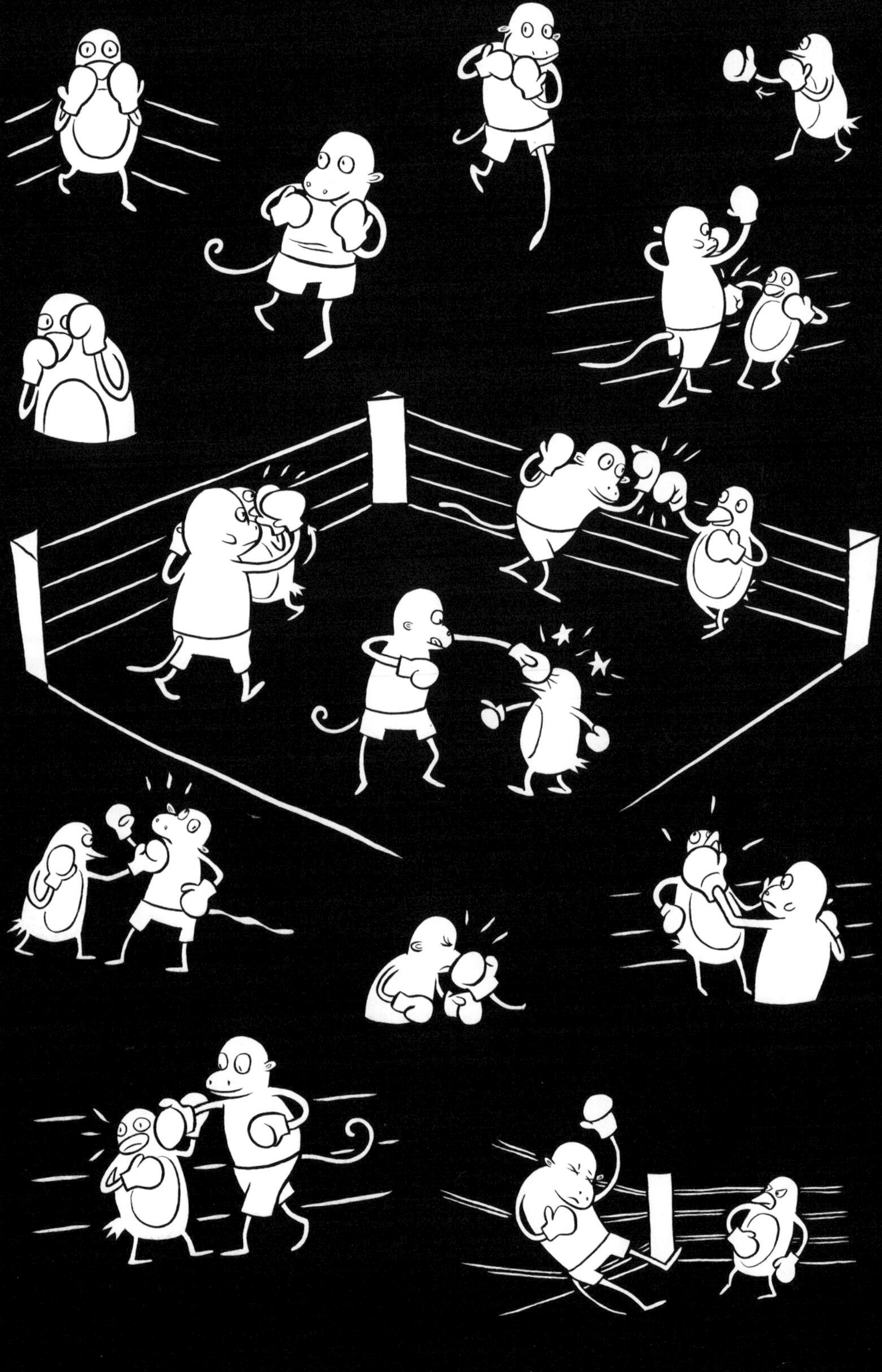

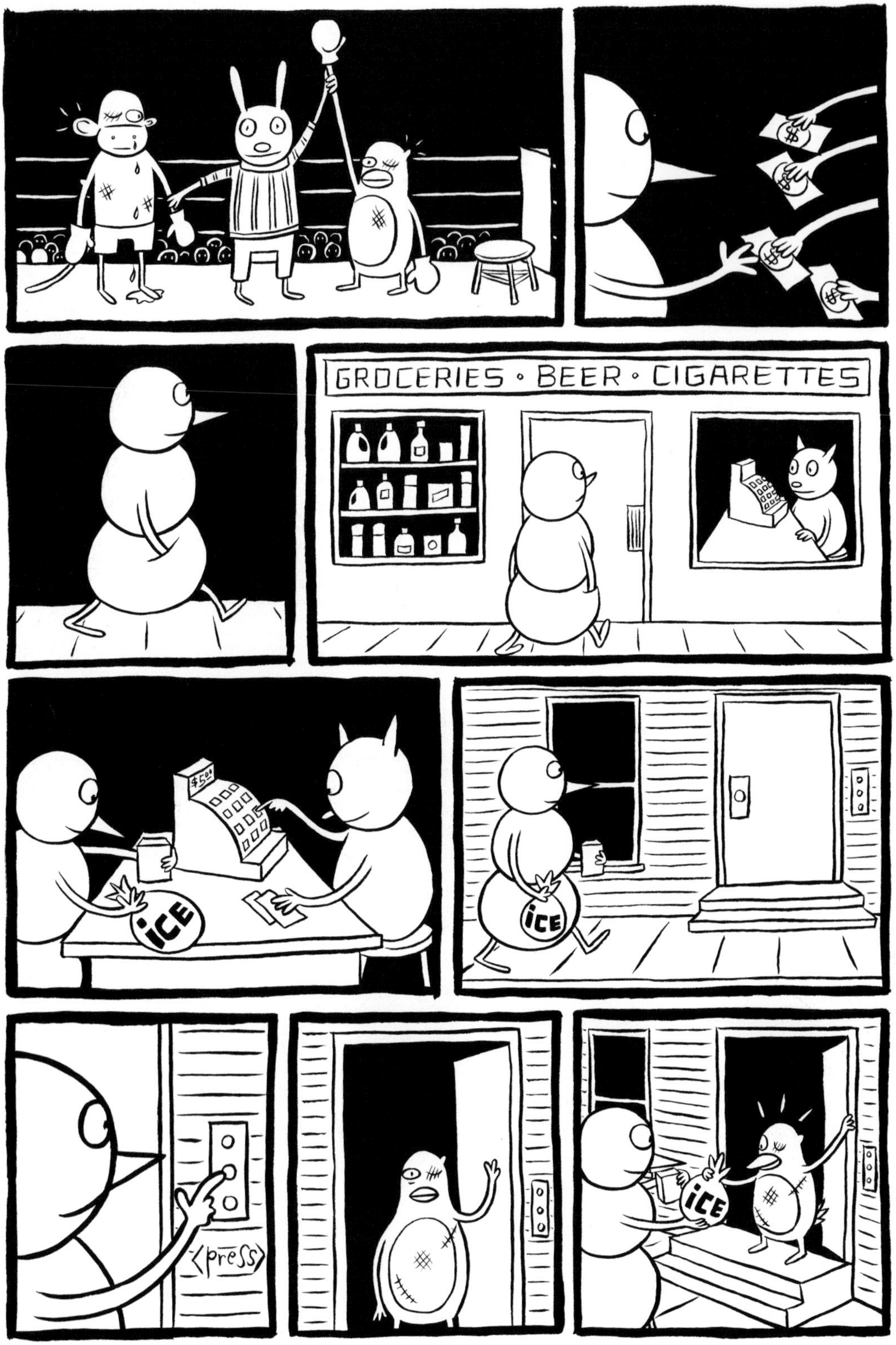
GROCERIES • BEER • CIGARETTES
$5.00
ICE
ICE
{press}
ICE

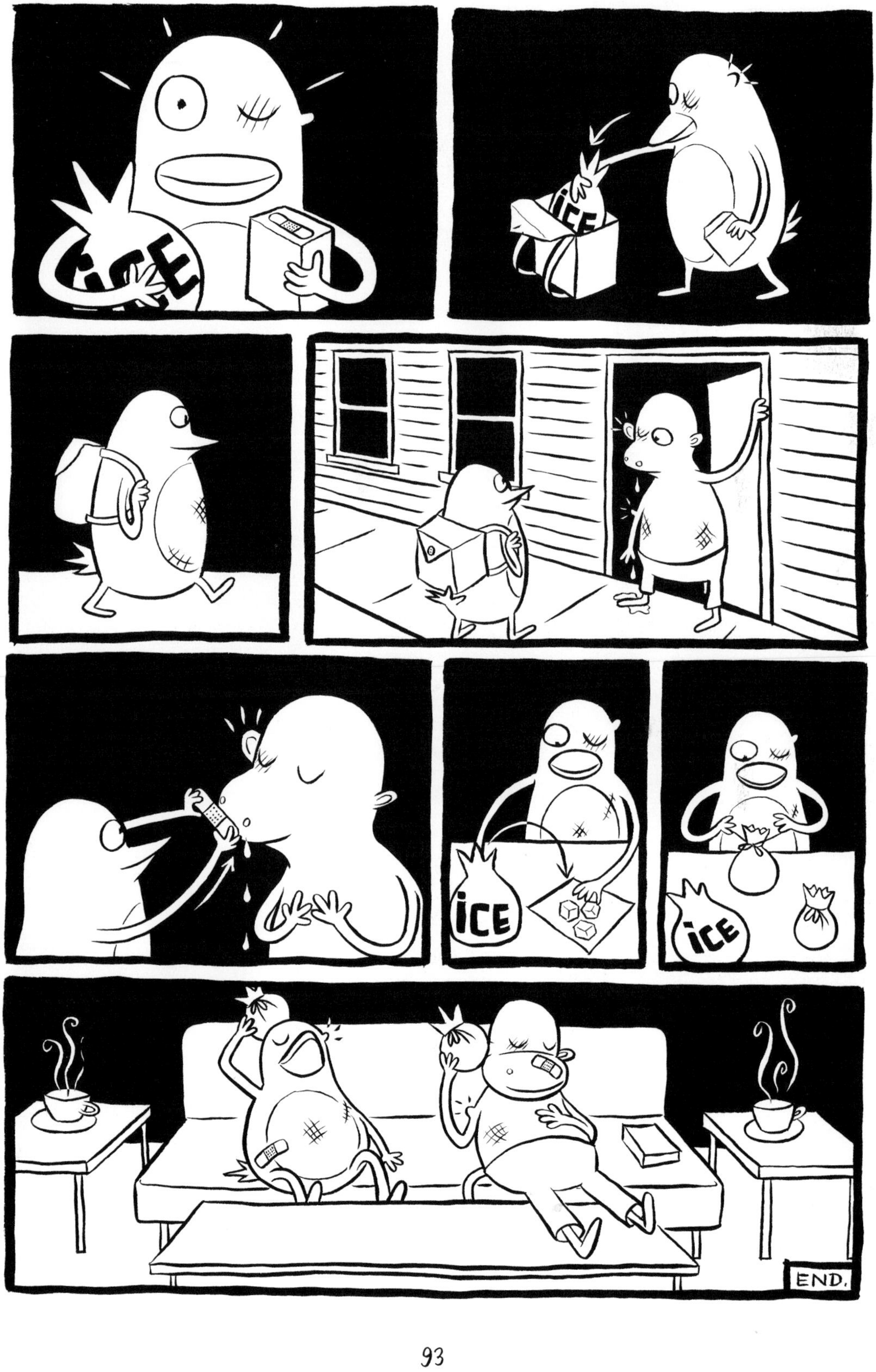
ICE
ICE
ICE
ICE
END.

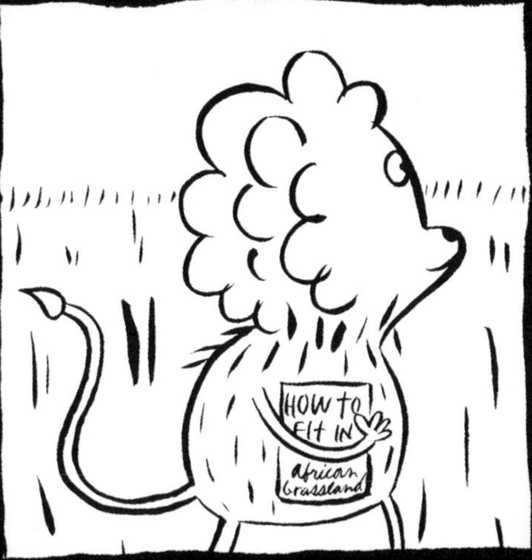
HOW to Fit IN
african Grassland

Lion Comic, February 2009

This was for an animal-themed issue of the Swiss comics magazine "Strapazin." At the time, I had this lion character who I drew a lot. I liked the idea that he was totally misguided, but also completely happy in his ignorance. In the story, he thinks he's succeeded in fitting in with the other animals. Not only does he not really fit in, but he doesn't seem to understand that, as a lion, he doesn't need to fit in because he's at the top of the social order.

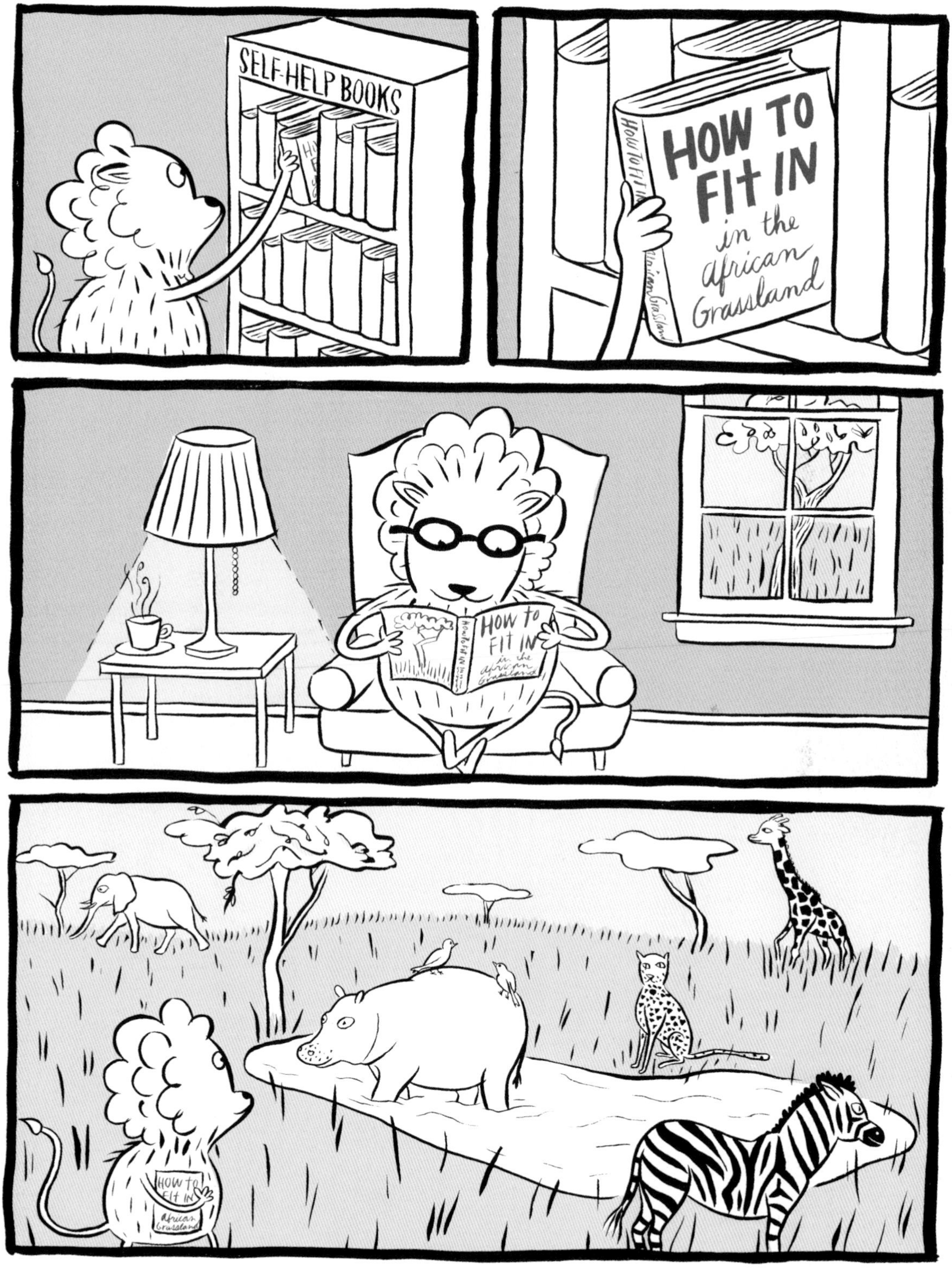
SELF-HELP BOOKS
HOW TO FIT IN in the African Grassland
HOW TO FIT IN in the African Grassland
HOW TO FIT IN in the African Grassland
HOW TO FIT IN African Grassland

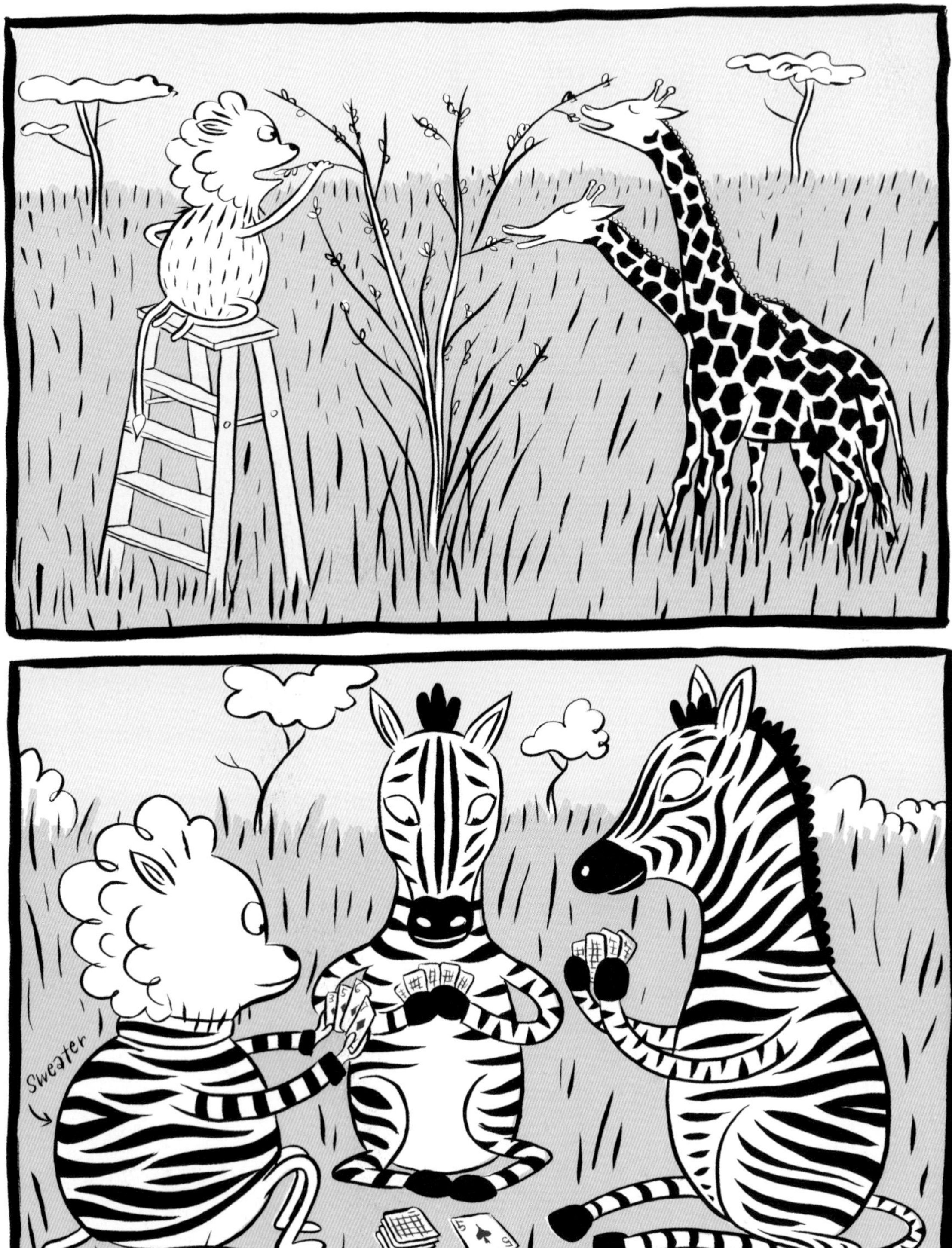
Sweater

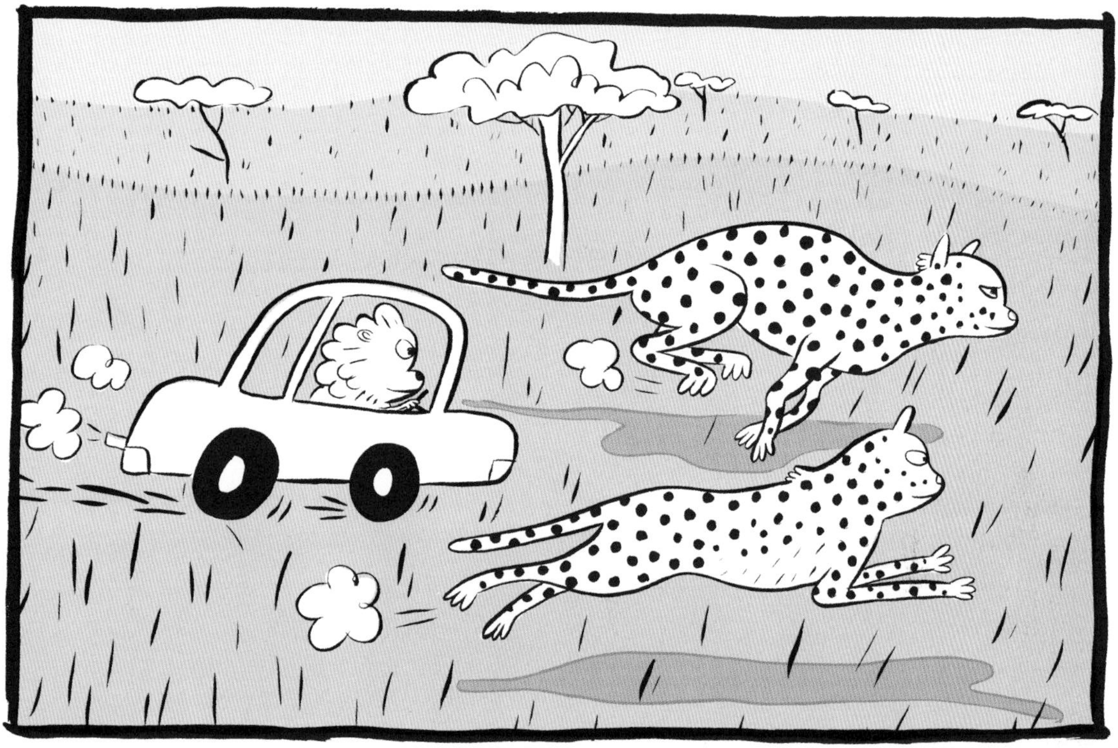

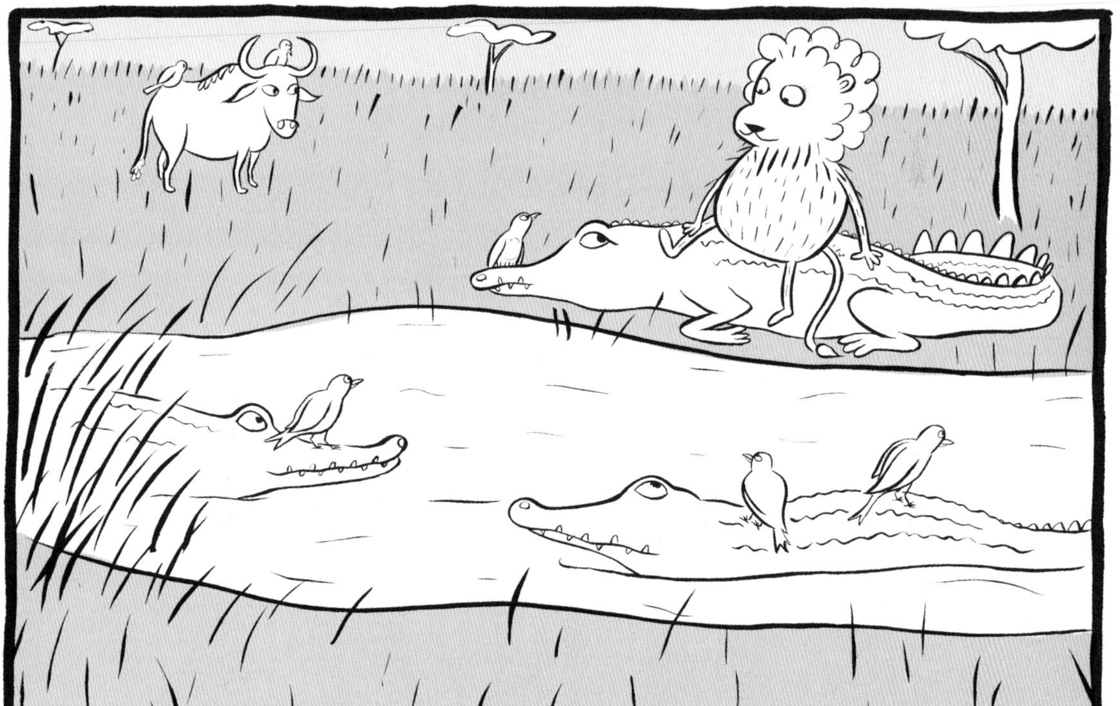

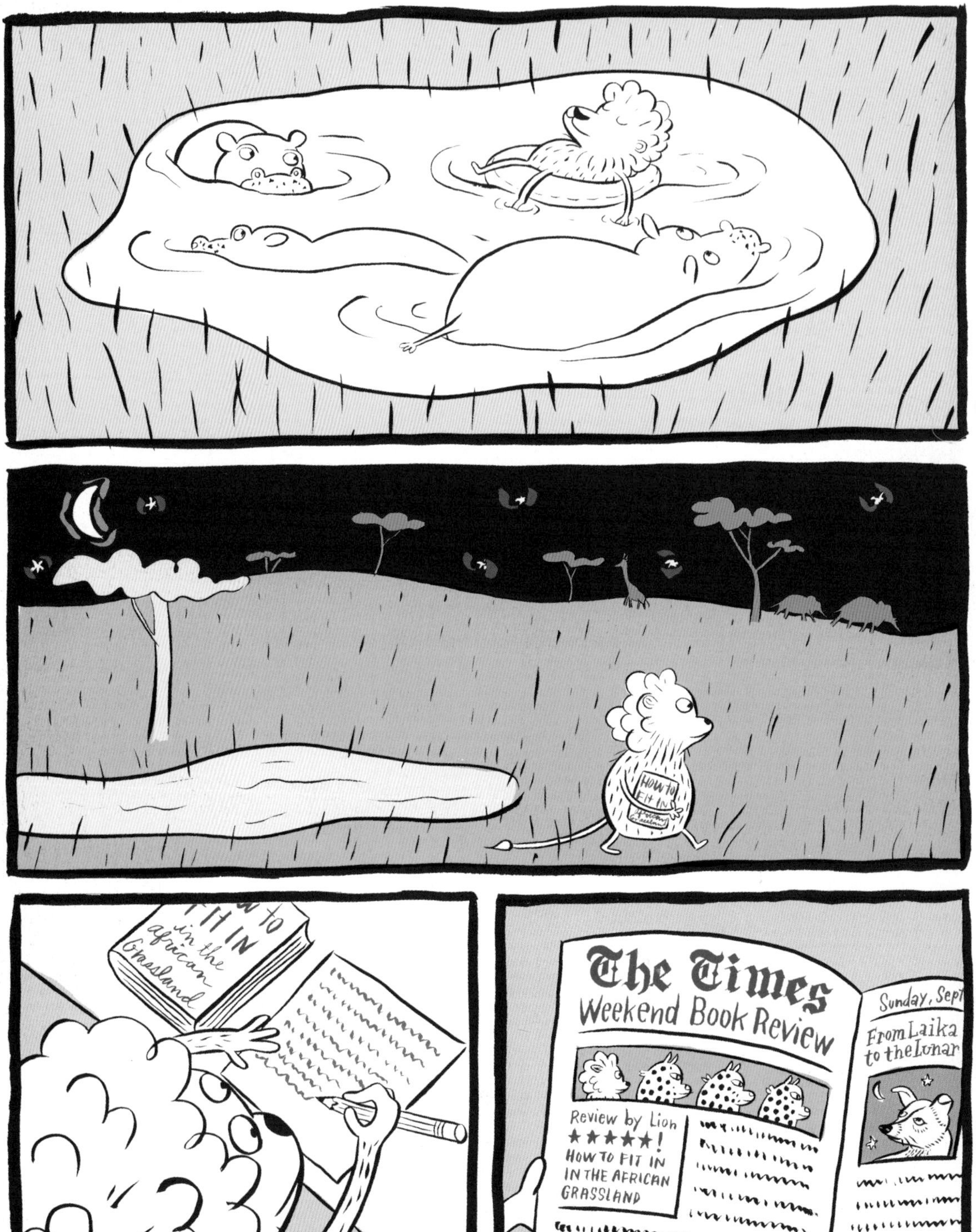
HOW TO FIT IN
in the
african
Grassland
The Times
Weekend Book Review
Sunday, Sept
From Laika
to the Lunar
Review by Lion
★★★★★!
HOW TO FIT IN
IN THE AFRICAN
GRASSLAND

Book Tribute, December 2010

Like many illustrators I know, I spend a huge amount of time listening to NPR. Unbeknownst to them, Brian Lehrer (10-noon on WNYC) and Leonard Lopate (noon-2, WNYC) are some of my best friends. (Terri Gross too.) It is from them that I get most of my book recommendations. I do read a lot, although I wouldn't say I'm a particularly critical reader. Mostly I'm just reading for a good story and nice pictures.

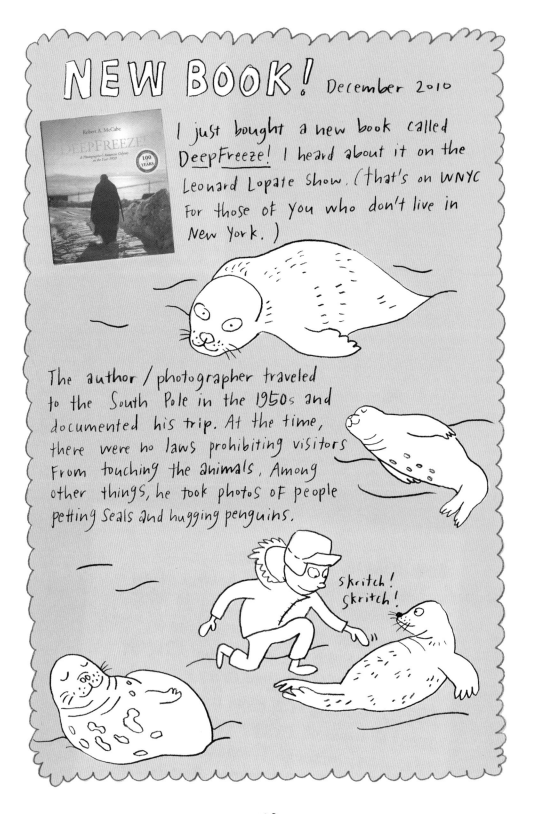

NEW BOOK! December 2010

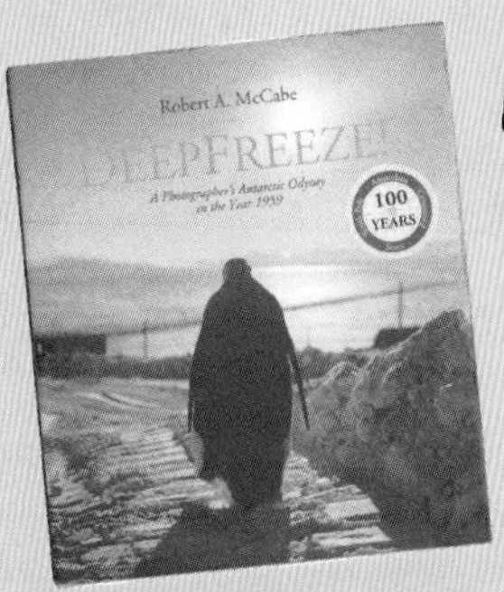
Robert A. McCabe
DEEPFREEZE
A Photographer's Antarctic Odyssey in the Year 1959
100 YEARS

I just bought a new book called DeepFreeze! I heard about it on the Leonard Lopate Show. (that's on WNYC for those of you who don't live in New York.)

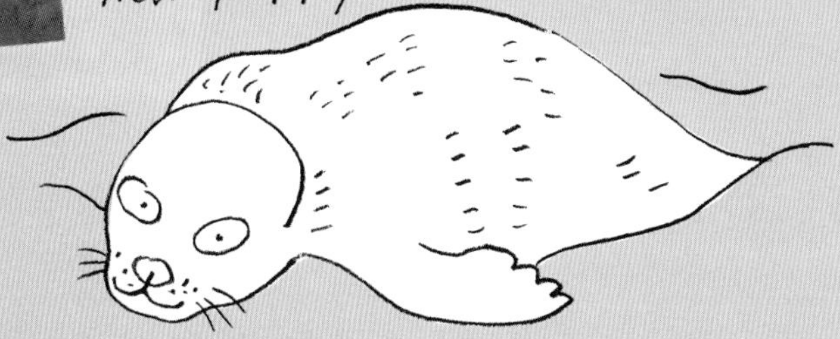

The author / photographer traveled to the South Pole in the 1950s and documented his trip. At the time, there were no laws prohibiting visitors from touching the animals. Among other things, he took photos of people petting seals and hugging penguins.

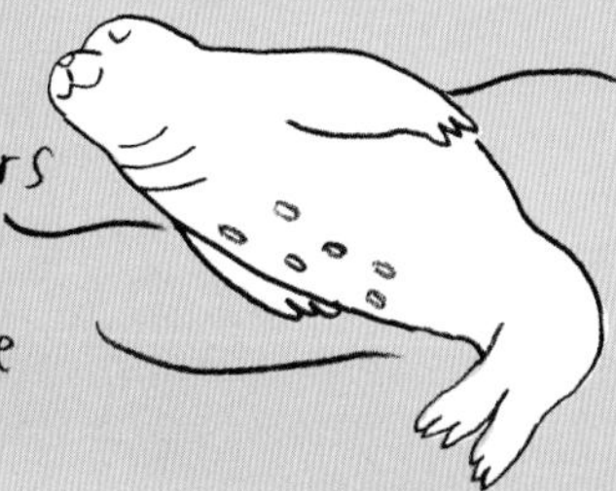

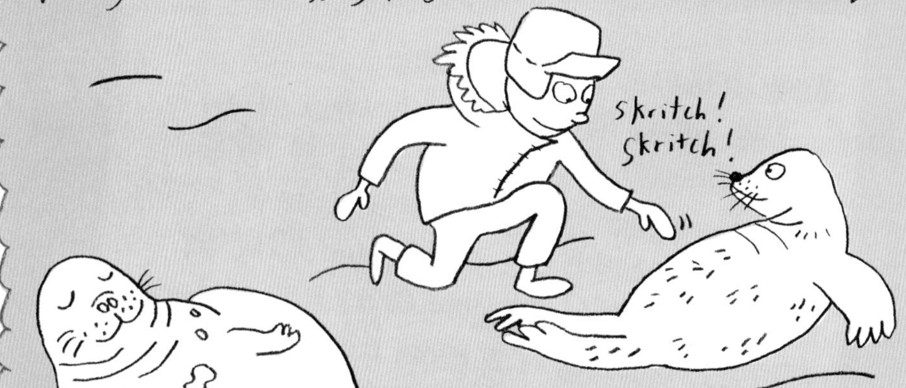
skritch! skritch!

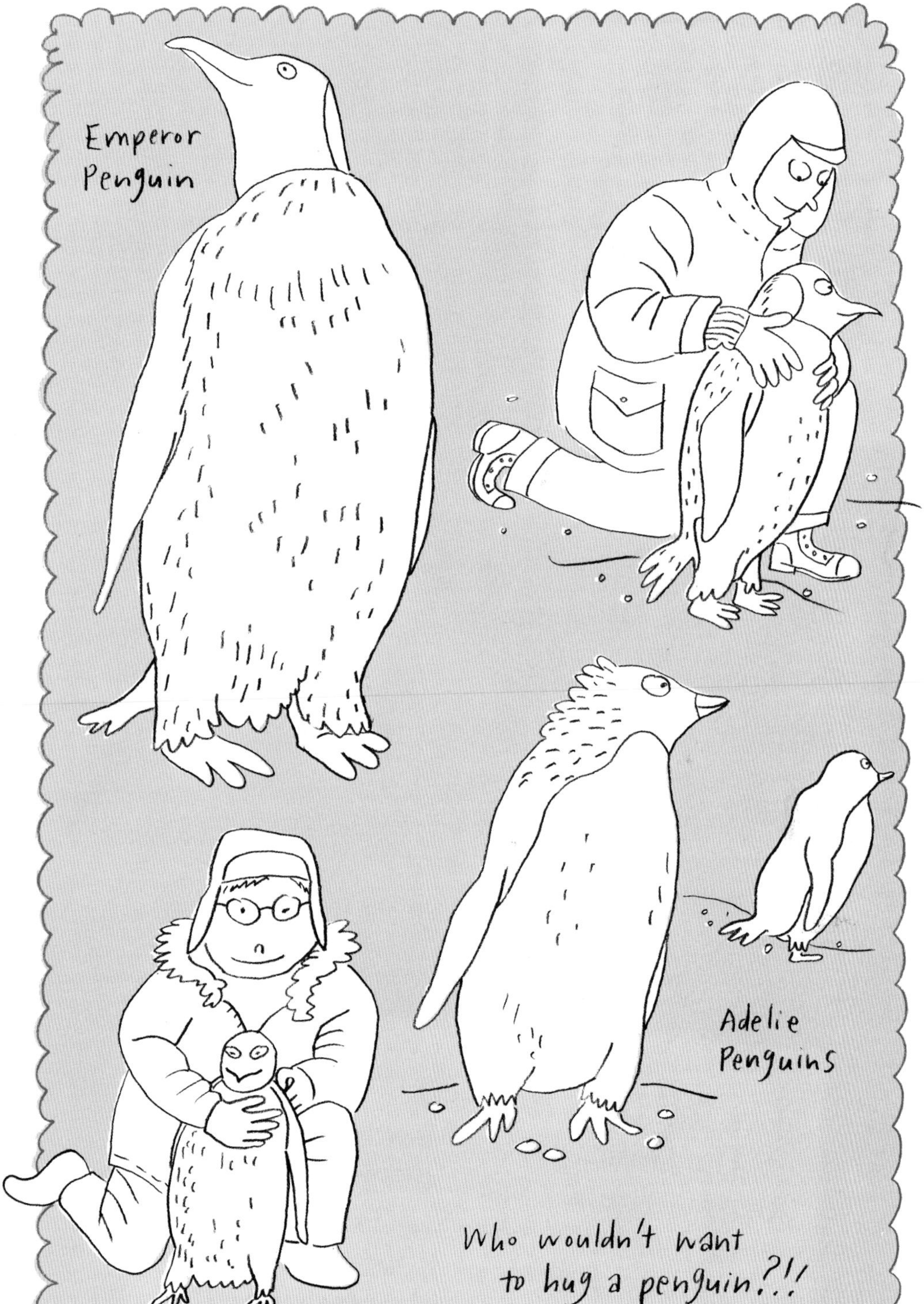
Emperor Penguin
Adelie Penguins
Who wouldn't want to hug a penguin?!!

Five Day Diary, May 2012
"The Comics Journal" invites artists to
make a Five day comic diary. (You can
Find more diaries online From plenty
of comics artists on their website.)
My life isn't always this exciting - it
happened to be a particularly
eventful week.

MONDAY, MAY 21, 2012 (DAY ONE)

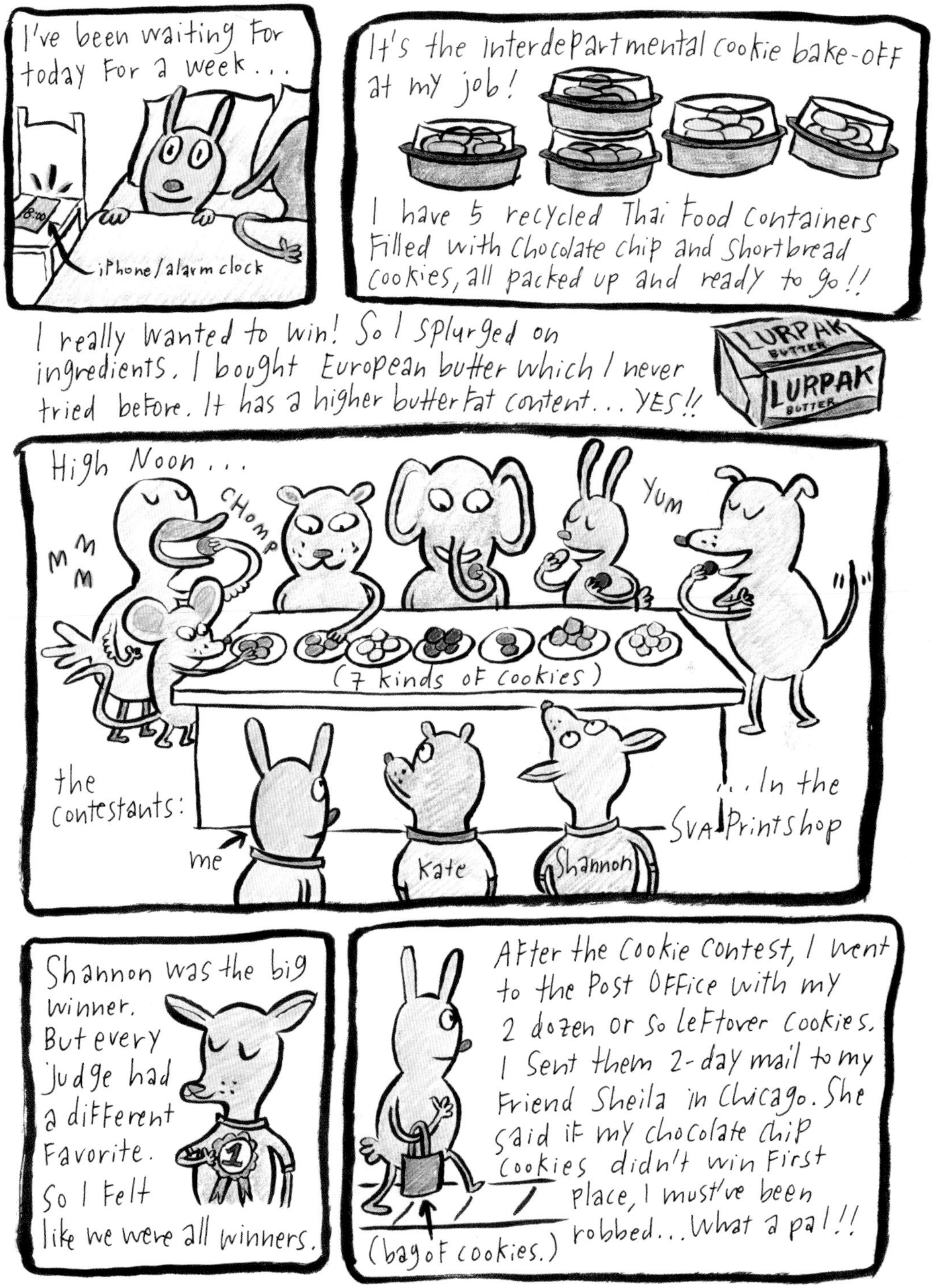
I've been waiting for today for a week...
8:00
iPhone/alarm clock
It's the interdepartmental cookie bake-off at my job!
I have 5 recycled Thai food containers filled with chocolate chip and shortbread cookies, all packed up and ready to go!!
I really wanted to win! So I splurged on ingredients. I bought European butter which I never tried before. It has a higher butterfat content... YES!!
LURPAK BUTTER
LURPAK BUTTER
High Noon...
MMM
CHOMP
YUM
(7 kinds of cookies)
the contestants:
...In the SVA Printshop
me
Kate
Shannon
Shannon was the big winner. But every judge had a different favorite. So I felt like we were all winners.
1
After the cookie contest, I went to the Post Office with my 2 dozen or so leftover cookies. I sent them 2-day mail to my friend Sheila in Chicago. She said if my chocolate chip cookies didn't win first place, I must've been robbed... What a pal!!
(bag of cookies.)

TUESDAY, MAY 22, 2012 (DAY TWO)

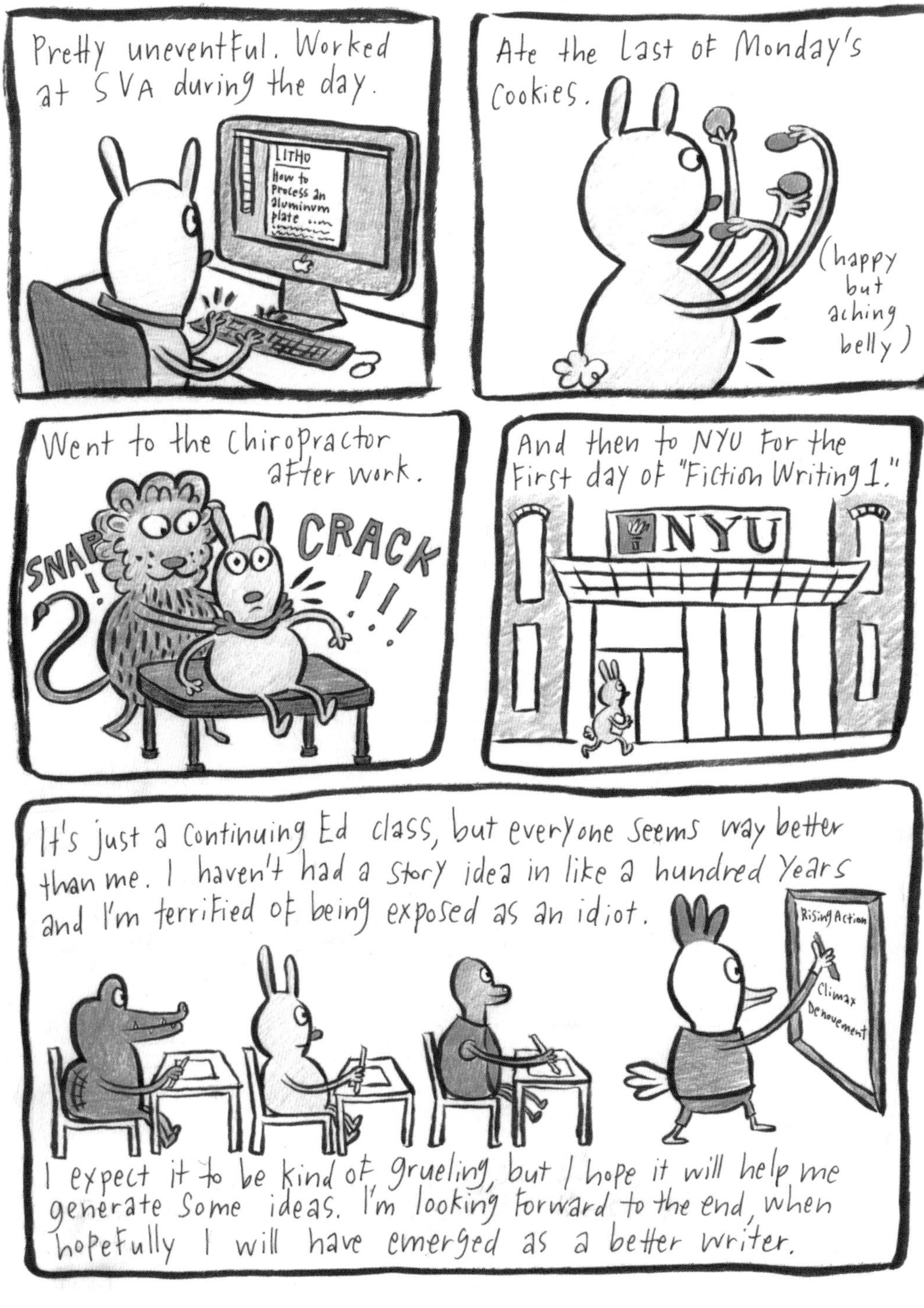

Pretty uneventful. Worked at SVA during the day.
LITHO
How to Process an aluminum plate ...
Ate the last of Monday's cookies.
(happy but aching belly)
Went to the chiropractor after work.
SNAP!
CRACK!!!
And then to NYU for the first day of "Fiction Writing 1."
NYU
It's just a continuing Ed class, but everyone seems way better than me. I haven't had a story idea in like a hundred years and I'm terrified of being exposed as an idiot.
Rising Action
Climax
Denouement
I expect it to be kind of grueling, but I hope it will help me generate some ideas. I'm looking forward to the end, when hopefully I will have emerged as a better writer.

WEDNESDAY, MAY 23, 2012 (DAY THREE)

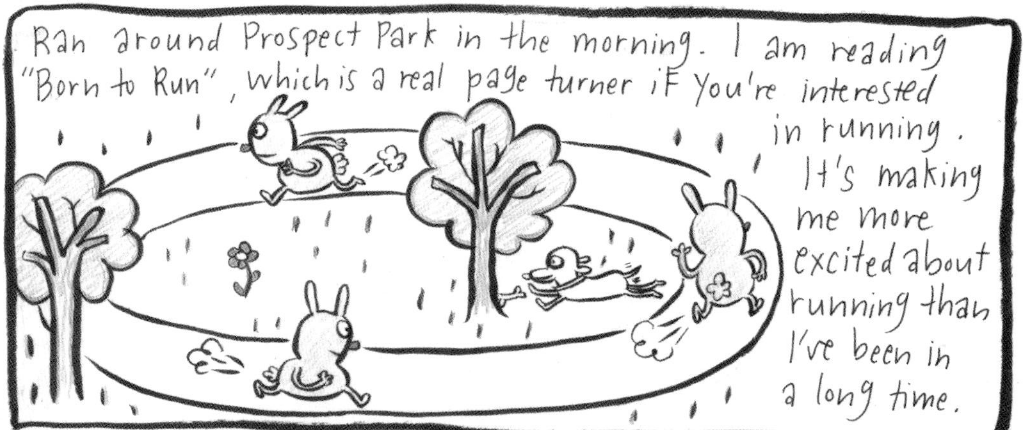
Ran around Prospect Park in the morning. I am reading "Born to Run", which is a real page turner if you're interested in running. It's making me more excited about running than I've been in a long time.

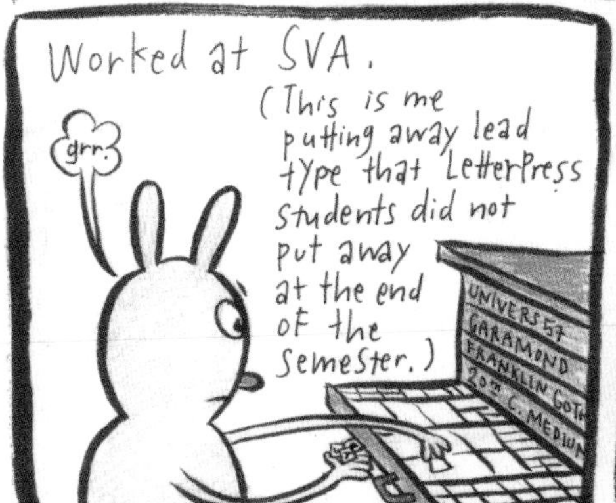
Worked at SVA.
grr.
(This is me putting away lead type that Letterpress students did not put away at the end of the semester.)
UNIVERS 57
GARAMOND
FRANKLIN GOTH

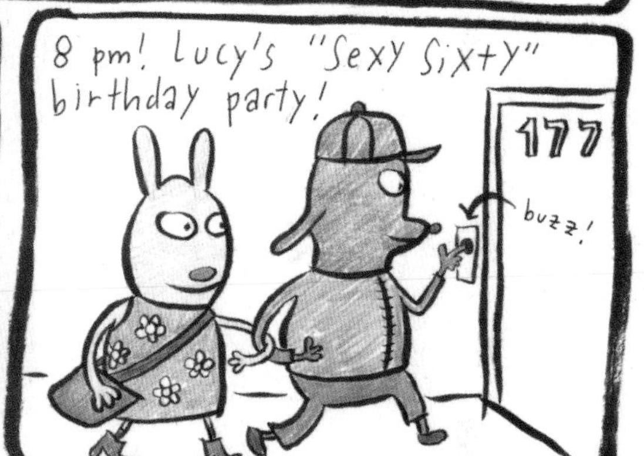
8 pm! Lucy's "Sexy Sixty" birthday party!
177
buzz!

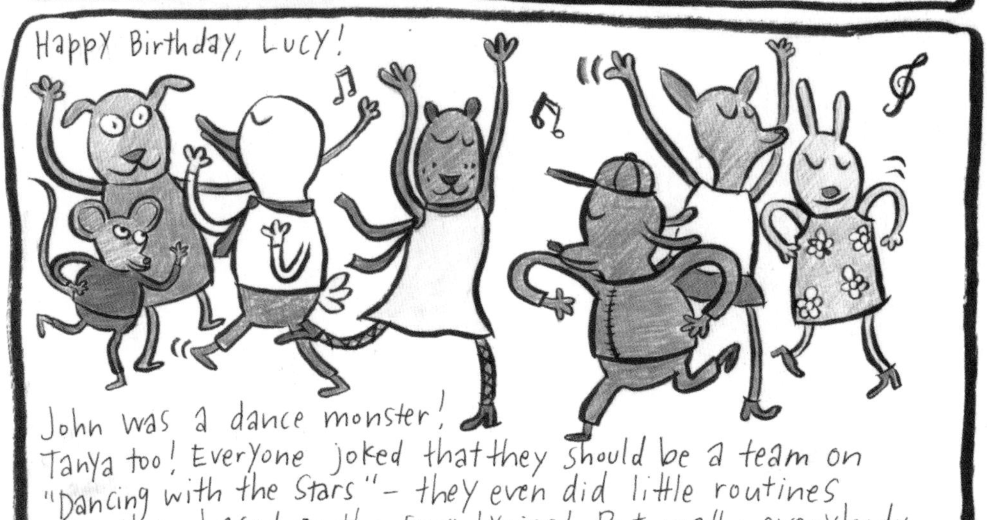
Happy Birthday, Lucy!
John was a dance monster! Tanya too! Everyone joked that they should be a team on "Dancing with the Stars" - they even did little routines together based on the song lyrics! But really everybody went all out on the dance floor - it was so much fun!!

THURSDAY, MAY 24, 2012 (DAY FOUR)

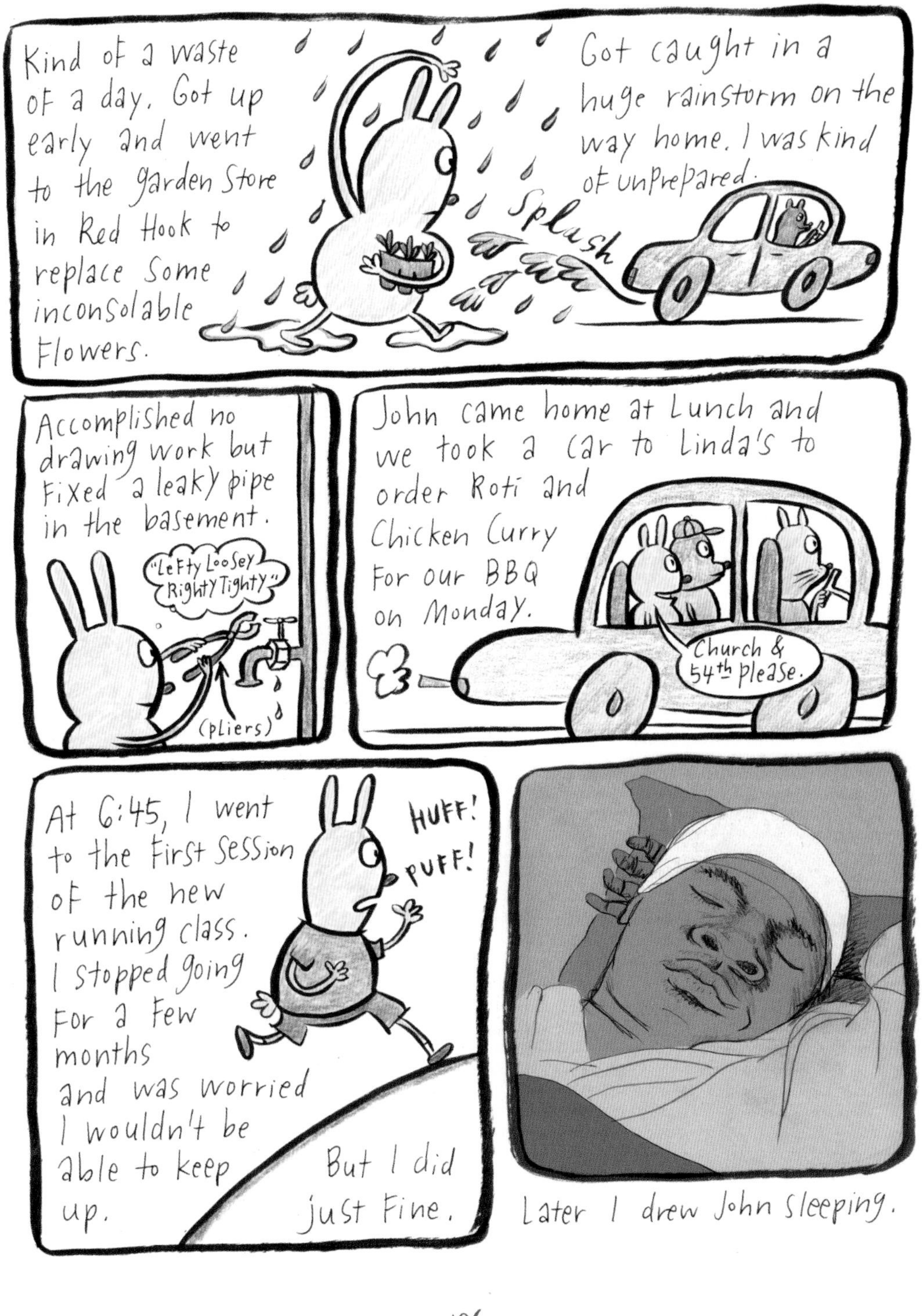
Kind of a waste of a day. Got up early and went to the garden store in Red Hook to replace some inconsolable flowers.
Got caught in a huge rainstorm on the way home. I was kind of unprepared.
Splash
Accomplished no drawing work but fixed a leaky pipe in the basement.
"Lefty Loosey Righty Tighty."
(pliers)
John came home at lunch and we took a car to Linda's to order Roti and Chicken Curry for our BBQ on Monday.
Church & 54th please.
At 6:45, I went to the first session of the new running class. I stopped going for a few months and was worried I wouldn't be able to keep up.
HUFF!
PUFF!
But I did just fine.
Later I drew John sleeping.

FRIDAY, MAY 25, 2012 (DAY FIVE & THE END!)

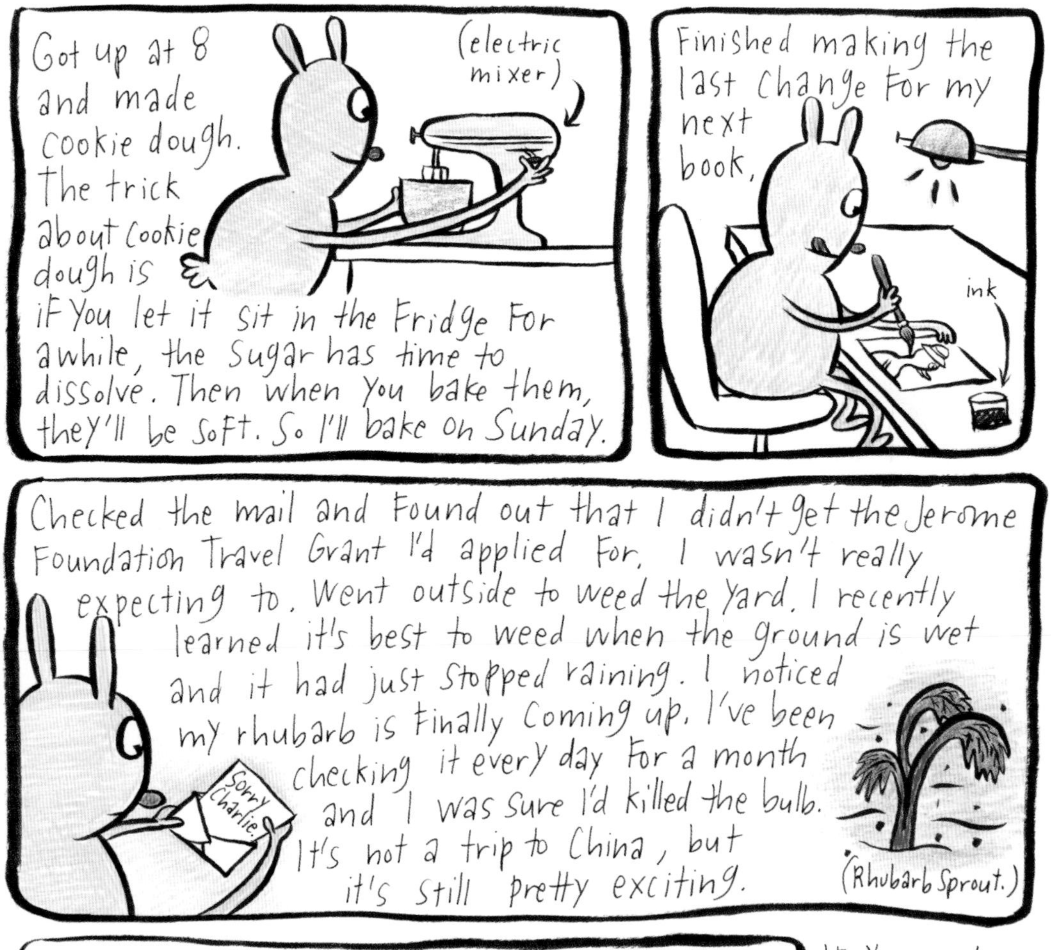

Got up at 8 and made cookie dough. The trick about cookie dough is if you let it sit in the fridge for awhile, the sugar has time to dissolve. Then when you bake them, they'll be soft. So I'll bake on Sunday.
(electric mixer)
Finished making the last change for my next book,
ink
Checked the mail and found out that I didn't get the Jerome Foundation Travel Grant I'd applied for. I wasn't really expecting to. Went outside to weed the yard. I recently learned it's best to weed when the ground is wet and it had just stopped raining. I noticed my rhubarb is finally coming up. I've been checking it every day for a month and I was sure I'd killed the bulb. It's not a trip to China, but it's still pretty exciting.
Sorry Charlie.
(Rhubarb Sprout.)

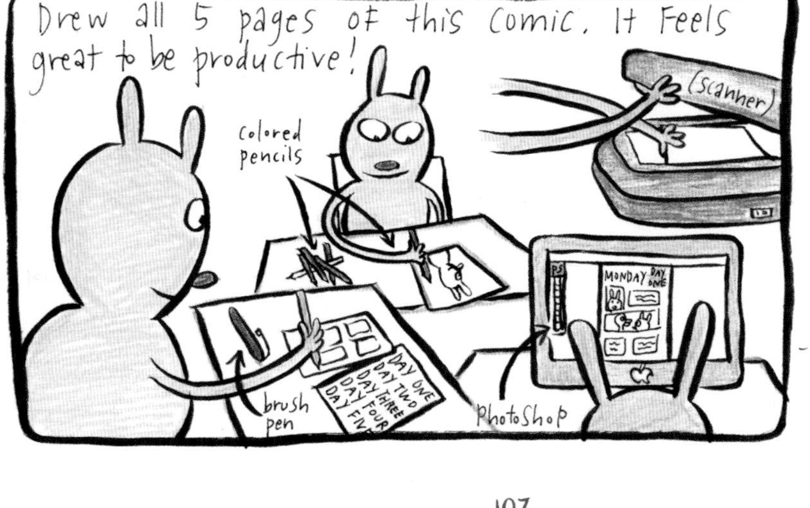

Drew all 5 pages of this comic. It feels great to be productive!
(scanner)
colored pencils
MONDAY DAY ONE
DAY ONE
DAY TWO
DAY THREE
DAY FOUR
DAY FIVE
brush pen
PhotoShop

If you made it this far, thanks so much for reading!

-SARA VARON

♡

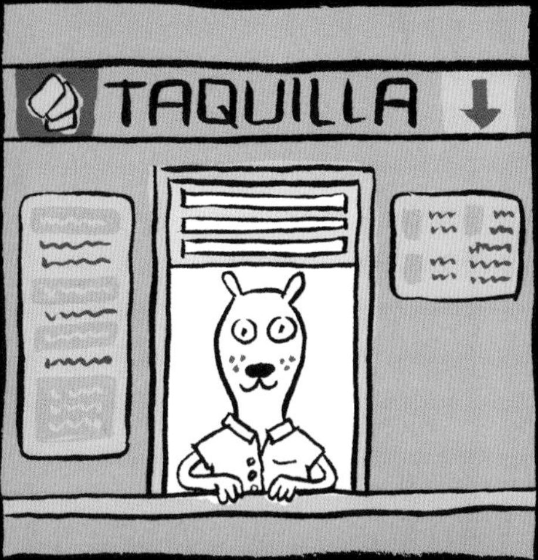
TAQUILLA

Mexico City, October 2013

In 2012, I went to Mexico City with my Friends Aya and Eun-ha to do an art Show. Mexico City was so much cooler than I expected!! The colors were great, the Food and people were great, the ruins were so Fascinating, the Folk art was amazing, and there were dogs everywhere! My Favorite dogs were those Spooky-looking hairless Aztec dogs, the Xoloitzcuintle. I don't know if I'd say the subway was great, but it was certainly a bargain. And very interesting.

EL METRO ES COMO UN BAZAR

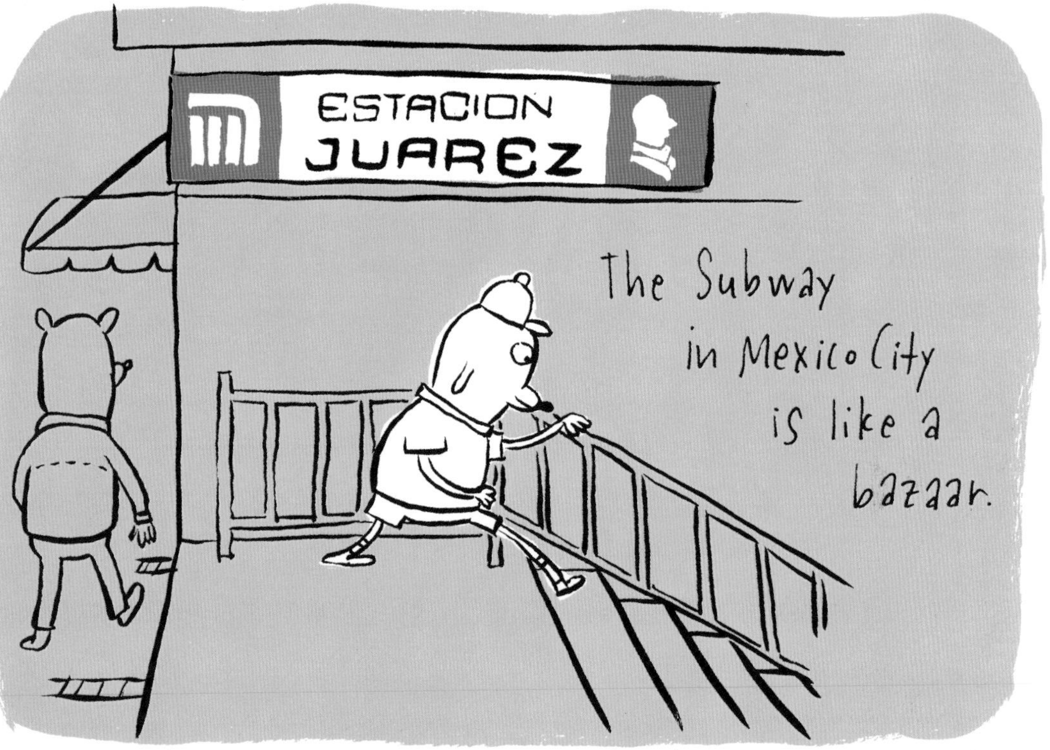
ESTACION
JUAREZ
The Subway in Mexico City is like a bazaar.

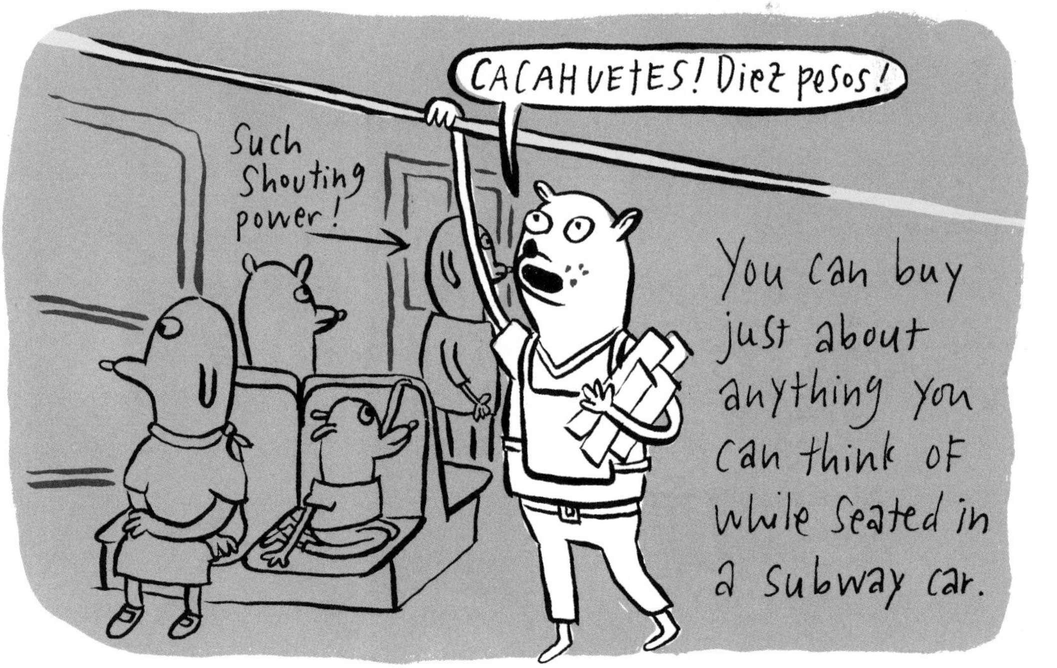
Such Shouting power!
CACAHUETES! Diez pesos!
You can buy just about anything you can think of while seated in a subway car.

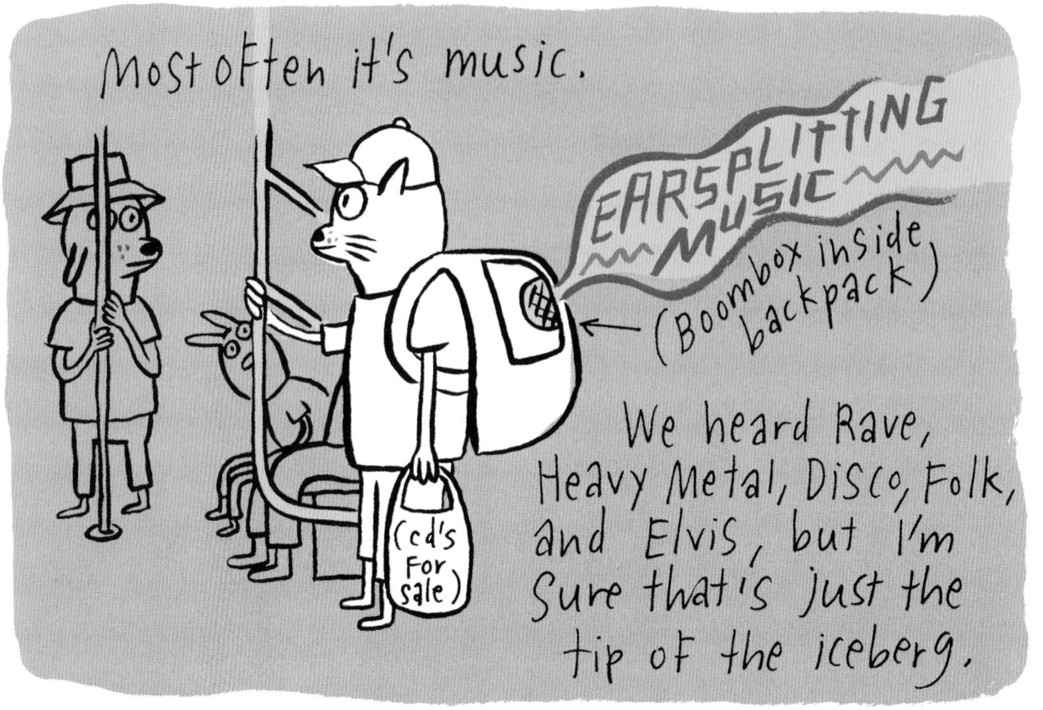
Most often it's music.
EARSPLITTING MUSIC
(Boombox inside backpack)
(cd's For sale)
We heard Rave, Heavy Metal, Disco, Folk, and Elvis, but I'm sure that's just the tip of the iceberg.

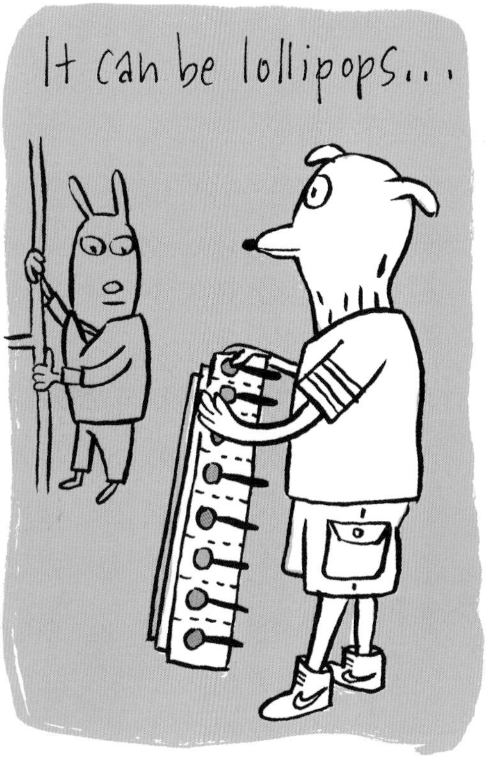
It can be lollipops...

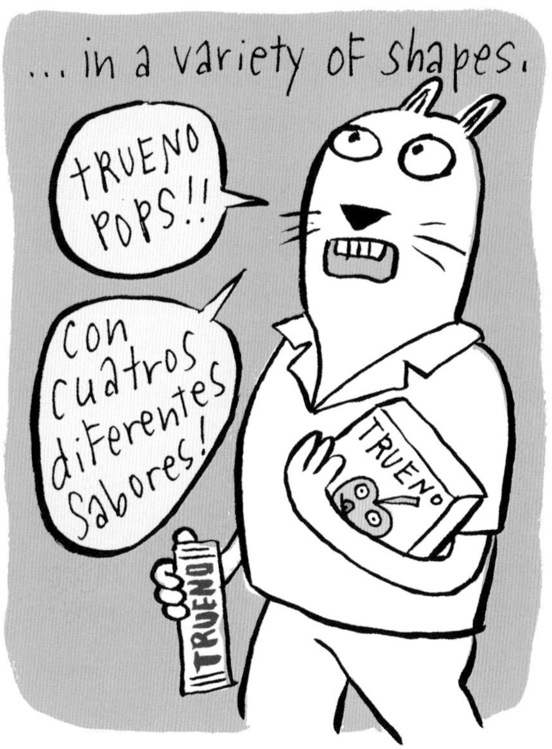
...in a variety of shapes.
TRUENO POPS!!
Con cuatros diferentes sabores!
TRUENO
TRUENO

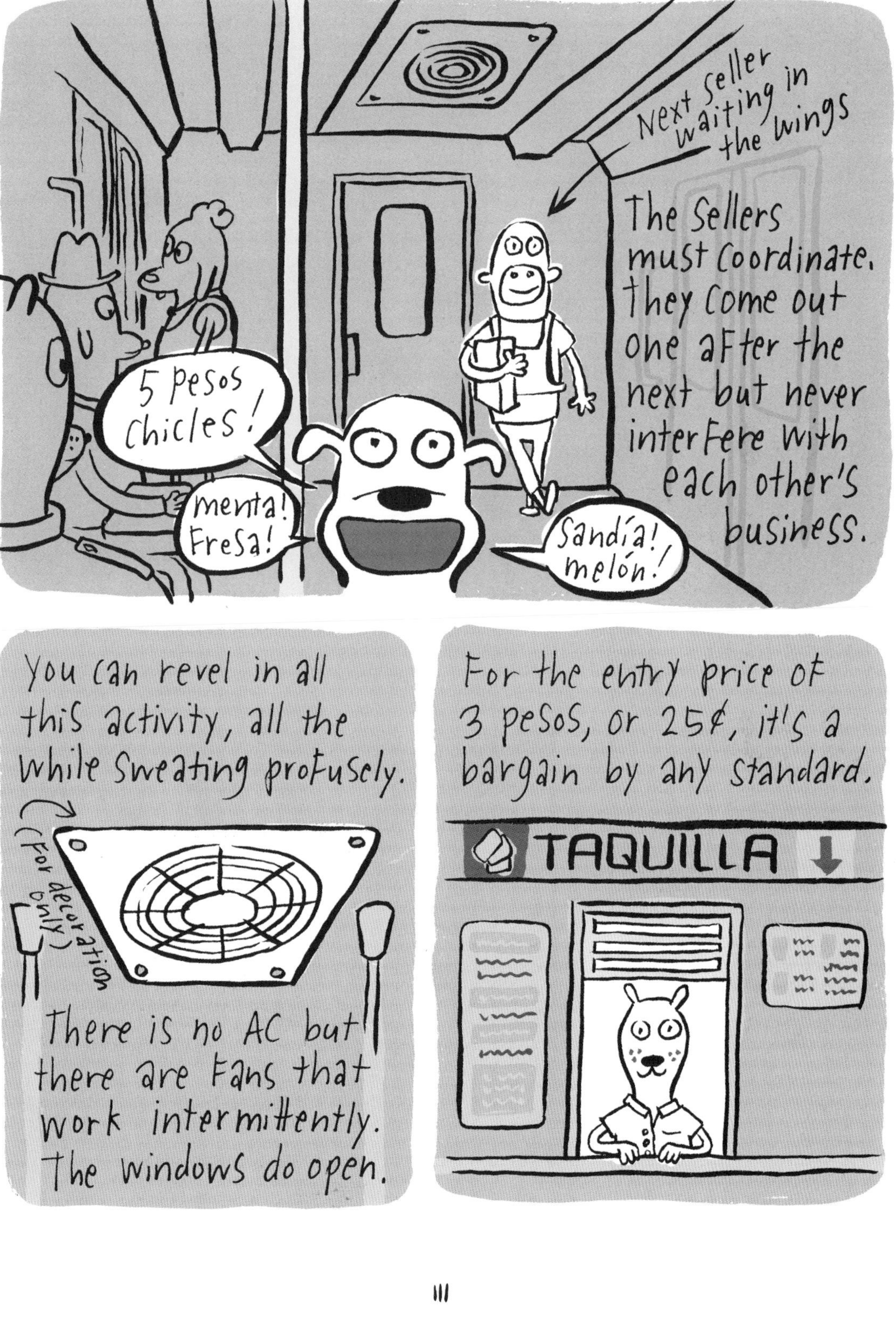
Next seller waiting in the wings
The sellers must coordinate. they come out one after the next but never interfere with each other's business.
5 pesos chicles!
menta! Fresa!
Sandía! melón!
You can revel in all this activity, all the while sweating profusely.
(For decoration only)
There is no AC but there are fans that work intermittently. The windows do open.
For the entry price of 3 pesos, or 25¢, it's a bargain by any standard.
TAQUILLA

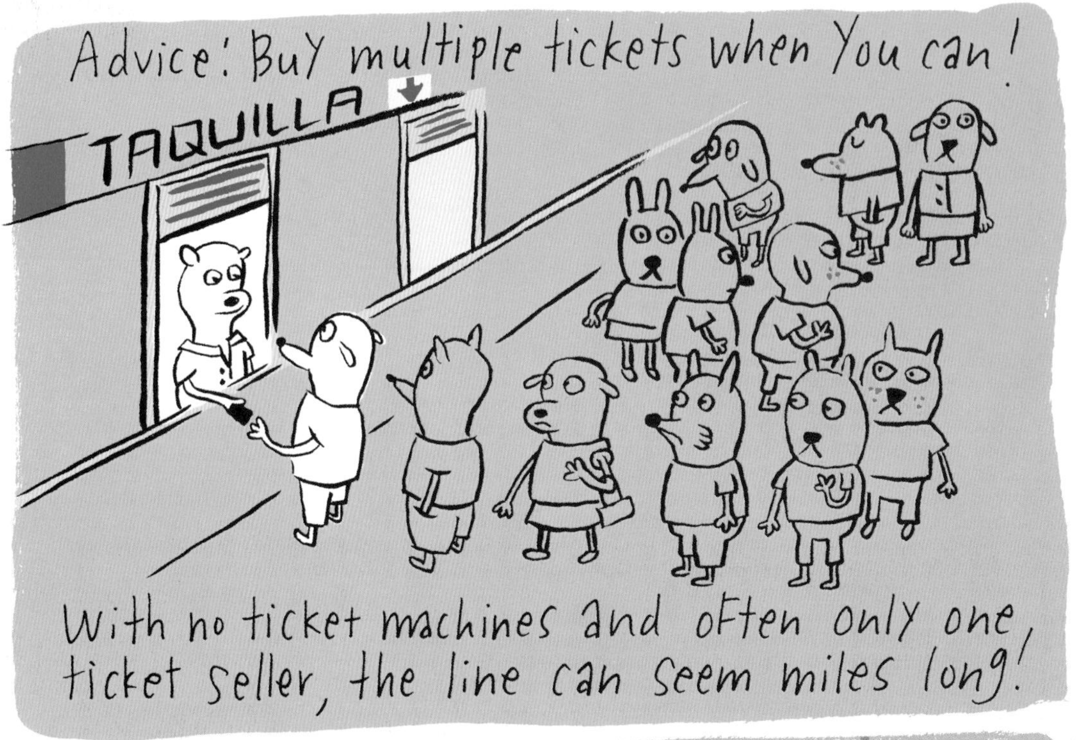
Advice: Buy multiple tickets when You can!
TAQUILLA
With no ticket machines and often only one ticket seller, the line can seem miles long!

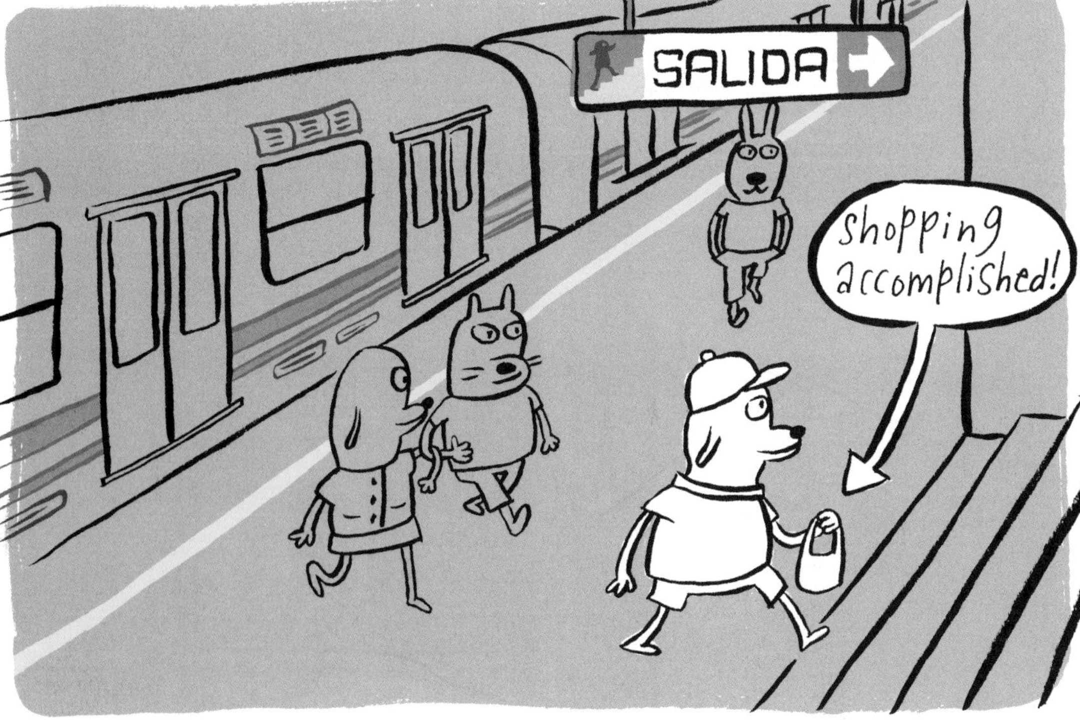
SALIDA
shopping accomplished!

three hairless dogs in front of a statue of a hairless
dog at El Museo Dolores Olmedo in Xochimilco, Mexico City.

Dinosaur Comic, thumbnails in August 2009
  Finals in July 2014
  This was submitted for the "Strapazin"
animal issue in 2009 but rejected. (The lion
comic took its place.) I used it in 2014
as a vehicle to experiment with using
two colors. (It was the first comic that I
colored for this book.) Ideawise, the
framework is a short story about dinosaurs.
I liked the idea that they look scary and
mean, but really they are just uncomfortable
and all they need is a little ice cream.

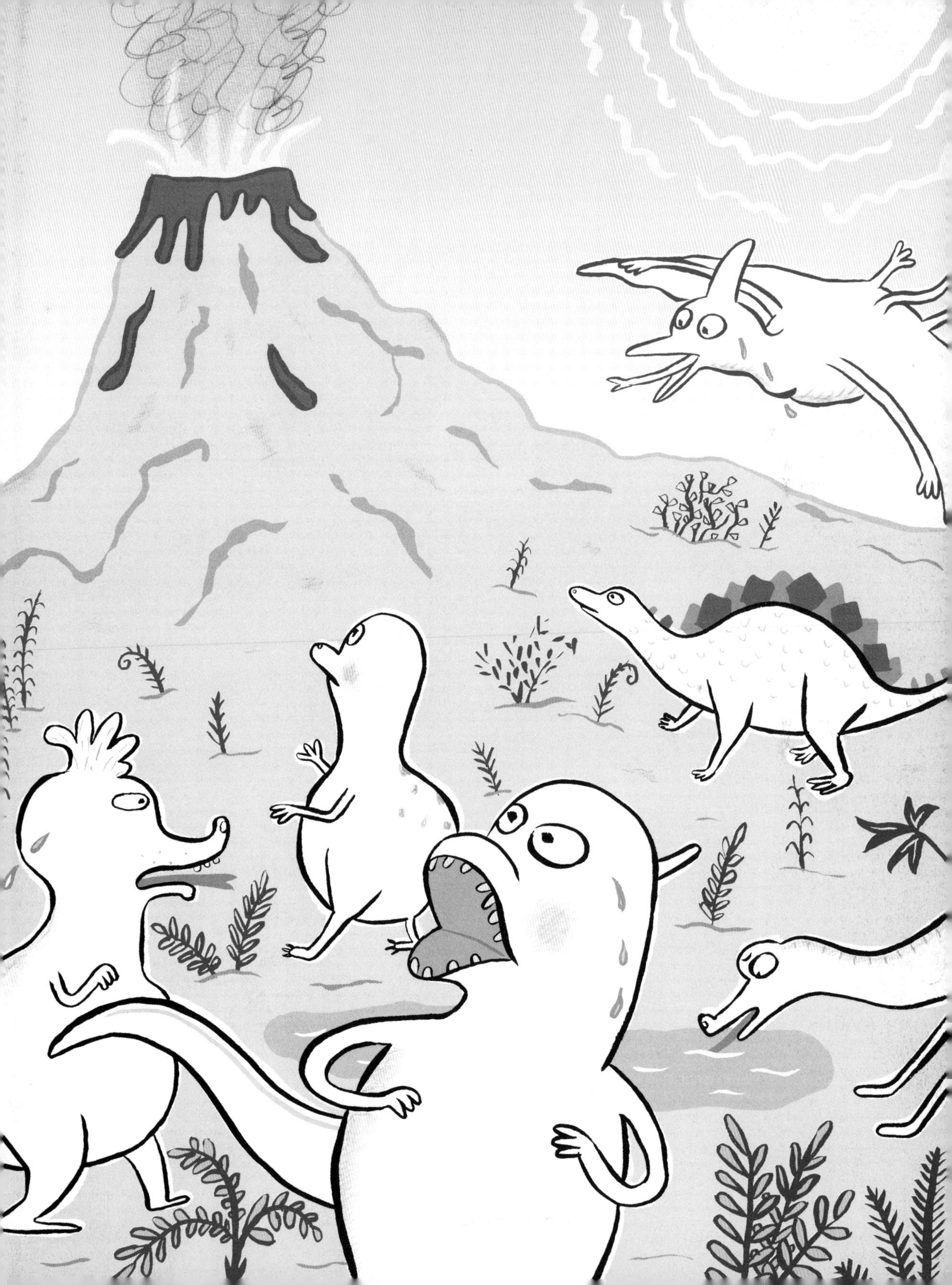

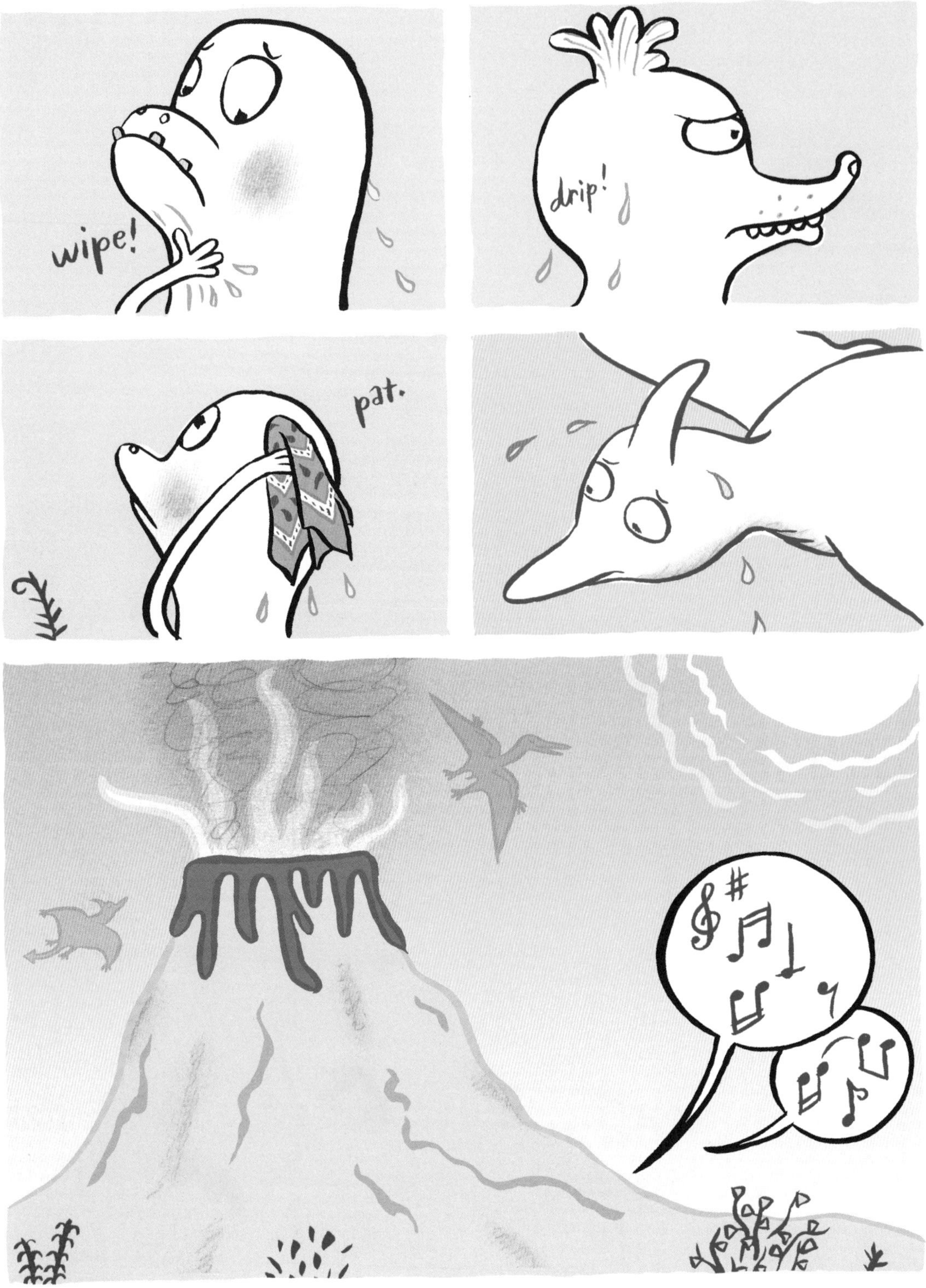
wipe!
drip!
pat.

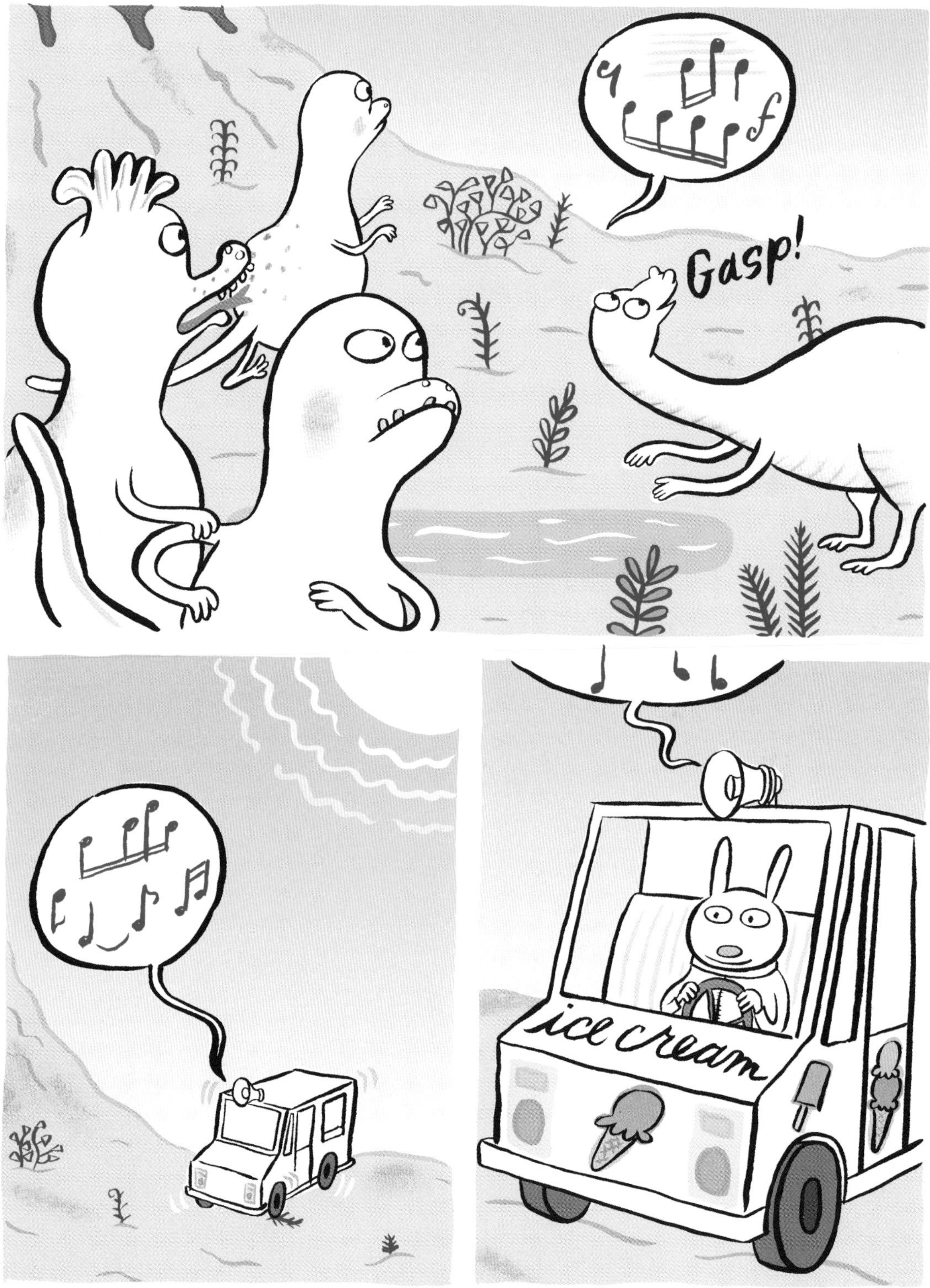
Gasp!
ice cream

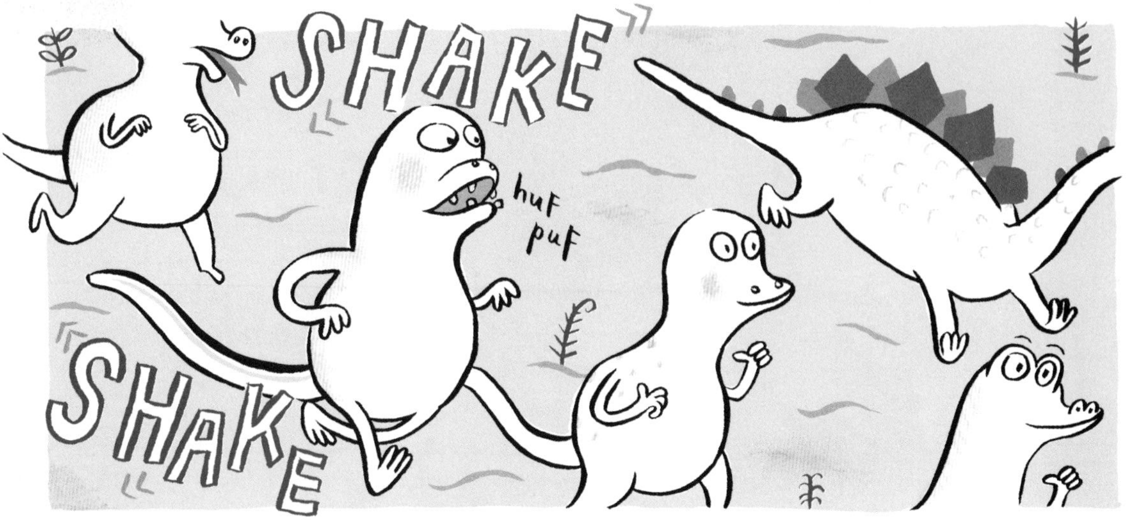
SHAKE
huf puf
SHAKE

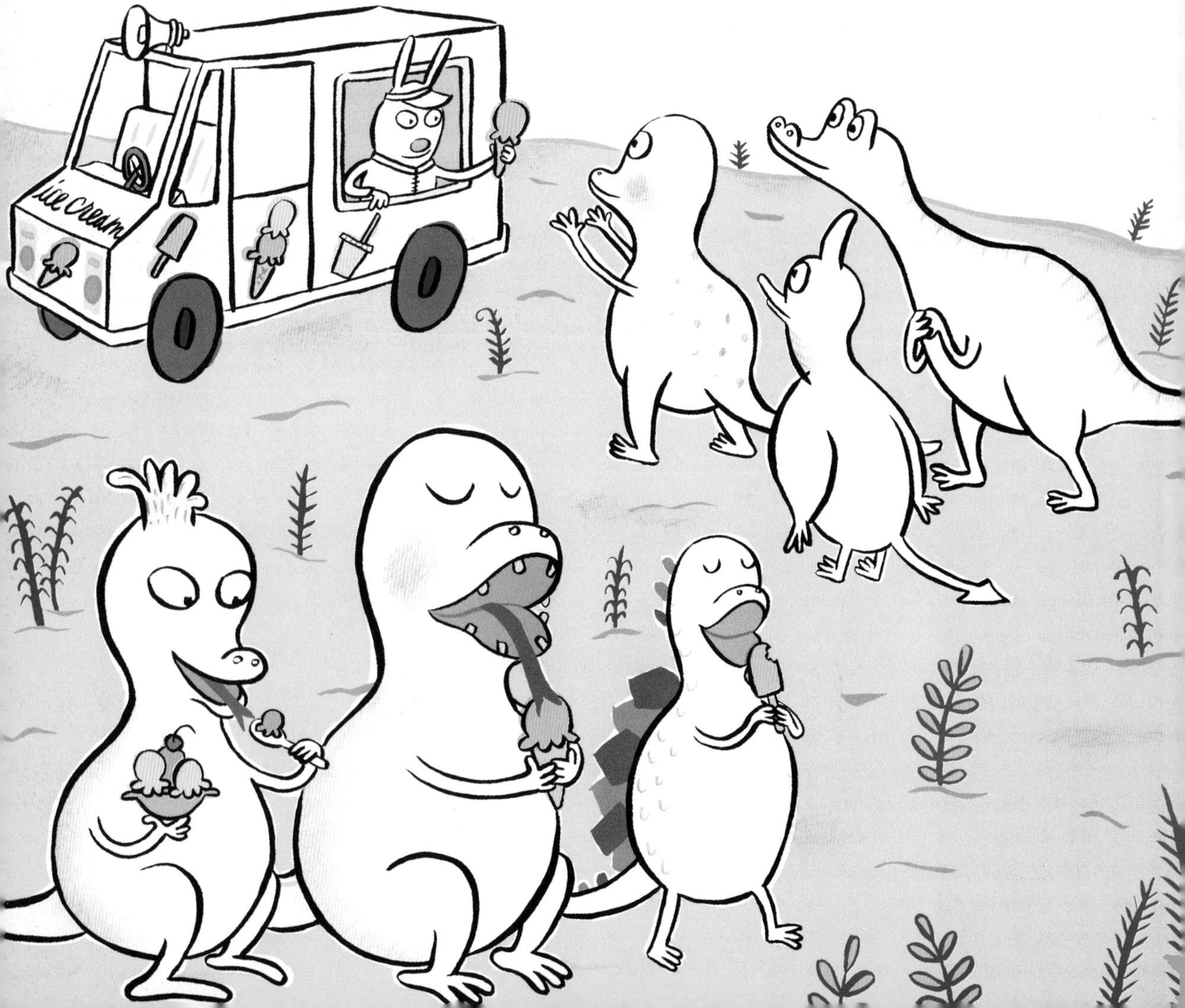
Ice Cream

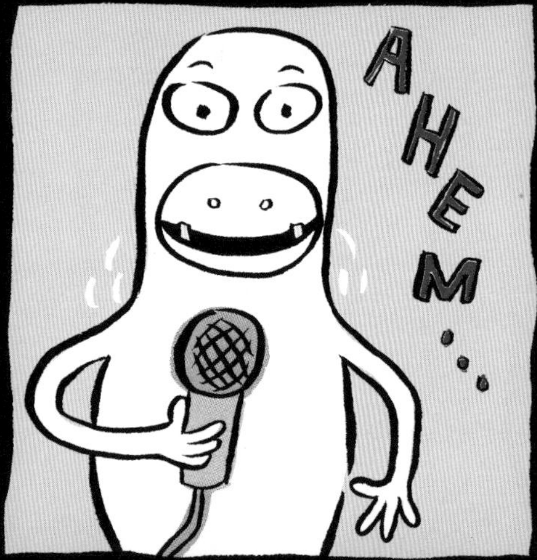
AHEM...

The Next Chapter, June 2014

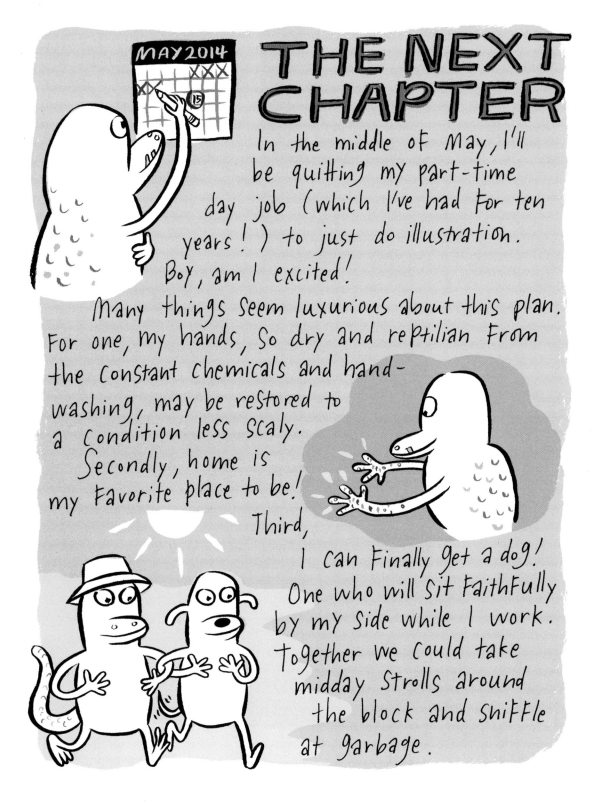

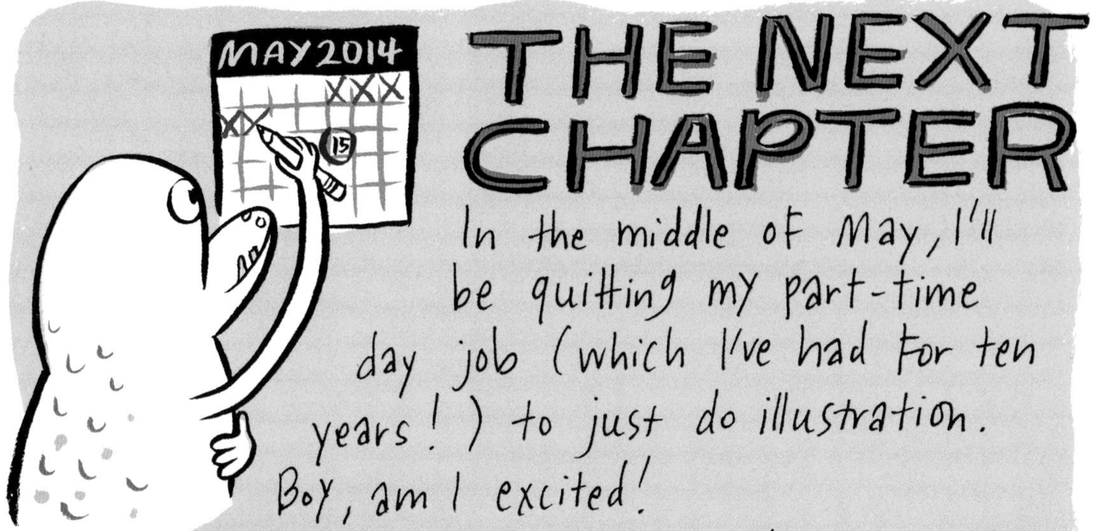
MAY 2014
15

THE NEXT CHAPTER

In the middle of May, I'll be quitting my part-time day job (which I've had for ten years!) to just do illustration. Boy, am I excited!

Many things seem luxurious about this plan. For one, my hands, so dry and reptilian from the constant chemicals and hand-washing, may be restored to a condition less scaly.

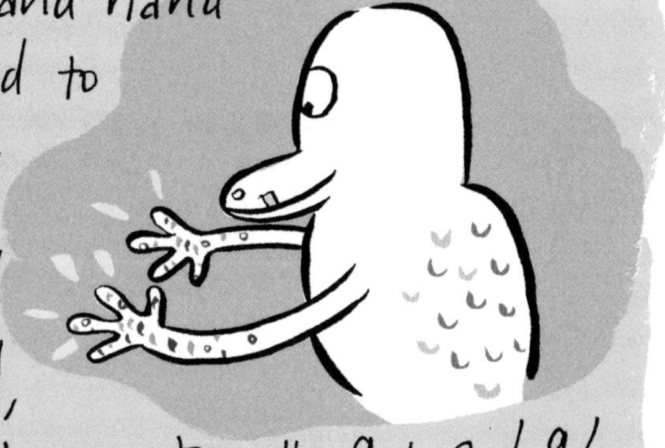

Secondly, home is my favorite place to be!

Third,

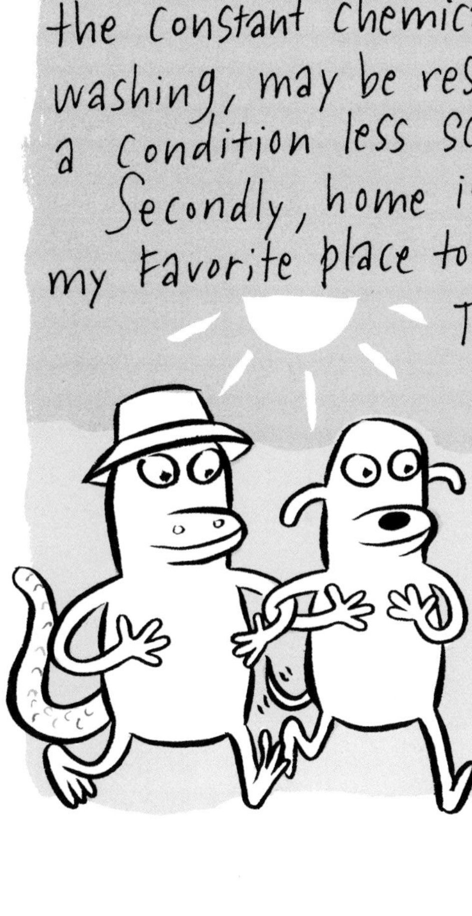

I can finally get a dog! One who will sit faithfully by my side while I work. Together we could take midday strolls around the block and sniffle at garbage.

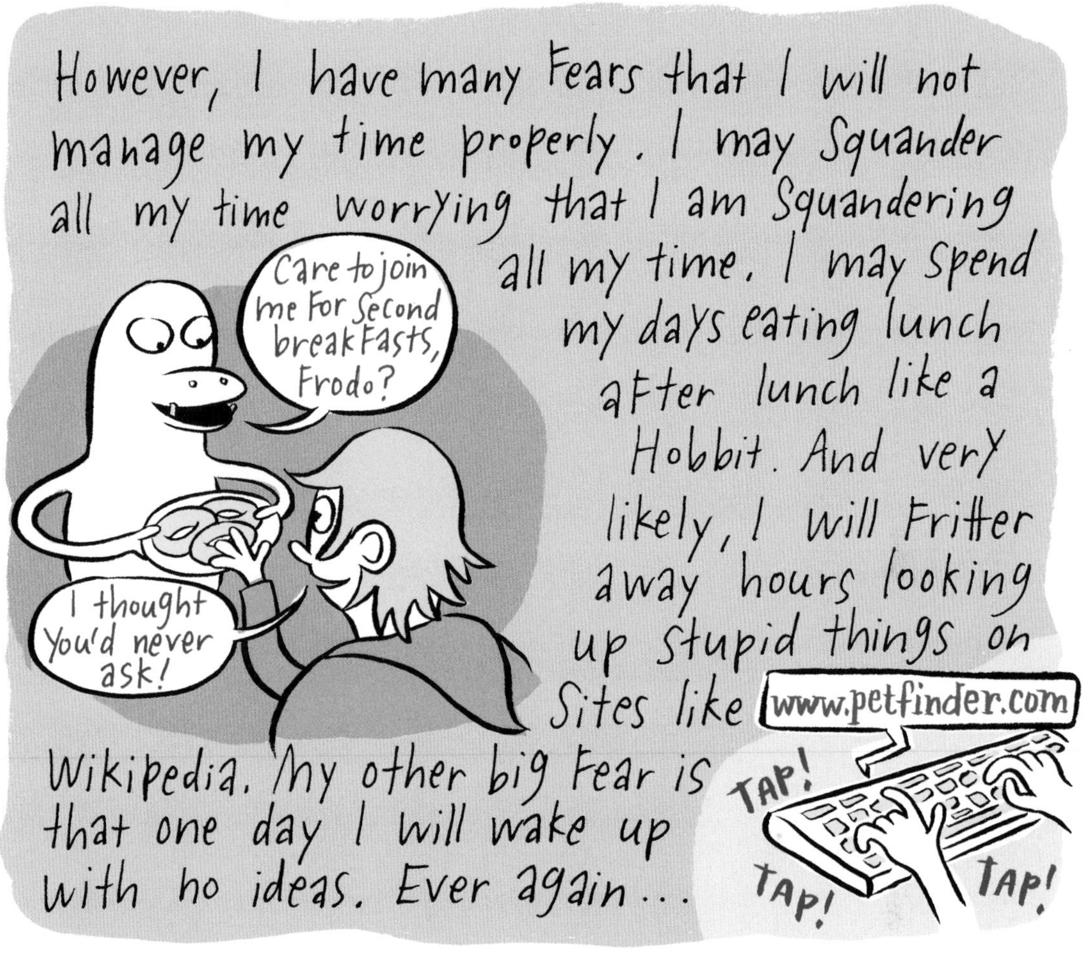
However, I have many fears that I will not manage my time properly. I may squander all my time worrying that I am squandering all my time. I may spend my days eating lunch after lunch like a Hobbit. And very likely, I will fritter away hours looking up stupid things on sites like
Care to join me for second breakfasts, Frodo?
I thought you'd never ask!
www.petfinder.com
Wikipedia. My other big fear is that one day I will wake up with no ideas. Ever again...
TAP!
TAP!
TAP!
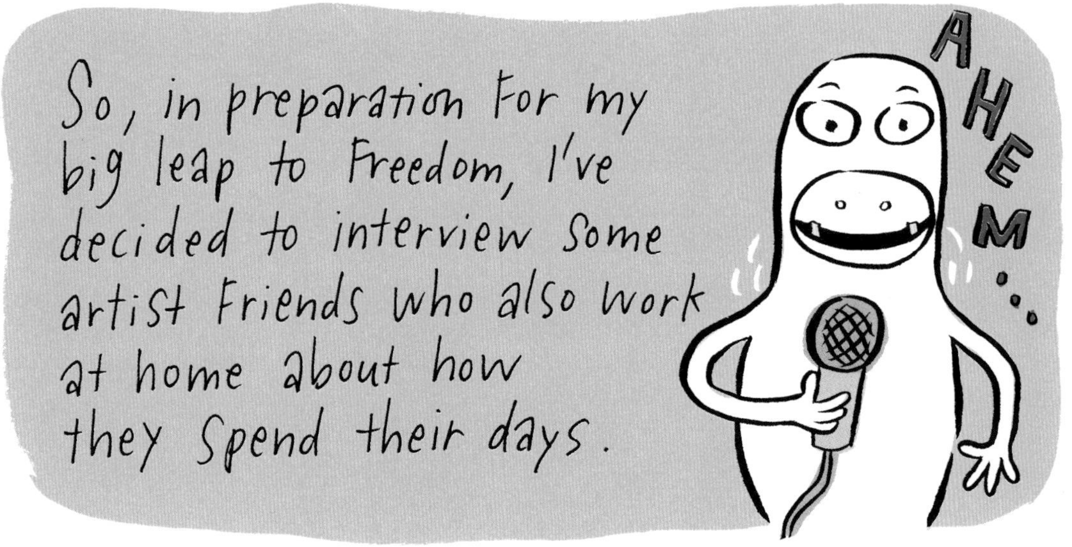
So, in preparation for my big leap to freedom, I've decided to interview some artist friends who also work at home about how they spend their days.
AHEM...

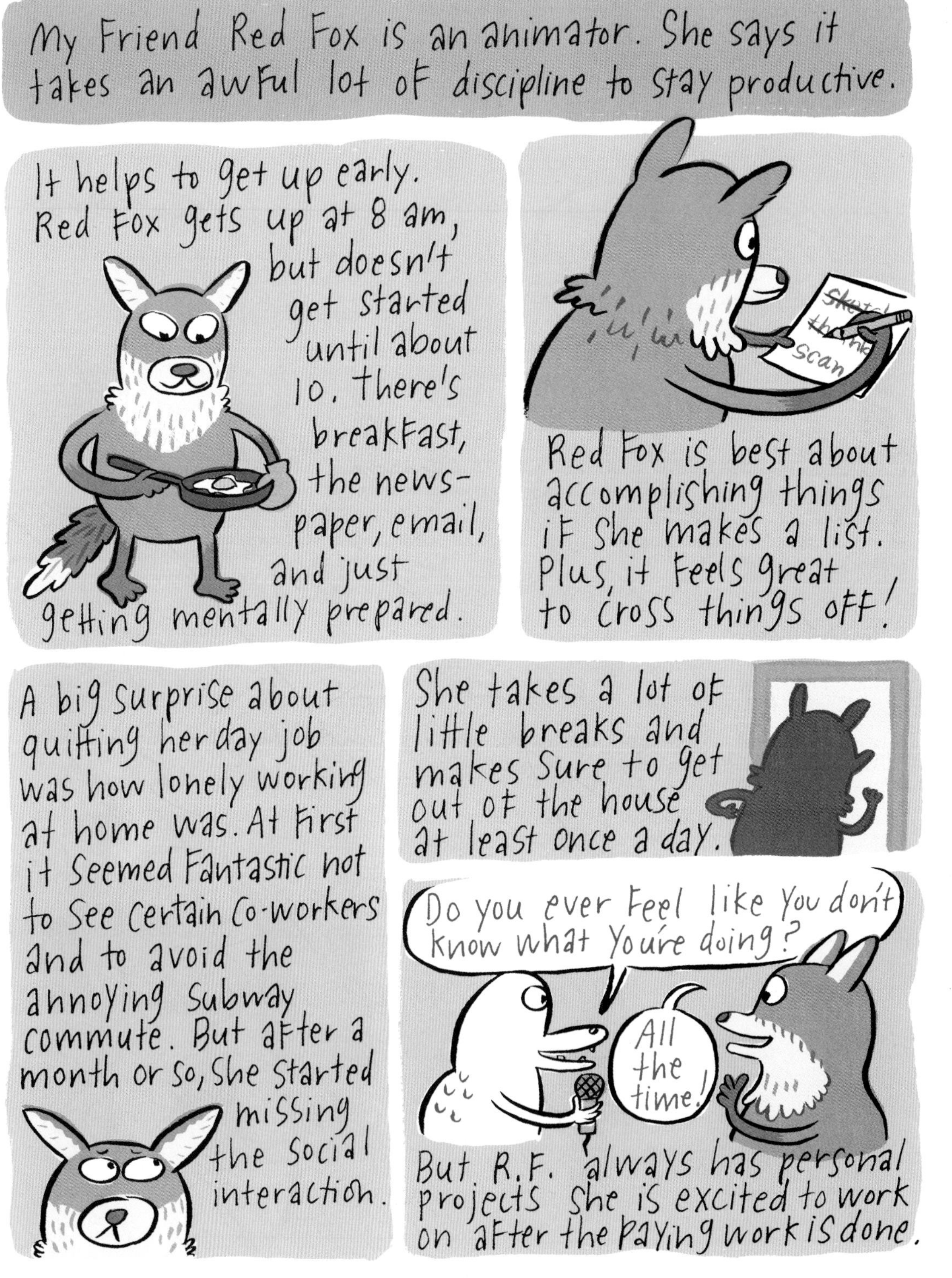
My Friend Red Fox is an animator. She says it takes an awful lot of discipline to stay productive.
It helps to get up early. Red Fox gets up at 8 am, but doesn't get started until about 10. there's breakfast, the news-paper, email, and just getting mentally prepared.
scan
Red Fox is best about accomplishing things if she makes a list. Plus, it feels great to cross things off!
A big surprise about quitting her day job was how lonely working at home was. At first it seemed fantastic not to see certain co-workers and to avoid the annoying subway commute. But after a month or so, she started missing the social interaction.
She takes a lot of little breaks and makes sure to get out of the house at least once a day.
Do you ever feel like you don't know what you're doing?
All the time!
But R.F. always has personal projects she is excited to work on after the paying work is done.

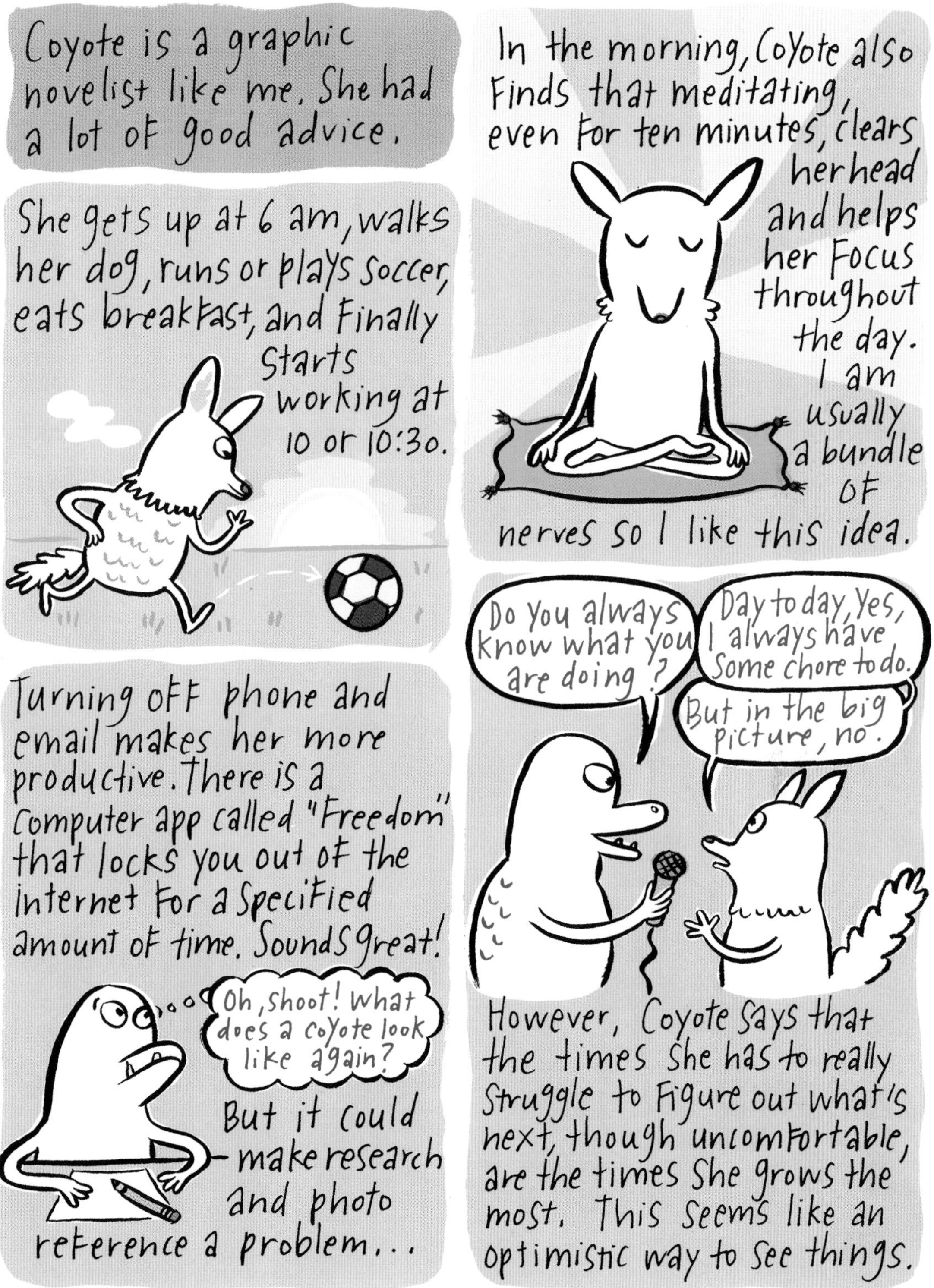
Coyote is a graphic novelist like me. She had a lot of good advice.
She gets up at 6 am, walks her dog, runs or plays soccer, eats breakfast, and finally starts working at 10 or 10:30.
In the morning, Coyote also finds that meditating, even for ten minutes, clears her head and helps her focus throughout the day. I am usually a bundle of nerves so I like this idea.
Turning off phone and email makes her more productive. There is a computer app called "Freedom" that locks you out of the internet for a specified amount of time. Sounds great!
Oh, shoot! What does a coyote look like again?
But it could make research and photo reference a problem...
Do you always know what you are doing?
Day to day, yes, I always have some chore to do.
But in the big picture, no.
However, Coyote says that the times she has to really struggle to figure out what's next, though uncomfortable, are the times she grows the most. This seems like an optimistic way to see things.

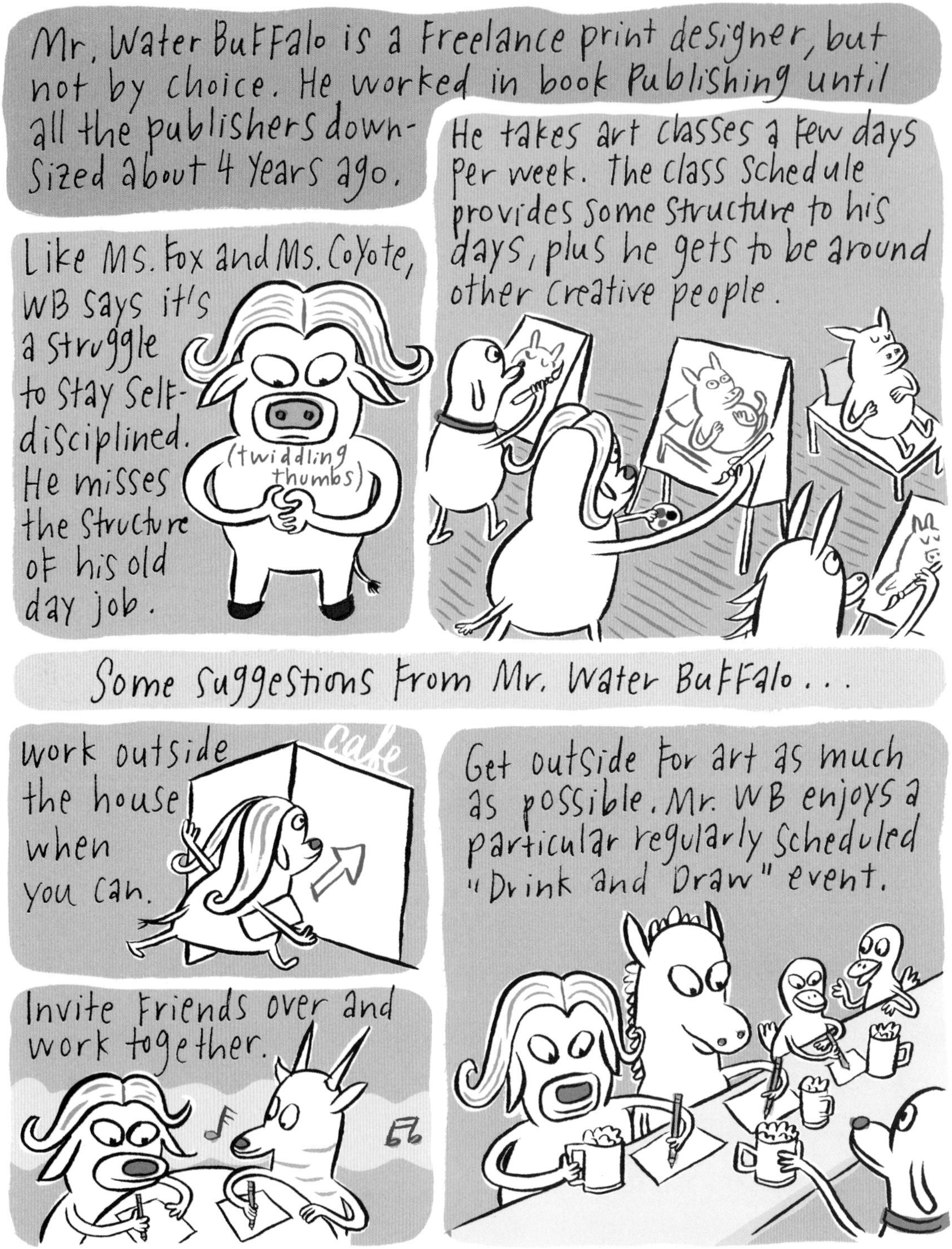
Mr. Water Buffalo is a freelance print designer, but not by choice. He worked in book publishing until all the publishers downsized about 4 years ago.
Like Ms. Fox and Ms. Coyote, WB says it's a struggle to stay self-disciplined. He misses the structure of his old day job.
(twiddling thumbs)
He takes art classes a few days per week. The class schedule provides some structure to his days, plus he gets to be around other creative people.
Some suggestions from Mr. Water Buffalo...
Work outside the house when you can.
cafe
Invite friends over and work together.
Get outside for art as much as possible. Mr. WB enjoys a particular regularly scheduled "Drink and Draw" event.
But for now, I'm looking forward to the solitude.

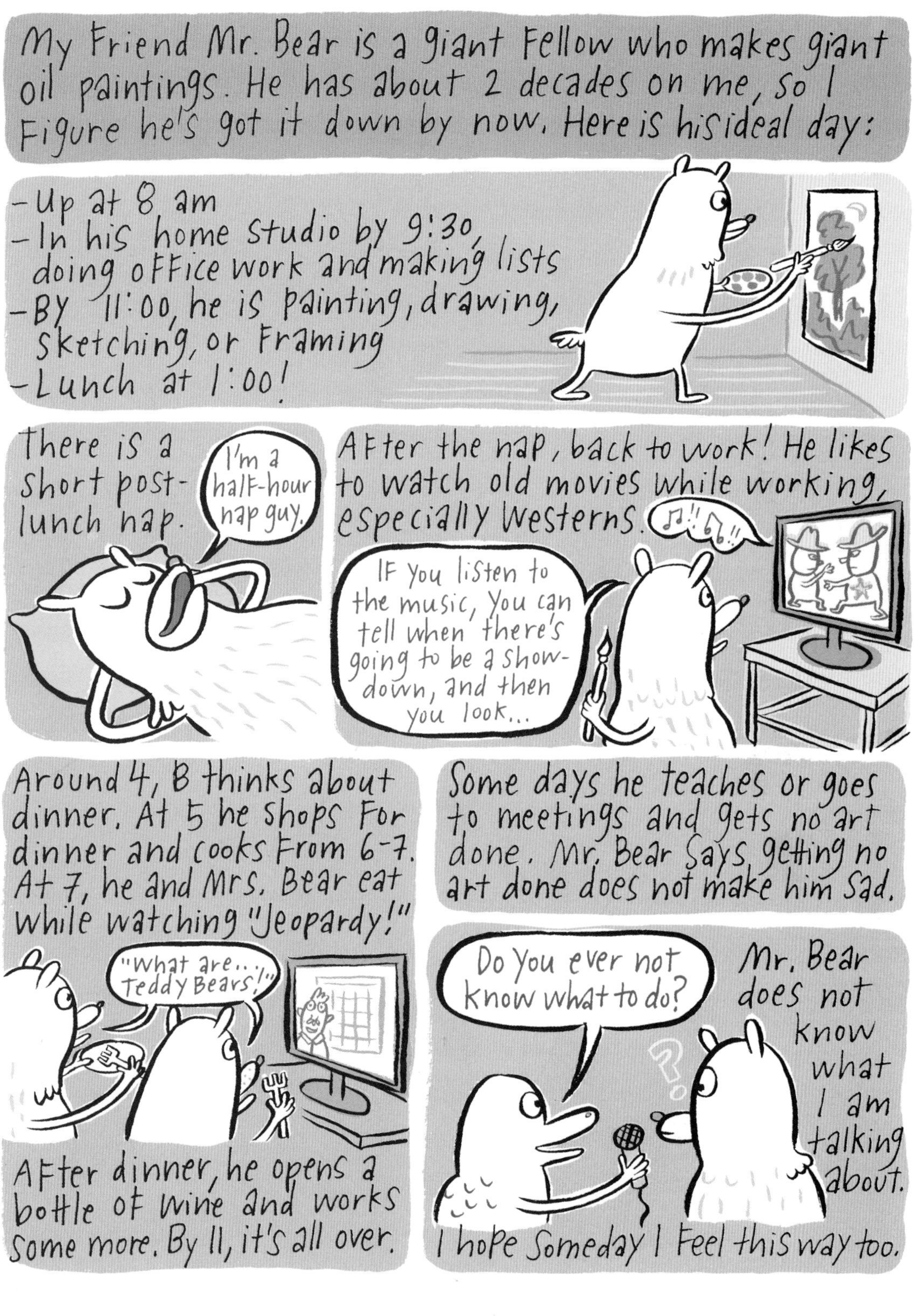
My Friend Mr. Bear is a giant Fellow who makes giant oil paintings. He has about 2 decades on me, so I Figure he's got it down by now. Here is his ideal day:
-Up at 8 am
-In his home studio by 9:30, doing office work and making lists
-By 11:00, he is painting, drawing, sketching, or Framing
-Lunch at 1:00!
There is a short post-lunch nap.
I'm a half-hour nap guy.
After the nap, back to work! He likes to watch old movies while working, especially Westerns.
♫!! ♫!!
If you listen to the music, you can tell when there's going to be a show-down, and then you look...
Around 4, B thinks about dinner. At 5 he shops for dinner and cooks from 6-7. At 7, he and Mrs. Bear eat while watching "Jeopardy!"
"What are... Teddy Bears!"
After dinner, he opens a bottle of wine and works some more. By 11, it's all over.
Some days he teaches or goes to meetings and gets no art done. Mr. Bear says getting no art done does not make him sad.
Do you ever not know what to do?
Mr. Bear does not know what I am talking about.
I hope someday I feel this way too.

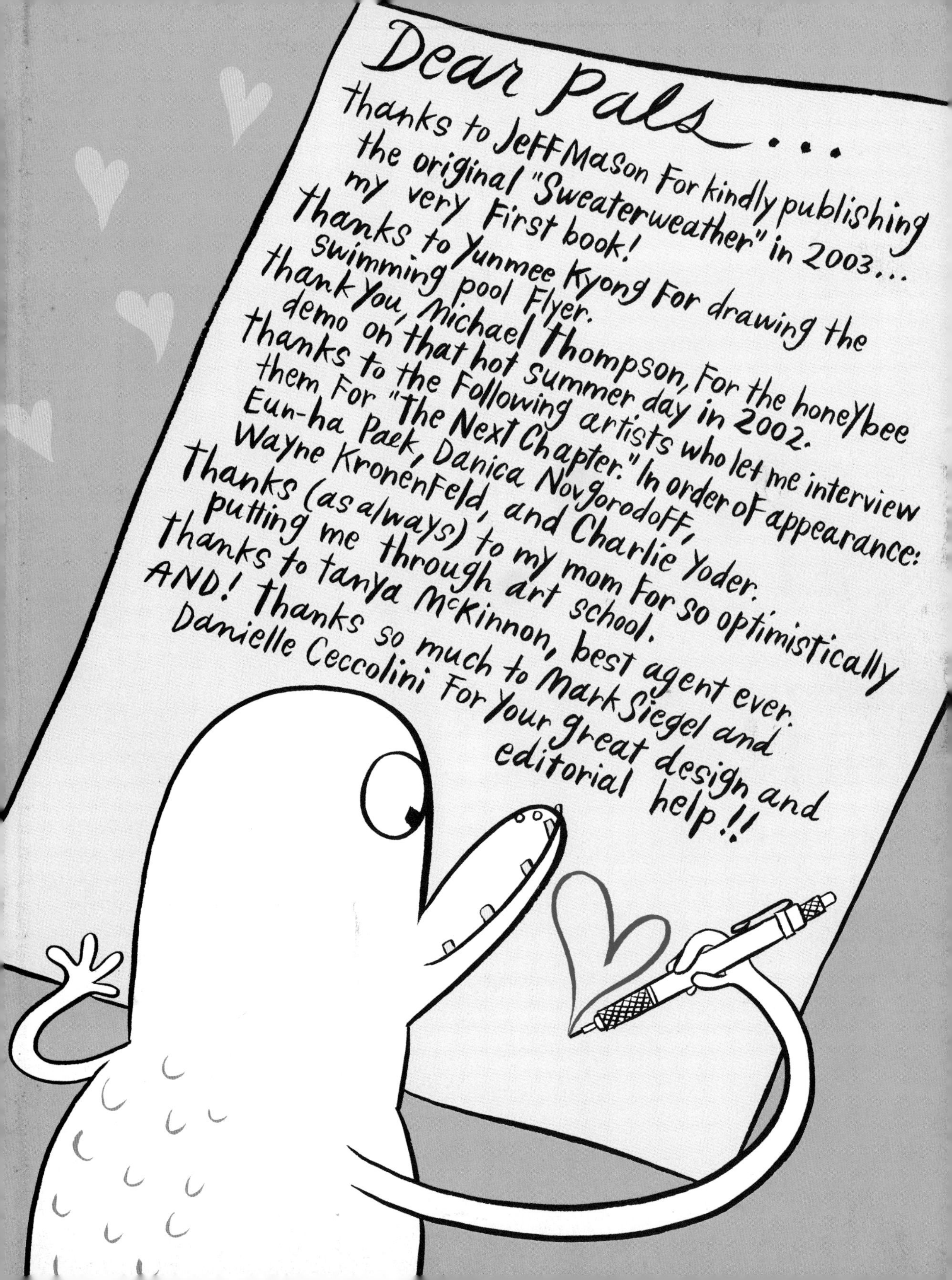
Dear Pals...
thanks to Jeff Mason for kindly publishing
the original "Sweaterweather" in 2003...
my very first book!
thanks to Yunmee Kyong for drawing the
swimming pool flyer.
thank you, Michael Thompson, for the honeybee
demo on that hot summer day in 2002.
thanks to the following artists who let me interview
them for "The Next Chapter." In order of appearance:
Eun-ha Paek, Danica Novgorodoff,
Wayne Kronenfeld, and Charlie Yoder.
Thanks (as always) to my mom for so optimistically
putting me through art school.
thanks to tanya McKinnon, best agent ever.
AND! Thanks so much to Mark Siegel and
Danielle Ceccolini for your great design and
editorial help!!

First Second

First Published in 2003 by Alternative Comics

Published by First Second
First Second is an imprint of Roaring Brook Press, a division of Holtzbrinck Publishing Holdings Limited Partnership
175 Fifth Avenue, New York, New York 10010

Cataloging-in-Publication Data is on file at the Library of Congress

ISBN 978-1-62672-118-0

First Second books may be purchased for business or promotional use. For information on bulk purchases please contact Macmillan Corporate and Premium Sales Department at (800) 221-7945 x5442 or by email atspecialmarkets@macmillan.com.

FIRST EDITION

First edition 2016
Book design by Sara Varon and Danielle Ceccolini
Printed in China by RR Donnelley Asia Printing Solutions Ltd., Dongguan City, Guangdong Province

1 3 5 7 9 10 8 6 4 2

Drawn with a combination of the following materials:
plain old office photocopy paper, Canson Bristol vellum, various brands of size 2/0 round brushes (for lettering), size 2 Windsor Newton Series 7 brush, Dr. Martin's Black Star Hi-Carb India Ink, Pentel and Kaimei brush pens, Faber Castell Pitt Artist Pen, crow quill pen, 0.9 mm mechanical pencil, Prismacolor colored pencils, Photoshop

All text is hand lettered, except page numbers and copyright page, which are set in Varon
Layout created in InDesign

BY ART WE LIVE

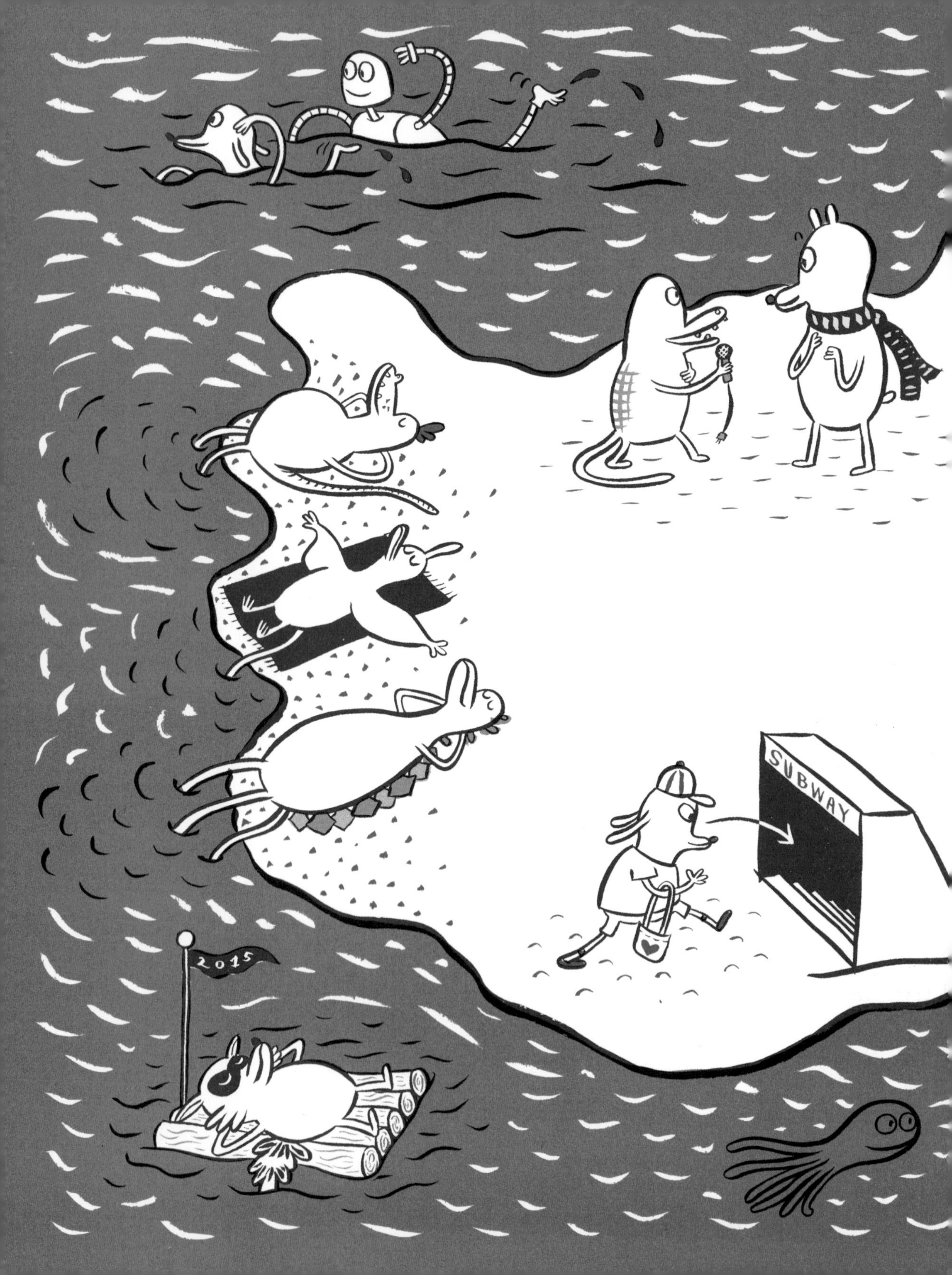
SUBWAY
2015